Vanessa Greene is the author of three previous novels, *The Vintage Teacup Club*, *The Seafront Tea Rooms* and *The Beachside Guest House*. She writes about (and believes in) the value of female friendship, as well as the restorative powder of tea and cake. She lives in north London with her husband and young son and daughter. She loves to hear from readers, so drop her a line on Twitter (@VanessaGBooks) or Facebook (www.facebook.com/VanessaGreeneBooks).

The Little Pieces of You and Me

Vanessa Greene

SPHERE

First published in Great Britain in 2016 by Sphere

1 3 5 7 9 10 8 6 4 2

A CIP catalogue record for this book
is available from the British Library.

ISBN 978-0-7515-6375-7

Typeset in Caslon by M Rules
Printed and bound in Great Britain by
Clays Ltd, St Ives plc

Papers used by Sphere are from well-managed forests
and other responsible sources.

MIX
Paper from
responsible sources
FSC® C104740

Sphere
An imprint of
Little, Brown Book Group
Carmelite House
50 Victoria Embankment
London EC4Y 0DZ

An Hachette UK Company
www.hachette.co.uk

www.littlebrown.co.uk

For James, Finn and Marlena

Prologue

The day that your life changes for ever, chances are there won't be a sign announcing it. The day that you choke on a fishbone, or circle the right lottery numbers, meet a drunk-driver head-on, or get that big yes in a phone call, most likely won't feel like anything special at all.

Nothing will be marked in your calendar, telling you that, by the time night comes, you'll be living according to different rules – that your previous life, the one that currently fits you like a faded T-shirt, is already on its way out. Your readiness for the change won't matter. The sun will rise, the sky turn from pale pink to blue, your alarm will sound, the radio will play a song you remember from your student days. You'll make toast, spread marmalade, check the milk. There'll be no sense that the boundaries of your world are about to shift. That this particular dawn is a new dawn.

That much Isla knew now.

Chapter 1

Tuesday, the 17th of May, was a morning that was just like all the others. If Isla had been aware that it would be a day she'd always remember, she might have worn something different, maybe not the jumper dress that had bobbled around the hem, or her scuffed biker boots. She would still have tied her wavy dark hair back with the purple scarf, the one her best friend Sophie had given her, but she would have put a brush through it first, at least. If she'd known.

But she hadn't. She had walked down the narrow steps of her Amsterdam apartment and, oblivious, stepped out into the hazy sunshine, anticipating nothing more than the usual run of things. She was on her way to the theatre to meet with her fellow actors, to talk through the previous night's performance. Their play, *In the Hands of Strangers*, a drama her friend Greta had written back in the UK and they'd all helped shape through improvisation, had been attracting good audiences. As she walked, at a fairly brisk pace, she looked up and around at the barges and the houses, taking in her surroundings. It had been a leap of faith coming out here, leaving her home in Bristol to come to Amsterdam, but she hadn't looked back. She felt totally present, in the now, in this city that had welcomed her as one of its own.

Isla arrived at Paradiso, her regular waterside coffee shop, to find the shutters down, and looked for an alternative along the stretch of canal. A few metres away she spotted a barge with a wooden hand-painted board: *The Floating Bookshop*. The door was ajar, and the aroma drifting out boded well – freshly brewed coffee. She hadn't noticed the place before, but she always enjoyed discovering somewhere new. She walked over and went inside. A striped rug covered the floor, slashing through the dim interior with bold colours, and every available patch of wall space was lined with books. A wooden table in the centre of the barge was covered with the latest bestsellers. Up at the counter, a dark-haired man in his thirties, who seemed to be running the shop, was caught up in quiet conversation with a woman a generation older.

Isla browsed the shelves until she spotted an old favourite. It was a novel by Elizabeth Bowen, *The House in Paris*, one that she and Sophie had both loved when they were at uni together back in Bristol. She pulled the book out and looked at it – an early edition, leather-bound with gold lettering. Paris. They'd always talked about going together. Sophie would love this, she thought, picturing her best friend opening the package back home.

The older lady walked slowly out of the shop carrying books in a bag, long white hair intricately pinned high on her head, leaving a trace of jasmine scent in the air. 'Until next time, Rafael,' she called back towards the counter.

'Take care, Berenice.'

Isla looked over at the man behind the counter, and her gaze met his. He was better-looking than she'd realised at first glance – tall, with dark brown eyes. She pushed past the discomfort of shyness and feigned her usual confidence, walking over to the counter with the novel in her hand.

'I couldn't see a price on this one,' she said, passing it over.

He handled the book gently, and opened the front cover to show her the price written in pencil. 'Here you go.'

'I see,' she said, wondering how she'd missed it. 'I'll take it.'

'Quite hard to part with this one,' he said, with a smile. His voice, the calmness of it, the trace of an accent she couldn't place, put her at ease.

Her hand made contact with his as she handed over the money, and a sensation akin to an electric charge ran through her. He must have felt it too, she thought. She felt certain she saw a flicker of acknowledgement in his face.

Today was one of those days, and it had arrived without warning. Tonight she would think of this man, and her plans, her sense of where she began and ended, would loosen a little.

She hadn't come to Amsterdam looking for someone to share her life with. She had had her fair share of love. Her twenties had been filled with passion that burned brightly but then burned out, nights of sleep lost in the pain of letting go. Those endings that had seemed unhappy weren't really – each one had reunited her with her freedom. She admired Sophie's commitment to Liam and Rebecca, but she didn't envy her family life.

But there in the bookshop, readying herself to turn and leave the stranger who no longer felt like a stranger, Isla sensed things had already changed. Her world had opened up.

Sophie woke early, with the daylight, and lifted the duvet gently so as not to disturb Liam. He lay with his back to her and she was tempted to drop a kiss on his shoulder, trace a trail up his neck to where his light stubble started. But he had stayed up late working on notes for one of his college lectures. She'd let him sleep a while longer.

She put on her dressing gown and walked down the stairs of their townhouse, a slice of Georgian architecture lined up against identical neighbours in the curve of Bennett Street in Bristol. It was a road they'd been lucky to afford. Ten years ago, when prices were lower, a doer-upper had come on the market, and Sophie had fallen in love with the potential of it the moment she'd walked through the door. She and Liam had put their combined energies into making it a home – it had felt good to have a project, something they could focus on together. Dropping out of medical school was the hardest thing she'd ever had to do, but when her parents said they would no longer fund her she'd had no choice. The distraction of making a home for herself and Liam was what she had needed. They'd enjoyed breaking away the plywood and revealing period fireplaces, tiles in almost perfect condition. Then there was all the time they spent picking out the small things that made it special – browsing the Clifton junk shops to find vintage clocks and coffee tables. This would be their new start, away from the whispers and judgement. Sophie and Liam were building a future.

Sophie got down the cafetière and made coffee in her white and oak open-plan kitchen. When it had brewed, she stepped out on to the patio. It was July, warm enough to be outside like this, in bare feet. A wood pigeon cooed, but aside from that the garden was quiet, just the way Sophie liked it. She looked out at the lawn and flowerbeds, the summer blooms brightening the space – her own small oasis of calm. If you didn't look too closely it could almost be something out of a lifestyle magazine.

Ha, she thought, smiling to herself. Perfectly styled dysfunction.

She and Liam were fine, that was the good part. But that was only half the story.

Rebecca, Liam's daughter, was sixteen now. She came for the weekends and holidays. They'd been friends once, or something close to it, but these days Bennett Street on the long stretch from Friday to Sunday had started to feel like a battleground.

Sophie missed Isla – she was the friend Sophie turned to for advice, and Sophie was sure that if she knew more about the situation with Rebecca, she'd be able to help improve things. Sophie loved to hear her friend's updates from Amsterdam, but she also longed for the two of them to be able to go out, and talk over a glass of wine – laugh the way they used to. Isla was like that – a burst of sunshine in the life of anyone lucky enough to know her, coasting along at her own speed, on tracks she laid down as she went. She'd always been like that. Sophie remembered how, as their first year at uni drew to a close with a hazy hot summer, they were sitting on the floor of Sophie's room in their shared student flat, biros and A4 pads in hand.

'This is the summer it all starts for us,' Isla announced. 'A list can be a powerful thing.'

'Right,' Sophie said, chewing on the end of her black pen. 'I'm ready. How many things?'

'Ten,' Isla said. 'Twenty. More if you want. Imagine you're a granny sitting in your rocking chair. Think of what it is you really, really want to have done in life.'

Sophie paused for a moment. There was only one thing, really. She started to write.

Be a doctor.

The dream she'd had since she was a kid with a toy stethoscope. She was finally on her way, at medical school in Bristol. She got on well with her fellow students, and her tutor, Richard, always made time for her. His passion for the subject reminded her during every lecture why she had chosen to study medicine, and filled her with hope and excitement about qualifying in the future. He even introduced her to a few of his friends, other tutors – and that made Sophie feel as if she was really part of things.

Isla looked over her shoulder. 'Not just career stuff, Soph. Fun things.'

'I know, I know. Give me a minute.'

She couldn't really think of anything else. Isla was scribbling furiously on her own piece of paper.

Girls like Isla hadn't existed at her boarding school, Sophie thought, and, even if they had, she was pretty sure they wouldn't have talked to her. Isla's hair was dyed bright red, with a blunt-cut fringe, and a solitary peacock-feather earring dangled from one ear. When they'd met for the first time, in the kitchen of their shared student flat, Sophie had struggled to think of what to say. Isla had filled the silence easily, though – and in just a few weeks they had become close friends. She turned back to her paper.

Read *Anna Karenina*.

Find a lost dog and reunite it with its owner.

'You're dreaming big, right?' Isla said, without looking up from her own list.

Sophie paused. No – not big exactly. She looked up at the posters on her wall. Roman Holiday, *her favourite Audrey Hepburn film.* Learn Italian, *she added. And,* Make pasta from scratch.

Complete a triathlon.

See the Northern Lights.

'Really big?' Isla prompted her.

Sophie bit her lip, then made herself write it.

Fall in love with someone who loves me for me.

'Done,' Isla said, a moment later, laying down her biro with a look of pride.

Sophie felt embarrassed about her own list, and instead looked over at Isla's. 'What did you write?'

'Number one you may already know, seeing as I talk about it almost every day,' Isla smiled. 'Perform on Broadway.'

'You'll do that,' Sophie said. Distant a dream as it might sound, Sophie felt sure that Isla could do it. She was a natural actress, and her amateur student plays had already got glowing reviews. 'What else?'

'Two – Live abroad. Three – Make chocolate in Paris.'

'Now that I like the sound of,' Sophie said.

'I always fancied the idea of doing a chocolate-making course there. Truffles, bonbons, macaroons ... then a stroll down the Champs-Elysées, sitting down at some gorgeous little pavement

café and ordering a citron pressé. *There's room for two in that dream, obviously.'*

'Pleased to hear it. I'm in. What else is on your list?'

'Four – Learn to fly on a trapeze.'

'You're kidding.'

'Not remotely. My grandma Sadie was in a circus. Did I ever tell you that? So I figure it's in my blood, somewhere. The half of my blood that I know about, that is.'

'Maybe your gran could join you for that one,' Sophie said. 'I've got a really bad head for heights, as you know. Swinging upside-down from a flimsy little swing is absolutely not my idea of fun.'

'Fine. Each to their own, then. Five – Learn to tango in Buenos Aires.'

'That sounds so romantic,' Sophie said.

'Doesn't it?'

Isla got to her feet and danced with an imaginary partner on the worn carpet, her eyes closed. Sophie got up and joined her, and they danced together, until they tripped over one another's feet and collapsed in giggles.

Isla resumed reading her list. 'These ones you'll probably like. They're fairly easy. Six – Wild swimming. A lake, a waterfall, wherever, just somewhere out in the open, where I can, you know, commune with nature.' She smiled.

'Doable. The next one?'

'See sunset and sunrise the same night. And this – this you'll like,' Isla said. 'Make a patchwork quilt.'

'That's a nice one.'

'My gran's got a lot of beautiful material in her house – it'd be a nice way to tell our family story. Something to pass down to future generations and whatnot.'

'Lovely. Have you ever sewn anything?'
'Badges. For Brownies,' Isla said.
'Fine – a walk in the park then.'
'Let's see yours,' Isla said.

Thinking back, Sophie sighed. Her list was in a drawer somewhere. She hadn't seen it for years. It wasn't that she didn't care about travelling, or learning Italian – and she'd even got as far as training for a triathlon a couple of years ago – but those ambitions didn't fit with her life as it was any more. Her priorities had changed after she and Liam had got together properly and Rebecca, her stepdaughter, had come into her life.

Back at uni, when the storm had hit and the truth came out about Sophie and Liam, Isla had weathered it with her. Sophie's father's job as a top MP meant the tabloids were all over the scandal – a married university tutor having an affair with a young student.

Isla had taken her out clubbing and told her in that dizzy drunken fog that, whatever Sophie's parents said – and they hadn't taken the news well – she was still a good person.

How simple things had seemed back when she and Isla had written those lists. That wasn't real life. The people you committed to, and the lives you were responsible for, were what would really guide your decisions in life, not the sun-chasing desires you had as a teenager. She enjoyed watching Isla meet her goals, but her own life was different now.

Sophie could hear Liam's footsteps on the stairs, and, out of habit, she got to her feet to make his coffee. Their life was made up of these small courtesies and routines, reminding them that they were together, a team, through it all, and after everything. When Rebecca slammed her door, or dinner was an interminable stretch of hostile silence, Sophie could look over at Liam, and there'd be an understanding there, a sense of solidarity they built up in small ways every day. And sometimes, he'd smile, and his eyes would crinkle at the corners. It wasn't perfect, their life, but it was full of love.

Love that hadn't been convenient, but love that was strong, and true, and meaningful. Love that had been worth the cost.

Chapter 2

'What's this?' Rafael asked, looking at a piece of paper pinned to Isla's fridge.

Isla looked over towards the kitchen, where Rafael was standing.

'That's the list,' Isla said. 'I've told you about that, right?'

'Not yet.'

It had been two months since Isla's first visit to the bookshop, the day she'd set eyes on Rafael for the first time. She'd found a reason to return the next day – to enquire about a novel by a prize-winning French writer. It was actually one that she already had sitting on her bedside table in the apartment, unread, next to a copy of *Grazia* (read) that Sophie had sent her. Rafael had found her a copy, and she bought it – they'd chatted for a little while. They were both foreigners making a home in the city – he'd moved over from Mexico, she had left behind a comfortable life in Bristol. He'd stayed on her mind all week – his easy humour, and kind smile. She went back at the weekend, and he told her a local reading group was going to discuss the literary novel she'd bought. He wondered if she might like to join them.

Caught unawares, she hadn't had time to formulate a response that was anything other than the truth. Instead, she'd smiled. 'I'm afraid I wouldn't have much to say,' she said. 'I've got two copies now, and I haven't read either. So, before I bankrupt myself—' she drew on all her courage '—I wonder if you'd like to go for a drink with me?'

He had laughed, and agreed, without hesitating. They'd gone out – and found they couldn't stop talking. At the end of their first date, he'd kissed her. The city changed for her then. Each road led to or away from Rafael – his home, his work – and every café and bar became a landmark imprinted on her mind, a place where they'd talked about their pasts, or future, or just kissed until she felt dizzy. The past two months had been a whirl, of long cycle rides in the countryside when the shop's opening hours and her rehearsal schedule allowed it, and of Sunday mornings spent barely leaving his apartment.

Now, she went over to him in her kitchen and put her arms around him from behind. Little by little he was starting to feel like hers.

'Well – let me introduce you,' she said, pulling the piece of paper from the fridge door and moving to his side. 'This list is a very good friend of mine, and you should meet her too.'

'I'm intrigued.'

'Sophie and I wrote these, years back. When we had no doubt I would be a famous actress and she'd be saving lives.' She smiled. 'It may not have happened yet, but I'm going to do them all.'

'Live abroad – that one's done.'

'Yes – and that turned out to be quite a good decision.' She kissed him on the cheek and he continued to read over her shoulder.

'The trapeze? Amazing.'

'One day,' Isla said, with a smile. 'No time limit on these things. Well, aside from the obvious. I just want to be a happy little old lady looking back and knowing I did everything I wanted to.'

'You're a born adventurer.' He smiled.

'I guess. Anyway, this list certainly kept me going when I was working at the biscuit factory back home, trying to scrape together enough money to bring the play out here.'

'And you did it.'

'Yes. Together with Greta and Alec, who were on my uni course with me, I founded the group in the UK and got us all out here. But you must have had a plan, too, coming here all the way across that big blue sea. You couldn't get much further from home.'

'A sketchy one,' he said, shrugging.

Isla pressed him – he was such a good listener that they'd barely talked about his life at all. 'I'm guessing you didn't speak Dutch when you arrived?'

'I'd never heard a word,' he laughed. 'I couldn't get by at all. I used the English I had – which I'd learned from the American movies I used to watch back home.'

'And now look at you – you've got your own business here.'

'I feel lucky,' he said. 'I got a few regular customers, like Berenice, brilliant B, who spread the word, then started running events, and things took off from there. It wasn't a plan, not really. A lot of it just happened.'

'Well, however you got here, I'm glad you came,' Isla said. She couldn't imagine being without him now – with the laughter and brightness that he brought to her days.

He put his arms around her and drew her in close to him. 'Me too.'

The following morning, Rafael left to open the bookshop and Isla cycled over to the theatre. The water on the canal of Prinsengracht sparkled in the July sunshine. She smiled to herself, recollecting the sensation of Rafael's hands on her skin.

Was there a name for it, she wondered, this feeling when you woke up and realised that this good life was your life? That the day you were starting was better than any you ever imagined yourself living? It was worthy of a name. Rafael seemed more than happy to be considered hers, and the independence she'd once valued above everything else in her life didn't seem as essential as it once had any more.

Sophie had called her late the night before. She'd seen her friend's name flash up on the phone but – and she never did this, not usually, not to Sophie – she'd reached over and pressed the red button. She'd see Sophie in person soon enough, and would make it up to her.

Sophie had texted last week to say she'd booked her tickets – in just a few days she'd be over here to visit, and they could catch up on everything properly then.

Isla arrived at the theatre, parked her bike and walked in through the stage door.

Greta was tidying up one of the dressing rooms, rearranging costumes and props. 'There's that sparkle in your eyes again,' she said, with a smile. 'God, it would be sickening, really, if it wasn't making your performances even stronger than usual.'

'Thanks,' Isla said, wrinkling her nose. 'I think.'

'You've been the best you've ever been these past few weeks, we've all noticed it.'

A glow of pride welled up inside Isla. She knew, deep down, that it was true. The last few weeks she'd truly come alive on stage, each response from the audience, or emotional silence, spurring her on to perform better and better in the next scene. The difference wasn't hard to figure out – Rafael was there with her, each night, sometimes in one of the unsold seats at the side of the theatre, other times just in her mind, urging her on.

'Come and get some coffee with me,' Greta said. 'The others are through in Alec's room. It's been a busy morning.'

'Sure,' Isla said, dropping her rucksack and following Greta through to the other dressing room.

Alec – their temperamental male lead – was definitely sunny-side-up today. He poured Isla coffee and motioned for her to sit down, an irrepressible smile on his face.

'Why do I get the feeling something's going on around here that I don't know about?' Isla said, suspiciously.

'Oh, it is,' Alec said. 'It totally is.'

'Go on, tell me, then,' Isla said, unable to restrain her excitement. She knew – they'd all known – that there were key local reviewers in the audience the previous night. 'Has a new review come in?'

'Better than that,' Greta said.

'We're going to New York,' Alec announced.

Isla furrowed her brow, unsure of what he meant.

'The show,' he explained. 'Get this. We're going to Broadway!'

New York. Broadway. The words danced in the air until she was barely sure she'd heard them right at all. Did Alec really mean them – their show? Her? Was this really happening?

'Us? Us including me?' Isla said, biting her lip to stop from smiling.

'Of course including you, you doughnut. You're the best thing we've got.'

'It can't be real. It's too good.'

She felt as if she was lighting up like a candle, her cheeks catching the glow and warming. This was IT, *the one*. What she'd always dreamed of. Being an actress was about more than just the glory, a glamorous setting, of course it was – she would have enjoyed it if she'd been acting in a pub theatre. But New York? That was something most people never got near – if she got there, she had made it. It would all have been worth it – the hard graft and late nights. She would have arrived.

'He's being serious,' Greta reassured her. 'I didn't believe him at first either.'

'How?' she said, a hesitant smile coming to her lips. 'I mean – I know the run's gone well, and we've had some great feedback ... but this? How?'

'Invited the right people at the right time,' Alec said. 'I've got some American friends in high places in the theatre world and while they were over here on holiday I asked them along. They came last night. And they were impressed. They've promised to arrange us some dates at the end of the summer. It'll be at a small theatre, obviously we'll need to start building up a name for ourselves ... but it's a good thing.'

'A good thing?' Isla said, almost feverish with excitement. 'It's New York!'

'I know,' Greta said, with a huge smile. 'It's insane.'

'It's incredible.'

Isla imagined the look Rafael would have on his face when she told him the news. She couldn't wait to talk to him and share the excitement that felt as if it might bubble right out of her. This was everything – *everything.*

He would be as excited as she was. Yes, it would mean time apart, but they'd laid the foundations of their relationship well enough. She was confident that they could cope with distance for a while, and he'd already shown that he was supportive of her pursuing her ambitions.

As the good news sank in, she thought of Sophie. The person who'd been there when she'd put performing on Broadway at the very top of her list. She couldn't wait another minute to share the news with her friend.

She picked up the phone and called her.

'Hey, Isla. I'm just—'

'Whatever you're doing, you have to stop it for a minute.'

'OK,' Sophie said, laughing. 'What's up?'

'You're not going to believe this,' Isla said. 'I've just had the most incredible news. We're taking the play to Broadway.'

Isla lifted the phone away from her ear slightly, anticipating Sophie's excited shouting. She could still hear it. 'You're kidding! That's amazing. That's more than amazing. That's *number one*, Isla.'

'It is number one. I know. I told you a list is a powerful thing.'

'I'm so proud of you.'

It meant a lot, to hear that from Sophie. Sophie who had supported her every step of the way in her journey towards making acting her career. 'Thank you. God, even I'm proud of me.'

'New York!' Sophie shouted.

'I know!' Isla said back.

Sophie lowered her voice. 'Oh, God. Everyone in the staff canteen is staring at me.'

'Let them,' Isla said. 'It's not every day I get to tell you news like this.'

'New York, eh,' Liam said, as he and Sophie stood in the hallway of their home in Bennett Street the next morning. 'Well, you've always said Isla was talented.'

'She's just really got it. The moment she steps on stage, you forget it's her – she inhabits the role. And she's seemed so happy working with the theatre group she's with. I'm not at all surprised that they got spotted.'

'When's she going?'

'In just over a month. She'll be out there for September.'

'Do you think you'll go?'

'I'd like to – I'll talk to her about it when I go over to visit.'

'Cool.' He put a ringbinder and a notebook in his bag and closed it.

'You've got everything you need for today?' Sophie said.

'Yes – I'm all set. I wish they could all be like this student, actually – his thesis is shaping up really well. It's the new term, and the freshers, I'm more worried about.'

'I'm sure they'll be more scared than you,' Sophie said, giving him a kiss.

'I don't know about that,' he said. 'It was easier when they weren't forking out so much money to do the courses. Students these days are so much more demanding.'

'You're worth every penny,' Sophie said, teasing him gently.

'Obviously I know that,' he said, smiling. 'But it's them I need to convince. There are the strong students, who give it their all and grab the opportunity with both hands – like you were, before ... ' His smile disappeared for a moment. Sophie knew how guilty he felt that he hadn't been able to support her financially himself. 'Sorry.'

'Ancient history,' Sophie said. 'Carry on.'

'But some of the others seem to think you can buy a degree. That they're entitled to a good pass, whether they've put the work in or not.'

'That's no good.' She paused. 'It really isn't. How do the other lecturers feel about it?'

'They're resigned to it, mostly. But if we roll over, give in to some of these students' demands and issue good marks to those who aren't deserving of them, then we're letting the truly talented and hard-working students down – and then comes the process of it devaluing degrees, full stop.'

'You have to put your foot down; it's too important.'

'Exactly, I agree. Which is why I'm not anticipating winning any popularity prizes this term. And why I'd quite like to go in wearing full body armour when September rolls around.'

She smiled, and took his hand. 'I can't supply you with that, I'm afraid. But I could ease the pain when you get home tonight. How about your favourite pasta bake, with a nice bottle of wine?'

'Sounds wonderful.' The smile returned to Liam's face. Thank you.'

'You'll be fine.' She stood up on tiptoes to kiss him. 'I love you.'

Sophie left the house shortly after Liam. She had been working as a clerk in the children's ward at Bristol Hospital for eight years now – dealing with patients and their families and handling medical notes – and she could almost drive there on autopilot.

It wasn't what she'd once pictured herself doing, but it was a job that had its rewards. She met the most incredible kids working there. They never ceased to amaze her with their energy, their resilience, their laughter. Their strength in the face of conditions that kept their parents awake at night. The best days were the ones when she got to see them go home, healthy and well. They'd leave the ward with their parents, all smiles, and she'd silently hope not to see them again. Sometimes she and Karen would get a thank-you card or a photo, and they'd pin it to the board proudly, a reminder of the happy stories they had played a tiny part in.

She went up to the fourth floor and to her desk, and took off her coat. Karen wasn't in yet, so she took some paperwork in to Rob, one of the doctors, in Room 8. He smiled when he saw her. 'Morning, Sophie.'

Rob had started at the same time as her, and he'd always been a supportive colleague. Over time, they'd become friends. Rob, broad-shouldered with dark hair, was considered by some of the staff to be harsh, and he certainly didn't mince his words. But when Sophie chatted with him she never felt conscious of hierarchy in the way she did talking to some of the other doctors. When they were working, or in the canteen, on coffee break, they were equals: simple as that.

Today Rob and a nurse were treating Milly, a little girl with chronic eczema who'd come in quite a few times. When Rob was with a patient, his gaze softened, and the sternness some knew him for disappeared.

'Hey, Milly,' Sophie said, greeting her with a smile. Milly held up her toy monkey and waved back.

'How can we help you today, Milly?' Rob asked, crouching down to talk to her at her level.

'My skin's all oww-y again,' she said, softly.

'Her eczema flared up badly this weekend,' her dad told Rob. 'She went to a birthday party and must have eaten something with egg in it.' The stress showed in his eyes. 'I should have stayed there with her, I know that . . . but—'

'You can't always be there every minute, especially as she gets older,' Rob reassured him. 'You do what you can. Now, Milly, let's do our best to get this sorted, shall we?'

Sophie looked at the red-raw patches of skin, and how delicately the nurse had to put on the tubigrip bandage in order to cause minimal discomfort to her. Even then Milly was wincing. Sophie couldn't offer anything more than a smile, and reassurance. At best a brightly coloured sticker. At times like these, she wished she could do more – that she could be the one to take the pain away. But she couldn't. She wouldn't ever be that person – that door had closed for her a long time ago.

*

An hour later, after Milly and her father had left the ward, Rob stopped by at the main desk.

'Have you got time for lunch?' Rob asked.

'I think so. That OK, Karen?' Sophie asked.

Her colleague nodded. 'Bring me back a KitKat, will you?'

'Sure, OK.' Sophie grabbed her bag. 'Let's go.'

They went through to the canteen, bought sandwiches and drinks, and found a quiet table over by the window.

'How's it going?' Rob asked.

'Truth?'

He nodded.

'Really glad I've got some time away booked in.'

He smiled in recognition. 'It's been pretty full-on here lately, hasn't it. You and Liam going somewhere nice?'

'It's just me this time. Liam can't afford the days off – and I really need to take them, as they've been stacking up. I'm going to Amsterdam, to see Isla, my best friend and partner in crime.'

Rob smiled. 'Is there a hell-raising side to you I haven't seen?'

'Hardly.' Sophie laughed. 'But the two of us had our moments, back when I could handle more than a glass of wine.'

'Always the life and soul of the staff parties,' Rob said, teasing. 'Curled up in the corner in an armchair by nine-thirty.'

'I think my partying days, what there was of them, are over. But let's see what this trip brings. It's a long time since I had a holiday.'

'Hopefully as soon as you're on the plane you'll forget about this place completely. You deserve a proper break.'

'Thanks.'

They fell quiet for a moment.

'It didn't feel right taking the time off, last year. After what happened – that little girl dying.'

'I know,' Rob said. A moment of silent mutual understanding passed between them. 'It was a tough year here, Soph. For all of us. But it wasn't your fault, and it wasn't mine. Dr Lyra accepted full responsibility. She was displaying classic signs of meningitis. Her parents were concerned enough to ask about it. He should never have sent her home that night. He made a serious error.'

'I just can't help thinking – I was in there, Rob. With her. Just for a few minutes – but perhaps there was something I could have seen when Dr Lyra did the examination. There was a chance . . .'

'Look, Sophie,' Rob said, his expression serious. 'You know I'd never normally say this, and forgive me if it sounds harsh. But you're a ward clerk. You're not a doctor. You're not qualified or paid to take on the responsibility that Dr Lyra had – and that means you can't spend another minute feeling bad about what happened.'

Sophie desperately wanted to undo what had gone wrong the previous year. It struck her to her core that she wasn't qualified to help avoid it happening again. But, as the words sank in, she realised they had also freed her a little. She'd thought, so often, that if she had acted differently, that girl might still be alive.

Sophie drove home that night, looking forward to the quiet evening alone with Liam. She stopped by the supermarket to pick up a bottle of wine to go with the pasta bake that was waiting in the fridge. She and Liam would have some unhurried time to catch up on their days.

As she drove up to the house, she saw a glimmer of light coming from the living room.

'Hey!' she called out, opening the door. 'You're back early.'

A trail of belongings in the hallway told a different story from the one she'd had in her head. Rebecca's handbag was tossed to one side on the carpet, mascara and a lip crayon spilling out. She went over to the living room and looked inside.

Rebecca was lying on the sofa in the living room watching TV, her long legs, in skinny jeans and mismatched socks, sprawled out.

'Hi, Rebecca.'

'Hey,' Rebecca said without looking up. 'Not quite who you were expecting, right?'

Liam came into the room, and put his arm around Sophie's waist. 'Sorry,' he whispered. 'I tried to call you. Véronique has a date tonight, so I said Rebecca could stay here with us.'

'Sure,' Sophie said, 'of course.'

'Sorry,' Rebecca said. 'For ruining your evening. He's only my father, after all.'

'Come on, Rebecca – you know it's not like that,' Sophie said. 'You're always welcome here.'

'I'm always welcome to be passed between the parents you broke up, you mean.'

Ten years, and Rebecca's resentment seemed only to have grown. Ten years, and those words still cut Sophie like a knife.

'It's not like that,' Liam said. 'There are a lot of people who love and care about you, and Sophie is one of them.'

'Yeah, right,' Rebecca said. 'You're just jumping to her defence, as always.'

'Enough, Rebecca,' Liam said, firmly.

The room fell quiet.

'I'll get the dinner on, shall I?' Sophie said.

An hour later, Liam finished preparing the meal in the kitchen, and Sophie and Rebecca sat together at the table.

'So Dad said you're going away this weekend,' Rebecca said, picking at a splinter in the table with her nail.

'I am, yes,' Sophie said, lifted by her interest. 'I'm going to see Isla. I've talked about her before to you, haven't I?'

'Yes. You've mentioned her. The only one of your friends who wanted to come to the wedding.'

Sophie felt the hit of the barbed comment, but stayed calm. It was true, after all – there was no getting away from the fact that Sophie had lost a fair few friends. Arguably, it had been with good reason. However she looked at it, denying it wasn't going to make it go away.

'She's been a good friend to me, yes. Not everyone understood why I did what I did when I got married to your dad, and I respect their opinions. They had the right to step away. But I also appreciate that Isla stood by me.'

'Whatever,' Rebecca said, pressing her nail into the wood until she'd made a dent. 'I was just saying what I remembered about her. I don't want to discuss all that marriage-wrecking stuff right now, before dinner.'

'Good,' Sophie said. 'That makes both of us, then. You'll be OK, won't you, you and your dad, this weekend?'

'Are you kidding?' she said, looking up, a smile on her lips. 'You think we're going to fall apart without you?'

'No – that isn't what I was saying ...' Sophie paused. Took a deep breath. It hadn't always been like this – a hopeless spiral in which everything she said seemed to lead them further into conflict. Rebecca had always been spirited, but this vitriol hadn't always been there. At the start of secondary school she'd taken on a slight edge, caught up in wanting to be cool, but she had still delighted in helping Sophie in the kitchen, or out in the garden. She'd still been a young, sweet girl in many ways. 'I just wanted to be sure that you have everything you need.'

'So that you can get out of here, have a break from me with a clear conscience.'

'That's not true at all,' Sophie said. As she said the words, she was conscious of the lie. She *was* looking forward to a break – from this Rebecca. This Rebecca with her underhand comments, her subtle passive aggression and her more overt digs.

'Don't pretend you actually like spending time with me,' Rebecca said.

Guilt nagged at Sophie. Perhaps she had neglected their relationship – given up too easily when the going got tough. 'I do.'

Sophie glanced over at Liam, silently willing him to return to the table. He was out of earshot, humming along to the radio and spooning their dinner on to plates.

'Liar,' Rebecca whispered.

Sophie realised she had to make peace now if they were to stand any chance of improving things. 'Look – next weekend when I'm back, how about you and I do something together?'

'Like what?' Rebecca said, flatly. She looked up and met

Sophie's gaze; her blue eyes were wide, challenging Sophie to impress her.

'Go out,' Sophie said, her voice wavering a fraction. This should not be intimidating her. A sixteen-year-old with an attitude problem should not be bothering her this much. 'Shopping maybe? Or to get our nails done?'

Rebecca rolled her eyes, and made no attempt to conceal her contempt. 'Original.'

'I wasn't trying to be original,' Sophie said, her voice rising in volume as her patience broke down. 'God, Rebecca – I'm just trying to do something – anything – to break down this hostile front. It doesn't have to be like this between us.'

'I don't want to go shopping,' Rebecca said, her voice level and calm. 'Thank you.'

Sophie didn't know how to respond – Rebecca's tone gave nothing away. 'Well, if you do change your mind, I'm here. I'd like to spend more time with you, whether you believe it or not.'

'Fine,' Rebecca said. She looked at her father. Seemed to want him to come over and break the tension just as much as Sophie did. 'I don't believe it.'

Sophie stayed quiet. There was no way of winning.

Rebecca's gaze returned to meet Sophie's, confronting her. 'And don't hurry home.'

'Sorry?' Sophie said. Rebecca's words stung.

'I prefer it, you know,' Rebecca said, whispering so that her father wouldn't hear. 'I prefer it when you're not here.' Rebecca lowered her voice so it was quieter still. 'Sometimes I think Dad does too.'

Sophie wanted to shout back. Let loose all the anger and frustration that had been building in her. What had she done to make this girl hate her so much that she'd say a thing like that? That she'd keep saying the very worst things she could? But she was the adult, she reminded herself. She couldn't sink to Rebecca's level.

'I'm sorry you feel that way,' Sophie said. She took a deep breath, glad that she'd managed to hold back all the other things she really wanted to say, for another day at least.

After dinner, Sophie took the empty plates over to the kitchen. Staying calm with Rebecca for the duration of the meal had nearly broken her. She'd continued to make digs, albeit more subtle ones when her father was sitting with them. Liam and Sophie had exchanged looks a couple of times, and she could see that he was picking up on the tension – but nothing that Rebecca said was quite obvious enough for him to challenge her directly.

'I'm sorry about that, the way she's been speaking to you,' Liam said. 'It's not OK. Not at all. I'll have a word with her about it.'

Sophie shook her head. 'You haven't heard the half of it.'

He looked surprised. 'Why, what else did she say?'

'I don't want to go over it. Not now.' Sophie felt raw and hurt thinking of their earlier confrontation, and she didn't want to cry. Even now, with Rebecca safely upstairs. 'She seems determined to create a rift between the two of us, even now. I've tried to offer an olive branch, but I'm getting nowhere. I don't know where I've gone wrong recently, Liam. She seems to really hate me.'

'You haven't done anything wrong,' he said, putting an arm around her. 'You've always been there for her. As much as she's ever allowed you to be.'

'I mean, granted it's never been the easiest relationship – she's always seen me as a rival, I guess. But it was OK, wasn't it, before? And now this.'

'I know,' Liam said, concerned. 'I can see it's got a lot worse.'

'What do you think's going on for her?'

'I don't know – school, friends, boys?' He shrugged, and it was obvious his guesses were no more than stabs in the dark. 'I guess I'm due a proper chat with her. I'll talk to her this weekend.'

'Being sixteen is crappy sometimes,' Sophie said. 'I know that. I can remember it. But I'm getting far too close, Liam, to losing it with her. And I don't want to do that.'

Sophie went upstairs and started packing for her trip away on Saturday morning. She felt better for having talked to Liam about Rebecca. A break, and some time with her friend, would give her time to build some kind of strategy. Or at least the energy to keep on going without losing her temper.

A message buzzed through on her phone, from Isla.

Only one more day. Can't wait to see you. Have planned a lot of fun things for us to do. x

Sophie smiled. After weeks of waiting, she was nearly there. She and Isla would be back together again and it would be like old times.

She texted back quickly.

Can't wait either. It's been too long. x

She was excited about going to a new city for a long week-end, but would have been just as happy if the two of them were holed up in a Costa around the corner, so long as they had a chance to chat.

Sophie returned to packing her things, layering clothes into her suitcase. She found herself daydreaming about the first completely free days in months – and the time that she and Isla would have to catch up. She picked up her new high heels – unworn – and hesitated for a moment before putting them into her bag.

Liam put an arm around her and kissed her. 'I'm going to miss you.'

'Me too,' Sophie replied.

'But I hope you enjoy yourself. I know things haven't been easy round here lately.'

'I don't ever seem to be able to say the right thing.'

Liam frowned. 'I'm sure it's just a phase.'

'I hope so.'

'Yes.' Liam held her for a moment. She felt complete, there in his arms, as if nothing could touch her. 'Anyway, back to us – I've booked us a table, Tuesday night, just after you get back,' he said. 'For our anniversary.'

Sophie smiled. It didn't feel like ten years since they'd got married. A simple town hall do, with a meal in an Italian restaurant afterwards. It wasn't the big wedding she'd once dreamed of, and yes, there had been a certain sadness about her family not being there – but it had been perfect nonetheless, because she'd been marrying Liam. And Isla and her mum Hattie had been there, signing the book as witnesses, and sharing in her happiness. That had meant a lot.

'Our Italian. Something to look forward to when you get back, to help you overcome those post-holiday blues.'

'That's sweet of you,' Sophie said, pulling back so that she could look him in the eyes. 'Thank you.'

'Got to give you something to make coming home seem worthwhile. I know how hard it is for you to be apart from Isla. I don't want you missing your flight home.'

'Don't worry about that.'

He stroked her hair and kissed her again.

'Any plans for this weekend?' she asked. 'Other than talking to Rebecca, I mean?'

'A quiet one, I think. Mark said he might drop around for lunch on Sunday.'

'Ah, that reminds me. It might not be that quiet around here,' Sophie said. 'There's going to be a party at the house across the road – one of the girls dropped by to tell us, and apologised in advance for the noise.'

'No invite, then?' Liam said, with a smile.

'She did ask us along, actually.' Sophie smiled. 'They seem like a nice bunch. Students. They thought Rebecca might like to join them, too.'

'I'll mention it to her. Anything to cheer her up.'

Sophie went back to her packing, organising her small bottles of cosmetics into a clear wash bag.

'Listen, Soph,' Liam said, sitting down on their double bed. 'I know we've been kind of caught up in the day-to-day lately, but I want you to know I love you.'

She smiled. 'What's brought this on?'

'I just want you to know that I don't take you for granted. That I never will. I know how much you've tried with Rebecca, and I appreciate it, I always have.'

She sat beside him, and he took her hand in his. 'I'll never forget what you gave up so that we could be together.'

She touched his cheek gently, ran it over the stubble there. 'We both made sacrifices,' she said. 'And, while I'm sorry that people got hurt, I've never looked back.'

'When we moved in together, what I said, about not wanting another family. I know that hurt you.'

'It was a shock, at first,' she admitted. Liam had made it clear then that he wanted to put the sleepless nights and nappy changes behind him. The stress of having a newborn had driven a wedge between him and Véronique and he didn't want the same thing happening to him and Sophie. 'But I understand. I know it came from wanting to put our relationship first. I'm used to it now.'

'There's no part of you that wonders?' Liam said.

Perhaps there was. Yes, there was. But Sophie had stopped lingering on those thoughts. 'It took a little getting used to, but I'm all right with how things are.'

'The thing is, I don't think I was being entirely fair, back then. I was selfish, ruling it out.'

'Are you saying you feel differently now?' she asked.

'Yes,' he said. 'I think a baby could make us really happy.'

'We are happy,' she said softly.

'I know. But I don't know – something's changed. I want this with you, a family. Our family.'

'Really?' She had to be certain. If she was going to consider this, she had to know for sure that it was what he really wanted.

'Really.'

Sophie had taken in what he'd just said, but still couldn't quite believe it. For years, having a child simply hadn't been an option. Liam, as kindly as he could, had made that clear. Sophie had accepted it as their only possible reality, and come to value the positive aspects of a child-free life. Now, in the space of a conversation, the potential for a different kind of future had emerged. Sophie realised she'd lost sight of what she even wanted.

'I'm going to need some time to think about it,' she said.

Chapter 3

Isla cycled around to Rafael's apartment after rehearsals. As she rode by the canal, she thought of Sophie. She couldn't wait to show her friend the markets, cafés and bars – and introduce her to the first man in years she'd really cared about.

Rafael opened the door of his ground-floor apartment and she greeted him with a kiss. 'Morning.'

'Hi,' he said. They went inside, down a hallway lined with photos that he'd taken. 'How did it go today?'

'Good, thanks. We got confirmation that we'll get our flights paid for, which is a relief. I was wondering how we were going to cobble that money together.'

'That's great.' His eyes lit up. 'Have you booked them yet?'

'No – we're going to do it all together next week.'

'*Then* will you start to believe you're really going?' he said, teasing her.

'Maybe.' She smiled. 'I don't think my feet have touched the ground since I found out.'

'And who could blame you? It *is* number one,' Rafael said.

'It *is* number one. Do you think you'll come? I mean, I know flights are expensive ...'

'Hopefully,' he said. She could see he was hesitant to commit, and she felt awkward about having put him in a position where he had to answer.

'I know it's a big ask,' she said.

'Running a bookshop doesn't quite make me the millions I'd like it to,' he said, with a smile. 'I wish it did.'

'And I wish I were Hollywood A-list already, so I could fly you out myself.'

'One day. And in the meantime, I will be thinking of you, no matter what.'

'Me too. And, either way, we'll be together again by winter.'

'Yes,' he said, bringing her close and kissing her. 'I haven't forgotten your promise to show me a proper English Christmas, you know.'

'Me neither. I'm only holding back on telling Mum so that she doesn't start preparing right now.'

'Does she know about me?' Rafael said.

'A little.' Isla felt like a kid saying it. It had only been two months but already she felt far ahead of where she'd been with previous boyfriends – both in terms of what they were planning, and what she'd told Sophie and her mum. She hadn't been able to resist mentioning Rafael to them: to talk about how she was without speaking about him wouldn't have been honest.

37

'What about you?' Isla said. 'I don't know that much about your family. Do you think you'll tell them?'

'Yes,' he said. 'I will. There've been a few things going on, though, back home. I want to pick the right moment.'

'Plenty of time,' Isla said. 'On to a different kind of family – you're free the day after tomorrow, right, to meet Sophie?'

'Of course. I've got a little something lined up for our day out together, actually. When's she arriving?'

'Intriguing,' Isla said. 'She'll be here tomorrow, around midday. Give us a night to get up to speed on gossip, then you guys can get to know each other the next day.'

'Perfect.'

'You're going to like her,' Isla said. 'She's one of the kindest people you'll ever meet.'

'I'm sure I will. I hope I live up to her expectations,' he said.

Isla ruffled his hair. 'Just be you, Rafa. That's more than enough.'

'A gin and tonic, please,' Sophie said. She recalled the way Rob had teased her the other day, about curling up in an armchair early while other people kept drinking. She didn't need to go overboard before she'd even left the country. 'Actually, maybe just a splash of gin.' The stewardess made the drink and passed it to her.

There was a party atmosphere brewing on the budget flight, and this way she could at least be part of it. A group of women on a hen weekend were chatting loudly in the rows at the front, and would occasionally burst out in laughter. They seemed so free, and relaxed – as if they had nothing to think about but having a good time. It was a while since she'd felt like that.

But that was the way of things, wasn't it – she wasn't eighteen any more. She'd grown up and taken on responsibilities. She wasn't footloose – able to head off on adventures on a whim – but she didn't really want to be. She liked that she and Liam had put down roots, that her workplace was like a second home, where she saw many of the same people each day. Since her parents had made their sharp exit from her life, she'd valued every bit of security she could find. It was something she'd never take for granted again. She loved hearing about what Isla was doing, loved her friend's approach to life, embracing new experiences and meeting new people, but they were different. They'd always been different.

She thought of the conversation with Liam. A baby. A *baby*. Their baby. It was exciting and terrifying all in one bundle. But perhaps it wasn't really such a leap. They'd already settled down. They had Rebecca. Sophie imagined herself holding a tiny, fragile newborn – entirely dependent on her – and felt slightly overwhelmed at the thought. She'd never changed a nappy before, never sung a lullaby, or rocked a baby to sleep. She enjoyed spending time with her niece and nephews – her brother Daniel and his wife had accepted her relationship far more willingly than their parents had – but she'd never been called on to look after the kids when they were very young. The newborn stage was a mystery to her. But Liam would know what to do. He'd done it before. And she'd learn.

Together, perhaps they did have what it took.

*

Isla was at the central train station, looking towards the ticket gates. There was Sophie, her thick light-brown hair up in a top-knot, dragging a suitcase behind her. She called over and waved, then looked at her train ticket, creased her brow and tried to ram the card into the wrong slot on the gate. Isla dashed over. 'It's that one,' she said, pointing out the way to put it in. 'Christ, you can always tell the tourists.'

Once Sophie was through, Isla embraced her friend in a warm hug. Sophie's hair smelled of honey, the way it always had, and it blended with the soap-clean scent of her skin. That freshness was part of her, even after a journey when she must have been crammed in with other travellers.

'Welcome to Amsterdam,' Isla said.

'So good to be here,' Sophie said, her eyes bright. She looked a little serious for a moment. 'And to see you. I've missed you.'

'Me too. Long-distance relationships are hard, eh.'

'Horribly,' Sophie said. 'And now you're going to make it even harder, what with flitting off to New York. And this gorgeous man I keep hearing about, threatening to steal your affections. I'm wondering now if we've really got what it takes to last.'

'I think we stand a pretty good chance,' Isla said, smiling.

They left the station and walked together through the red-light district, with its tourist emporiums and smoke-filled coffee shops, chatting and laughing as they caught up on recent events and gossip about mutual friends. By three, they were back in Isla's apartment and settled on the sofa, and they were soon halfway through a box of macaroons and on their second round of tea.

'So – when am I going to meet Rafael?' Sophie asked,

impatiently, a glow of excitement in her cheeks. 'Please don't tell me I've come all this way and now you're going to hide him away from me.'

'I'm not hiding him,' Isla said, laughing. 'I just wanted you all to myself for a little while first. We'll go out with him tomorrow.'

'Well, I'm glad to hear it. He looks absolutely gorgeous in the photos – all dark and brooding.'

Isla laughed. 'He's not that brooding in real life. I'm trying to train him out of that photo-face. He's good fun really.'

'That makes a change,' Sophie said.

'I'm tired of bad boys. All that sulking and drama, it's exhausting, Soph. Perhaps I'm becoming a grown-up at last.'

'Oh, don't say that,' Sophie said. 'I rely on you for the vicarious adventures.'

'I guess you must,' Isla said. 'Dependable, loyal, reliable, yes. Adventurous? Not so much.'

'What is this, back-handed compliment hour?' Sophie said, laughing. 'And anyway, I can sometimes be spontaneous . . . I mean, I would be far more, if it weren't for my job.'

Isla raised an eyebrow, disbelieving.

'Well, and Liam. And Rebecca.'

Isla stayed quiet.

'What?' Sophie said, feigning fury. 'Are you suggesting I was always like this?'

'You *were* always like this, yes. Even when we were footloose and fancy-free in Bristol. Or have you forgotten? Even at parties you'd creep upstairs and be tucked up in bed and asleep by eleven p.m.'

'I had a lot of work to be getting on with. Not all of us were doing arts degrees, you know,' Sophie teased.

'It paid off, I guess. Steady job, own house.'

'Yes. With more family than I bargained for.'

'How is Rebecca doing?'

'Hard work. Pretty horrible, quite often. We are going through kind of a difficult period.'

'Why – what's she been doing?'

'She makes sly comments. So for instance just before I came here, she made it clear that she was much happier in the house when it was just her and Liam. Then sometimes she'll pretend she hasn't really said anything, that I'm just imagining it. And I do question myself. Because she's the kid, isn't she? She's still a kid. And I should be able to see past the digs and find a way to support her through whatever else it is that she's going through.'

'You said a while back that Véronique is dating again. Do you think that might be part of it? Accepting that both her parents have lives beyond her.'

'Possibly, yes. I guess that must be tough for her.'

'Hopefully it's a phase that'll pass. You always seemed to get on all right, before now.'

'We did,' Sophie said, casting her mind back. 'There were even times when we'd sit up late in her bedroom, chatting, watching stupid video clips on the iPad. Laughing together. God, I can't remember the last time we laughed together.' She felt a rush of warmth towards Rebecca, remembering how it had once been between them. All relationships needed work. This one was no different.

'How's Liam been dealing with it?'

'He's supportive.' She thought of Liam and was grateful for the way he never hesitated to back her up, and managed to do it without taking sides. 'He's firm with her – and she seems to listen to him slightly more than me. I'm hoping he might get to the bottom of it this weekend; they'll have a bit of space with me away.'

'That sounds like a good idea. Are you guys getting on OK, aside from this?'

'Yes. He's got a few issues with the way the university is run these days, with students getting to call the shots that bit more. But he's fine. We're fine.'

Sophie thought about the night she'd left, and the discussion that the two of them had. 'Liam threw me a bit of a curveball, actually – just before I came out here.'

'Yes?' Isla asked, curious.

Sophie felt uncertain about saying it out loud. It still didn't seem quite real to her that Liam could have changed his mind. 'He wants us to have a baby.'

Isla raised her eyebrows. 'Wow. That's quite the turnaround.'

'Isn't it?' Sophie said. She found she was smiling. It had been a shock. But it had been a good surprise, she was more sure of that now. 'It came out of nowhere.'

'And how do you feel about it?'

'I like that it gives us options,' Sophie said. 'I haven't completely made my mind up yet.'

'Oh, come off it,' Isla said, warmly. 'I can see you're excited.'

'OK. I am,' Sophie admitted. 'I don't quite trust in it all yet, but I am excited.'

'That's great,' Isla said. 'I'm glad for you that he's thought again about it all. Always thought you'd make a lovely mum.'

'Thank you,' Sophie said. 'I can't say I'm brimming with confidence after all this stuff with Rebecca, but hopefully it'll be different this time.'

'It will be.' Isla glanced up at the clock on her wall, showing half-eight. 'Now, all this grown-up talk is making me crave a proper drink.'

'Good idea,' Sophie said. 'I'm pretty sure it's time we switched up from tea.'

Sophie and Isla walked out into the moonlit evening, the city coming to life around them. Bicycles filled the pathways, skilfully dodging them as they walked, and tramlines criss-crossed the road ahead.

'I'll take you to my local. Lovely guy from Valencia runs it.'

They went to a Spanish bar around the corner and sat chatting as they waited for their drinks.

The owner put a carafe of wine in front of them, and a couple of plates of food. 'A few snacks for you to enjoy, on the house. I'll leave you to it. Looks like you have quite a bit to catch up on.'

'Plenty,' Isla said. 'It's been a while.'

He gave them a wink, and left.

'So what does Rafael think about you going out to the States?' Sophie said, unable to hold in her curiosity.

'I think he's more excited than me, if that's possible. He's been so supportive of my acting from day one. It makes a change. I think, deep down, that Dino always felt quite threatened by it.' Isla thought back to the days with her ex, who had sometimes made snide remarks about her acting and whether it was really going anywhere.

'I think you're right,' Sophie said. 'It takes a strong man to let a woman go out and potentially be more successful than him. I mean – who knows where New York might lead for you.'

'It's the biggest opportunity I've had so far, that's for sure. And I'm so glad Rafael's different. He's – I don't know – comfortable in his own skin, I guess. He doesn't have anything to prove.'

'He sounds great.'

'He is kind of great.' Isla smiled, recalling his response to the lists they'd written. 'He found my list on the fridge earlier this week.'

'Oh, yes? What did he make of it?'

'He liked the idea.'

'It was fun, writing those,' Sophie said, reflecting. 'Well, for me it was a bit of fun – for you it's turned into a design for life, hasn't it?'

'In a way. Don't tell me, yours is in a box somewhere. Forgotten. Am I right?'

'Oh, come on, Isla,' Sophie said. 'You know how it is . . . '

'You started that triathlon training, though, right? Do you think—'

'I don't get much time for those things these days.'

'OK, I'll lay off you,' Isla said.

'I could start the training up again, I suppose,' Sophie said.

'You should. I'd come and cheer you on if you did it. And Italian lessons. That one was doable, you could—'

'One day,' Sophie said, cutting Isla off.

'Yes. No hurry.'

Isla looked at her best friend, as she toyed with the olives on her plate. She couldn't help wanting to push Sophie to reach for the things that she'd said she wanted to do.

She knew Sophie was happy – with her job, with Liam. Things were so much better than they'd been. But sometimes Isla wondered if her friend had settled – she'd been so passionate about pursuing a career in medicine once, but, when that fell through, she'd just seemed to accept that her life would take a different path. Sophie loved Liam – you only had to spend a few hours in their company to see that their connection was real. They had something good, but Sophie still seemed to see herself as having done wrong. As if she felt she had to make reparation, give up her own happiness, to pay back for what she took. And that saddened Isla – because as people went, Sophie was one of the very best.

Sophie settled into bed that night, sleepily content and a little fuzzy-headed. It had been so good to chat with Isla, as she'd known it would. In the past ten years, no one had even come close to understanding her the way her best friend did. Whether they were talking or silent, it didn't matter. She always felt at ease around Isla.

The talk about the list had made her think, though – it had brought her face to face again with the ambitions she'd once had. Occasionally she felt as though she'd missed her chance of doing so many things. Her drive to climb her way back up to respectability, to be liked again after getting together with Liam, had consumed her for so long.

The headlines that had ended her time at medical school still sometimes rang in her ears: TOP POLITICIAN'S DAUGHTER IN UNIVERSITY AFFAIR SCANDAL.

That wasn't how it had felt to Sophie at all. Liam, a tutor from a different faculty, had always shown an interest in her. When a drink in his office ended with them together on the sofa, she hadn't really known how to stop it. She hadn't been sure she even wanted to. They'd never spoken about his family. It was only when she was already in deep that she'd seen the whole picture.

When Sophie's mother found out, she had been furious. Sophie knew that, though her mother had tried hard not to let it show – no trace of human emotion in her features, not even a twist of her thin-lipped mouth to indicate how she was feeling. Her father compensated, showing feeling enough for the two of them. To him, Sophie was a disgrace. He was a respected MP and couldn't afford for her actions to jeopardise his good reputation. He did what he could to gloss over it, and over time most people forgot the story – but he never did.

Sophie's parents had shut the door behind her. Those years of sitting nicely at dinner, studying hard, getting onto a good course – none of it meant a thing now. Aside from the contact with Daniel, she'd said goodbye to being part of her family again a long time ago now.

Some days she felt she was doing pretty well in her life. Other days, it didn't feel much like that at all.

Having a family of her own might finally change things. That was something that she could do to truly wipe the slate clean.

The next morning, Isla woke her friend gently by delivering a cup of tea to her bedside.

'Rise and shine,' she said. 'We've got a big day ahead of us.'

Sophie rubbed her eyes. She'd woken with Isla's voice but still thought she needed to be ready to head over to work. Then it dawned on her, pleasingly, that she was on holiday, with nothing to do that day but relax.

After breakfast they headed downstairs, to where Rafael was waiting by the front door. 'Hey!' Isla called out to him.

Sophie went to shake his hand, but he brought her in towards him in a warm hug. 'Nice to meet you at last,' he said, kindly. She felt instantly at home with him. 'So, Isla told me it's your first time here, is that right?' he asked.

'Yes – it is. It's been a while since I went abroad.'

'I thought we could see it the way it's meant to be seen – from the water,' he said, with a smile. He motioned to a red and yellow boat moored a couple of metres away.

'Great. Is that yours?' Sophie said.

'It's a friend's. Borrowed it for a day. I stick to the book-shop variety.'

They climbed on board, Sophie steadying herself against Isla as she left the safety of the canalside.

'I brought a few things for lunch,' Rafael said, motioning to a large hamper overflowing with food and bottles.

'That's Rafael's usual idea of a bit of lunch,' Isla said, laughing. 'Hence why I've put on half a stone since I met him.'

'I believe in enjoying life,' he said. 'Don't you agree, Sophie?'

Sophie looked around her at the sun glinting off the water, the beautiful narrow houses that lined the banks, the city laid out for them to explore. It had been a while, but in that moment a new resolution formed.

'I do,' Sophie said, with a smile.

They spent hours out on the water that day, Rafael point-ing out the local sights and landmarks, and Sophie and Isla listening while they contentedly ate their way through the hamper. When day faded into evening, they chose a restaurant by the waterside. Sophie got to talk to Rafael a little more then – about the bookshop, and how it had been getting started up in a whole new country – and she warmed to him. He seemed always to be looking out for Isla – giving her his coat when the temperature dropped, making sure she had a full glass – Isla was right, he was very different from the men she'd chosen before. In place of ego was a natural kind of caring. She and Liam were far past that honeymoon stage, where small gestures and affectionate hugs could light you up from the inside, and, while she was happy for Isla, she also found herself missing it a little.

At midnight, Sophie and Isla said goodbye to Rafael and went upstairs into Isla's apartment.

'So – what did you think?' Isla said, as soon as the front door was shut and Rafael was no longer in earshot.

'Gorgeous. Like you described him, but better.'

'You think so?'

'Absolutely. You guys are great together, and he seems like a keeper.'

Isla felt a warm glow spread through her. 'That's kind of what I'm hoping too.'

'Not that you really care,' Sophie joked, repeating back Isla's mantra of the past few years when it came to romance.

'Exactly. Not that I really care.'

'OK, well, I don't know about you, but I think I'll sleep well tonight. I'm wiped out.'

'Same here,' Isla said. 'See you in the morning.'

Sophie went to the bedroom and Isla sat back on the sofa. She felt content and relaxed after the day they'd had together. Out on the boat with Sophie and Rafael, she'd felt as if her whole world was there. The little pieces of her were falling into place.

The things that mattered were going well. There was only that small thing that she kept pushing to the back of her mind.

She shifted to try to stop the tingling sensation in her feet. It was part of what she'd started to think of as 'the strangeness'. The minor physical quirks that were short-stay tenants in her body, their visits over the past year or so fleeting, but unsettling. Almost as soon as she noticed them – the tingling, or numbness in her hands and feet – the moment she tried to pin them down and identify them, make sense of them, they would pass. She'd forget about them, get back to her daily life. But then they would come back. They kept coming back.

The following morning, a Monday, Sophie and Isla went out for breakfast, cycling across the city. They found a little coffee shop and ordered hot chocolate and blueberry pancakes.

'I wish I could go to the gallery with you today,' Isla said. 'But I promised the others I'd spend the morning flyering for the show. We really want to get a full house over the weekend, when we should have some more reviewers coming in.'

'Don't worry, I understand. I didn't expect normal life to grind to a halt just because I've come to visit,' Sophie said. 'And I know it's an important time for you.'

'Mad really: six months here and there are so many places I still haven't seen. I haven't got to the Rijksmuseum or the Anne Frank house yet.'

'Craziness,' Sophie replied. 'Clearly you haven't been

prioritising properly. All that time, you know, falling in love and stuff, and totally ignoring the culture.'

A warm feeling spread through Isla's chest. They hadn't said it out loud yet. She thought she'd seen it in Rafael's eyes recently – and she was surer each day that she felt it herself. But it was good to hear it said out loud, even if it was someone else saying it.

'You can tell, then.'

'Of course I can,' Sophie said. 'Hard to miss. The way you're staring at each other dewy-eyed. Already finishing each other's sentences. It's pretty obvious.'

'We haven't actually said it to each other yet,' Isla said, feeling suddenly shy.

'It won't be long, by the looks of things.'

'God, I feel about thirteen right now,' Isla said, laughing. 'He's special, Soph. No flashiness, nothing to prove. No games.'

'How refreshing.'

Isla thought back on all the energy she'd wasted trying to second-guess what other boyfriends had been thinking. 'Yes, it is.'

'You told your mum about him yet?' Sophie asked.

'Yes, a bit. I didn't want her getting too excited – you know what an old romantic she is.'

'I miss your mum. It's been a while. I don't have as many excuses to see her these days.'

'You know she'd love to hear from you. She always asks how you're getting on.'

'I should call her. I'll call her. How is she, anyway? Any romance of her own at the moment?'

'No – nothing. Just working long hours at the

supermarket, I'm not sure how much chance she gets really. She's coming over before I go to the States – she wants to see the show again. Or at least that's what she's saying. I suspect it might have a little to do with wanting to check Rafael out.'

'Probably a little of both.'

'I think so.'

'I'm looking forward to seeing the show tonight,' Sophie said. 'Rafael tells me it's brilliant.'

'Totally biased,' Isla said, laughing. 'But it's not bad, I'll say that much. There must be something in it anyway, what with us going to New York and everything.'

'I'll come back to the apartment later. Catch you for an early dinner then, before you head over?'

'Sure. Enjoy the cultural highlights. And tell me everything so I can bluff my way next time someone asks me what I've seen over here.'

Later that morning, when Isla had finished handing out flyers for the show on the main street, she called in to see Rafael at the boat.

Berenice was there with him. 'Hi,' Isla said. 'How are you?' Berenice was often in the shop, and Isla had come to know her quite well in the time she'd been with Rafael. She was a kind woman, and a true British eccentric, and Isla always enjoyed their chats.

'Very well, my dear,' Berenice said. 'I've made some flapjacks.' She patted her bag. 'Thought they could probably find a welcome home with you two.'

'Thanks, B.'

'When I arrived here from England – twenty-five years

ago now – I had a Dutch husband back then, and there were times when I missed home. Flapjacks were my way of travelling there,' Berenice said.

'I know exactly what you mean,' Isla said. 'I've been known to cook up batches of scones far too big for me to eat, just so that I can get that smell of home.'

'Ha. Yes – that's why I need my surrogate grandson here,' Berenice said. 'I can do the cooking, but I certainly shouldn't do all the eating myself.'

Berenice opened the tin, and they all took one to eat. It melted in a pool of sweetness on Isla's tongue, energising and reviving her after the busy morning.

'They're good,' Rafael said.

'How did you manage to get so lucky, Rafa?' Isla said.

'All I did was sell her a few books, and then the cakes started to come in.'

'Oh, you've done a lot more than sell me books, Rafael, and you know it.' Berenice smiled. 'When this shop opened, it changed this stretch of canal. It used to be so quiet. I don't like quiet, Isla. Never have. When Hans died there was suddenly far too much of it. But Rafael's door was always open. We got talking, over morning coffee, and, well ... '

'The rest is history,' Rafael said. 'She's my favourite customer but a whole lot more too.'

'The only problem is, he's too good a listener,' Berenice said. 'Sometimes I realise I haven't asked a thing about him.'

'I know the feeling,' Isla said. She still felt as if she'd barely scratched the surface with Rafael. He insisted that there wasn't much to tell, when it came to his life, his past, his family – that he believed in living in the present. But

53

she was curious all the same, and hoped that over time he'd start to open up.

'How is your acting going, Isla?' Berenice asked. 'This one tells me you're off to America soon.'

'Good, thanks,' Isla said, feeling proud of her news. 'And I am – in September. I've a friend staying at the moment – Sophie – but after that I'll be starting to get things ready. It's something I've always dreamed of – well, same goes for all of us in the theatre group.'

'It sounds wonderful. And you must do these things, while you've got youth on your side. He'll miss you though, that's for sure.'

'Berenice,' Rafael said, embarrassed.

'It's true,' Berenice said. 'Listen, I can't stay here chattering this morning: the market will be closed soon and I've got my veg still to buy. You enjoy your friend's visit, Isla, and make sure to save her a flapjack, won't you.'

After Berenice left, Isla and Rafael were alone in the shop together. He looked at her, his gaze intense, then reached out to take her hand. He brought her in close to him and held her there. She savoured the connection, curled into his chest and took in the warm, slightly spicy smell of him. Two months – it wasn't a long time, not at all. But in that short period of time her life, and her happiness, had become inextricably linked with his.

'She's right, of course,' Rafael said, pulling away a little and stroking back a strand of Isla's hair. 'I will miss you. A lot.'

'Same here,' she said. With someone else, pride might have crept in and kept her silent, but she didn't feel the need to hold back with Rafael.

'In the meantime,' he said, 'seeing as you are still

here – could you do me a favour? I've got to run to the bank and get some change. Mind the shop for twenty minutes? I don't think it will get much busier than this.'

'Sure,' Isla said.

He went over to the till and opened it, getting some notes out, then shut the drawer again.

Isla joined him at the counter and played with the buttons on the till, causing the tray to jump out again with a loud ping. 'I've always liked playing shop.'

She picked up the telephone, and answered, mimicking Rafael's accent. 'Good afternoon, the Floating Bookshop.'

'OK, great. You're hired,' he said, putting the euro notes in his wallet. 'See you in a bit. I'll bring us some lunch back.'

'I've heard about this, you know, foreigners over here getting exploited for cheap labour . . . '

'Not cheap. Free.' He silenced her protest with a kiss, and then said goodbye.

With the shop to herself, Isla put on some music and tidied the display tables, placing each book carefully and smiling to herself.

Then, with no prior warning, a wave of dizziness swept over her. The room spun, and Isla held on to the edge of the table in an attempt to regain her balance. Her heart raced as she tried to work out what was happening to her. Her control over her legs had gone. The colours of book spines and posters blurred into one, then she lost her grip and fell to the floor. There was a knock as her head struck the corner of the table, but she heard the sound distantly, as if it were all happening to someone else. Then the pain hit. Finally, a thud, as her body met the floor.

*

Sophie was looking at *Sunflowers*. Bright yellow and uplifting, full of energy and colour, giving little clue to Van Gogh's tormented mind. She'd been walking around the museum for most of the morning, enjoying the peace, and the luxury of having her phone switched off. Anything Rebecca needed was in Liam's hands this week, and, with the responsibility lifting from her shoulders, she felt light.

What would it be like – being pregnant, if that happened for them? Being parents, watching their own daughter or son grow up from a baby to a toddler and then into a child of Rebecca's age? Here, on her own, away from everyday life, the vision formed, and it made her smile. Perhaps there was time still, for them to have another kind of life.

She turned to walk into the next room in the gallery, caught up in her thoughts. Then a feeling stopped her. Something wasn't right.

Without pausing to question what it might be, she left the gallery and walked, her pace almost a jog, in the direction of Isla's home.

Chapter 4

Isla drifted back to consciousness on the floor of the book-shop and saw an elderly lady leaning over her. She could make out the blue of her eyes, the gently wrinkled skin and the concerned expression on the woman's face. Then the hair, a white-grey, came into focus.

'Berenice,' Isla said, softly.

'Oh, Isla. What happened?'

'I fell, I think.' Isla summoned every last trace of energy in her body and pulled herself up to a seated position. She rubbed her temples, trying to wake herself up again.

Berenice brought over a glass of water and Isla sipped at the cool liquid.

'How long was I lying there like that?'

'Can't have been more than five minutes. I left my bag here and I realised on the way over to the market. I came back and found you.'

'Thank you,' Isla said, feeling dazed.

'I think we should call you a doctor.'

'I'm fine,' Isla insisted.

Rafael came in through the door, and when he realised something was wrong he was by Isla's side in a moment.

'She says she's fine, but I don't believe her,' Berenice said. 'Took a nasty knock to the head.'

'You're bleeding.' Rafael went to the sink out in the back of the shop, and brought out a clean wet cloth. He bathed the side of her head carefully, the touch reassuring and refreshingly cool. Isla felt her strength coming back little by little.

Berenice made tea and Rafael slowly helped Isla up and into a chair. Isla spotted a familiar figure walking past the doorway of the shop and nudged Rafael. 'That's Soph. Go and call her in, will you? She doesn't know I'm here.'

He nodded and went over.

'Sophie!' Rafael called out from the door of the bookshop, beckoning her inside. 'Isla's in here.'

Sophie dashed over.

Isla was propped up in a chair, her face pale and her lips so light they almost blended into her skin. 'I'm fine,' she said. She pointed to the biscuit in her hand. 'Bit of sugar will sort me out. It was the shock more than anything.'

'She fell,' Rafael explained. 'Hit her head.'

'Thank God you're OK,' Sophie said, wrapping her arms around her friend. 'I had this feeling. This weird feeling. Anyway, I don't usually believe in this stuff, but I just knew.'

'And I always thought I was the hippy one.' Isla forced a smile. 'Anyway, you don't need to worry. Just a knock.'

'If you say so.'

'You'll have something to drink too, right, Sophie?' Rafael said.

'Thanks,' Sophie said. She turned back to her friend. 'How are you feeling now, Isla?'

'OK, I think. Still a little bit dizzy, but mostly fine.'

'You fell, and then hit your head, right?' Sophie asked.

Isla nodded.

'So, what – you tripped over something?'

Isla looked confused. 'No – I don't think I did. One minute I felt fine, then my legs gave way. Everything went blurry, and then I fell.'

Sophie's concern grew, but she didn't let it show. She didn't want to worry Isla or the others unnecessarily.

'Have you been feeling OK in general?' she enquired gently.

'Yes . . . a bit more tired than usual, I suppose – but then the performance schedule has been pretty full on.'

'We should go and get you checked out,' Sophie said. 'It's probably nothing, but obviously you don't want to mess around if this is concussion.'

'Really?' Isla said, wrinkling her nose. 'I mean – I know you're probably right, but Sophie – I don't want to waste the time that you're here sitting in a germ-filled waiting room.'

'As it happens, that's *exactly* what I want to do today,' Sophie said, smiling. 'Come on, let's get it out of the way. I'm sure we'll still have time for sightseeing.'

When Sophie and Isla arrived at the hospital, Isla had initial checks for concussion, which she was cleared for. She'd remained slightly unsteady on her feet, though, and the doctor sent her for a CT scan.

59

'You've come from one hospital back in England and just ended up in another,' Isla said to Sophie, wryly. 'And after all those promises I made of the fun we'd have.'

'I feel right at home,' Sophie said, smiling.

'This scan seems a bit unnecessary,' Isla said. 'So I'm still feeling a little wobbly, but that's hardly unusual, surely? They said I wasn't concussed, didn't they?'

'They just want to be certain.' Sophie said. 'You were unconscious for a while, and you've not bounced back completely yet. They need to check there isn't any bleeding on the brain – sounds a bit scary, I know, but I'm sure you'll be fine. It's a precaution.'

'I'm not worried,' Isla said. 'I'm actually too tired to be worried. Just frustrated. Aside from the time I hoped to spend with you, I'm missing a performance to be here.'

A message buzzed through on Isla's phone, from Rafael.

Hi. Everything OK? Rx

Yes, she typed back. **I should be out soon. I'll call you. xx**

'He really wanted to come in with you,' Sophie said.

'I know.'

'Maybe you should have let him.'

'No – he's got the shop to think of – and this is taking forever. Anyway, I'm pretty sure nothing kills the honeymoon period like a hospital gown.' She looked down at hers, and the two of them laughed.

'Miss Rafferty?' A nurse called out.

Isla looked up.

'If you could just follow me, I'll take you through to the scanning room.'

'Do you want me to come with you?' Sophie asked.

'Yes.'

In the scanning room the technician talked Isla through the procedure. She could hear Sophie chatting with someone, and the familiarity of her friend's voice soothed her.

A doctor came in, and assured her there wasn't any sign of a bleed. 'We'll have a closer look, and call you next week with those details.'

'Thanks,' Isla said. 'This was all just a precaution, right?'

'Yes,' he said. 'There's nothing else you wanted to tell us, is there – anything physical you've experienced recently that's been out of the ordinary?'

Isla thought of the occasional numbness and tingling she'd felt in her hands and feet over the past few months. The way a couple of times her legs had weakened and given way – as they had the day of the fall. Those weren't the kind of symptoms he was talking about, though – they could have been anything. He was clearly looking for signs of something serious. 'No, nothing. Other than the slight wobbliness after the fall, which was probably shock. I'm well.'

'OK. Right,' he said straightforwardly, closing her file. 'We'll be in touch, then.'

Isla and Sophie walked back to the apartment together. The cool breeze was a welcome change after the time spent in the airless hospital.

'I want to stay,' Sophie said. 'At least until you get the all-clear.'

'There's no need.' Isla shook her head. 'Really. I'll call and let you know.'

'I want to. It's only a couple of days extra, and it'll mean leaving with my mind at rest, knowing that everything's all right with you.'

'But what about your work?'

'I'll call and speak to my boss this afternoon. I haven't had a holiday in years; hopefully extending it by a day or two isn't going to make much difference. I guess being away – and things not falling apart, or at least not that I know of – has made me realise I'm not completely indispensable.' She smiled. 'Close to it, but not completely.'

'Well – if you insist, it would be nice to have you here a little longer,' Isla said.

'I do. More time with you, and the certainty that I'm leaving you fit and well. It's an entirely selfish choice really.'

Isla looped her arm through her friend's. The thought of Sophie staying with her a while longer lifted her spirits a little. She still felt in shock at the turn the past few hours had taken – one minute everything calm and normal, and the next her having a brain scan. Sophie was a steady, familiar presence, and she needed that. 'Thanks, Soph.'

'Let's stop for coffee and cake on the way home,' Sophie said. 'I think we've both earned it.'

Sophie called Liam that evening.

'Hey, how's Amsterdam?' he asked brightly.

'Beautiful. Nice people, good food, tons of culture. I can see why Isla's so attached to this place.'

'Sounds perfect – and a damn sight more exciting than my weekend. I can't wait to have you back.'

'I'm afraid that's why I'm calling,' Sophie said. 'I'm really sorry about this, but I'm going to stay a few more days. It's a long story, but Isla had an accident—'

'God – what happened? Is she OK?'

'Yes, she's fine, but she fell over and had a nasty knock on the head, and they've done a CT scan to be sure.'

'Right ... OK. I understand. We can always celebrate another time.'

'Oh, jeez.' It clicked. 'I'm sorry. Our anniversary. The restaurant.'

'It doesn't matter,' Liam said. 'This is more important. You stay there with Isla; it's not long. We can rearrange.'

Sophie felt a pang of guilt. 'I'll make it up to you, I promise.'

'Sure,' Liam said. 'We can work something out when you're home.'

It wasn't just any anniversary, Sophie realised, biting her lip – it was their ten-year anniversary. Ten years since they'd taken those first steps into married life together, defying the people who disapproved of their relationship. Ten years in which they hadn't failed, as some friends and relatives had predicted, but instead carried on loving each other, being there for one another and enjoying each other's company. Yet Sophie had been so caught up in worrying about Isla that she'd completely forgotten about it.

Isla was grateful that Sophie had stayed on. Small things made a big difference, like Sophie cooking her dinner and choosing films for them to watch in the evening. Her friend was proving to be the perfect distraction while they waited for the scan results. That night, Rafael came by and joined them.

'I brought popcorn,' he said, holding up a box.

'Great.' Isla took it from him and gestured to a space on the sofa.

She went into the kitchen to get them all drinks. Sophie and Rafael greeted each other. They were talking, but in whispers, and with music on in the background Isla could barely hear them.

She stood closer to the doorway and caught the occasional word from Sophie – *results, precaution, hospital*. She didn't mind that Sophie was talking to him about what had happened. She'd meant to herself, just hadn't really found the moment to fill Rafael in. It was easier to have him assume she was just making the most of her last days with Sophie.

Then she heard Rafael's voice, soft and sincere. 'When you leave, you know, don't you, that I'll be here for her.'

On Tuesday morning, Isla got a call from the hospital asking her to come in for an appointment to discuss the CT scan.

She turned to Sophie, who was sitting with her coffee by the window, looking out at the canal. 'That was the hospital,' Isla said, feeling a little numb. 'Eleven-thirty, they want to see me.'

'Right, let's go and get this over with,' Sophie said. 'Then you can get back to packing your bags for New York, and I can get back to romancing my husband and pretending I didn't forget our anniversary.' She smiled, and took Isla's hand. 'It'll be fine, you know.'

They took the long route to the hospital, winding through the bustle of the weekday fruit and vegetable market on the way. They'd stayed up till around midnight the previous night, talking with Rafael.

'Rafael really cares about you,' Sophie said. 'He seems very genuine.'

'I know,' Isla said. 'I think he is.'

Sophie paused. 'You'll let him in, won't you? Tell him how today goes? I know he'll be thinking of you.'

'Of course,' Isla said.

The previous night in bed they'd talked about the film, laughing together as she explained some of the bits he hadn't understood. His English was good – if you spoke to him for a short time you might not even notice his accent – but there were still nuances in his second language that he missed, phrases and slang, and she liked that she could shed light on those. He hadn't asked her about the hospital, and she hadn't said anything – he knew enough from what Sophie had said, and it was nicer for her to be able to relax and forget about it for a while.

Sophie looked at Isla, and smiled. 'I'm glad you met him. I know you were happy before, but it seems like he's been good for you.'

'He is,' Isla said. 'I never thought I'd say this about a man, Soph, but I think he might be the best thing that's happened to me.'

At the hospital, Isla and Sophie met with a consultant, a man in his fifties. He got Isla's details up on screen.

'Thanks for coming in this morning, Miss Rafferty. I've had a chance to look at your CT scan more closely, and that's why I've called you back in today. Something doesn't look quite right – there are no signs of a bleed, but there are a couple of shadows. We'd like to do an MRI, to be sure.'

'But why?' Isla asked. 'Because really, I'm absolutely sure I'm not concussed. I think that was a false alarm. I'm feeling OK now.'

'No, it's nothing to do with that. But there's something showing up here I'm not entirely happy with, and I'd like to explore it further. I'm going to book you in for the MRI scan later this week,' the consultant said. 'So that we can get to the bottom of this.'

'I can't,' Isla said, instinctively.

The consultant looked surprised.

'I'm busy,' she said, quickly. She turned to Sophie. 'You know, rehearsals and then—'

'I think you might have to make time,' the consultant replied, gently.

'Can we arrange this for a few weeks' time? I'm going away for a while. That's if you really think it's necessary – I feel fine, honestly.'

She couldn't help thinking that if she hadn't come in to hospital after the fall, if they hadn't insisted on scanning her, she would be carrying on with her life, exactly as before. 'There's no need.'

Sophie looked at her, concern in her dark brown eyes. 'Isla,' she said, softly. 'This is important.'

'So's the play. I'm not changing my plans, Soph. You know how much this means to me.'

'We can't make you do anything you don't want to do,' the consultant said.

'Exactly,' Isla said to Sophie. 'Hear that? They aren't going to force me.'

'But, Miss Rafferty, I really would strongly advise that we look into these apparent anomalies properly, to rule out anything serious.'

'Isla,' Sophie said, quietly but firmly, 'I know you don't want to hear this. But please listen to him.'

Isla could almost ignore the consultant's words – but not Sophie's.

'What's going on?' she said to Sophie, fear rushing in. 'Why is this happening?'

Sophie put a hand on her leg, and tried to calm her. 'It may well be nothing.'

Tears welled up in Isla's eyes and she brushed them away roughly. 'It doesn't sound like nothing,' she said. The autumn months she'd pictured – out in New York, performing on Broadway – seemed to be fading before her eyes. 'The show ... what if I can't go?'

She turned back to the consultant. 'When do you think you'll have the answers you need?'

'It might be immediate, or it might take longer. I can't say at this point,' he replied.

'Don't take a chance with this,' Sophie said. 'You have to find out if there's a problem.'

Sophie was the voice of reason, of sense – and her friend was pleading with her to take the consultant's advice seriously. Isla wanted desperately to walk away; she wanted to go somewhere quiet and calm and forget all about hospitals and scans. But the concern in Sophie's eyes told her it was already too late. She couldn't hide from this.

On the walk home from the hospital, Isla was quiet. Sophie tried to lift the atmosphere, talking about anything but the hospital appointment, but Isla's replies were monosyllabic and distant. Finally she suggested they got a takeaway from the local Thai restaurant and Isla agreed. Half an hour later they were back at the apartment, sitting in Isla's living room on the sofa, eating noodles and sipping from bottles of beer.

Sophie could see the worry etched into her friend's brow, and she longed to be able to take it away. But all she could do for now was be there. And perhaps, she thought, to make sure that Isla had support if the tests were to go on after the time she'd left.

'Do you think you should call Rafael?' Sophie asked, gently. She knew it was probably not what Isla wanted to hear – but she also felt sure Rafael would want to know what was going on, and how Isla was feeling. She didn't want to think of Isla being alone during the medical processes after she went home.

Isla shrugged. 'Nope.'

Sophie looked her friend in the eye. 'So he doesn't know anything?'

'No. But do we?' Isla said, a little snappily.

Sophie raised an eyebrow at her friend's tone.

'Sorry,' Isla said. She rubbed her forehead. 'Today threw me a bit, I guess. I'll call him. Let him know I'm OK. That there's another scan they want to do.'

'Look, I don't want to interfere, it's your life – but I just know he'll be thinking about you, wondering if everything's OK—'

Isla frowned. 'I don't have that answer, though, do I? All I know is that there's some ... what? ... *anomaly*. Something they don't understand yet. Something that might throw a massive spanner in the works when it comes to this New York trip.'

'Or might not—' Sophie said, softly.

They fell quiet for a moment.

'I wish I could stay longer,' Sophie said. 'I don't like leaving you with things still unresolved.'

'Don't worry about it,' Isla said. 'You need to get back to work. And Liam.' She smiled a little, and while the curl of her lips clearly hadn't come easily, it seemed genuine. 'And all that baby-making stuff.'

Sophie wrinkled her nose. 'Don't put it that way. God, you're like an embarrassing mum.'

They laughed, and the tension eased. The strain in Isla's face lessened, and she looked calmer.

'But it's true, Soph. You have your own life to be getting on with. Don't worry about me. I'm a big girl.'

Sophie looked at her friend in her checked pyjamas and fluffy slippers, curled up on the sofa. Her dark hair was held back from her face with a wide hairband, her face free of make-up. There was a vulnerability in her eyes. In that moment, she didn't look much older than when they'd first met.

'I'd feel better about going if I knew you were going to talk to Rafael about this,' Sophie said. 'He wants to support you.'

'I know,' Isla said. 'I will.'

'Promise me you won't try and do this by yourself?' Sophie said. 'I don't want you going through this on your own.'

'I'll tell him,' Isla said.

Sophie tried to read Isla's expression, but it didn't give anything away. She didn't want to leave, not until they had more answers. She put her hand on her friend's arm. 'I might be in a different country but I'll always be there. Any time. Don't forget that.'

Chapter 5

Sophie got back to Bennett Street on Thursday night, just past midnight. The house was quiet and she wheeled her suitcase into the kitchen. Her eyes met with chaos – a sink full of dishes, and countertops heaving with dirty plates. She took a breath and tried to shake off her irritation. It didn't matter that Liam hadn't cleared up. And if they were going to start trying for a baby, she'd have to get used to a bit of mess.

Sophie went up to the bedroom, Liam's sleeping figure diagonal across the bed. She laid her things down on the carpeted floor quietly and slipped into bed beside him, embraced the familiar warmth of his back and shoulders.

She wanted to relax into being back home but she felt restless. As she lay there in the near-blackness, all she could think of was Isla. *Please let this be nothing. Let her be OK.*

*

The next morning, Liam woke Sophie gently and brought her in close. 'You're back,' he said, kissing her head. 'I didn't even hear you come in.'

'Yes, I sneaked in last night. You were dead to the world.' She'd lain awake for a while, and then finally dozed off holding him. He hadn't woken, but his presence was enough to silence her worries for just long enough for her to drift off to sleep.

'Did you miss me, then?' she asked, cheekily.

'A ridiculous amount.' He kissed her, and she felt glad to be home.

'Me too. I'm so sorry ... about the dinner. Not getting back in time for us to celebrate together.'

'Don't worry about it.' He smoothed back a strand of her hair. 'You had a good reason. How did things go, with Isla?'

Sophie recalled the meeting at the hospital and how Isla had been afterwards, shocked and quiet. 'There's nothing conclusive yet.'

'But what, there's definitely something the matter?' Liam looked concerned.

'They don't know. The consultant saw something on a CT scan that he wants to investigate. She's going in for an MRI.'

'God. What about New York?'

'Her plans are a little up in the air at the moment.'

'Poor Isla. She must be gutted.' He shook his head. 'It's good that you were there with her to keep her spirits up.'

Sophie hoped that – if nothing else – she'd been able to do that for her friend. She couldn't fix things, but she could distract her. Even from here, she could do a little of that.

'How was everything here?' Sophie asked.

'Good. Pretty quiet. The weather was awful. Me and Rebecca mostly stayed in, watched DVDs.'

'Did you have a chance to talk to her properly?'

'Kind of.' He looked a little defeated. 'Can't say I really made much progress, though. I mean, I asked how things were at school, with friends ... but she was quite vague. I'll talk to Véronique this week, see if she knows anything more.'

'That's a good idea.' There wasn't a magic solution, but at least they were moving forward, Sophie thought. 'I'm sure Rebecca enjoyed being with you, anyway. Maybe that's what she's been crying out for.'

'You might be right. I guess I have been quite consumed by work lately.' He paused, glancing over at his laptop, open next to a pile of papers on the desk by the window. 'It was good to have some quieter time with her.'

'The party over the road didn't keep you up, then?'

'No, thankfully – we barely heard a thing.'

'They call themselves students,' Sophie said. Memories came back to her, bringing about a smile. 'Even Isla and I partied hard enough to get a couple of noise complaints, back in the day.'

'You two were quite something, back then. Was it good to see Isla again?'

'The best,' Sophie said. 'I wish we hadn't had to be in hospital for some of it, obviously, but we still had some really good time together.' It had been a wrench leaving her, not knowing when they might next be in the same country together. 'I miss her, Liam – you know that. But I've left her in safe hands, at least – she's met a really nice guy. Rafael.'

'He's good enough?' Liam asked, surprised.

'I actually think so,' Sophie said, with a smile.

'I never thought I'd hear you say that.'

'Come on, it's not just me. She had a real knack for picking them – you met a few. Remember Dino?' Sophie said, raising an eyebrow.

'Yep. I wasn't particularly sorry to see him go,' Liam said. 'Did he talk about anything other than his motorbike?'

'I guess she wasn't ready to settle down back then. She's certainly in a different place now.'

Sophie went quiet for a moment, thinking about Isla. Everything was going so well for her – the play, Rafael. Please don't let anything ruin this for her, she thought to herself.

'Have you thought about what I mentioned?' Liam asked.

Sophie's thoughts returned to her own life. The baby. He was talking about the baby. 'Yes, I have. A lot.' She had started to warm to the idea, and felt surer now that it was something she wanted. Another week or so, and she was fairly sure she'd be ready.

'And?' he asked. There was hope and excitement in his eyes.

It was the same hope and excitement that she felt.

'Give me another week,' she said. 'just to think things over. But my heart says we go for it.'

After Isla had waved Sophie off at the train station, everything felt different; heavier somehow. She went along to rehearsals as normal, performed as well as she could. The buzz was building in the theatre group about their upcoming trip, and she joined in with that excitement. But inside she felt slow and tired. Only half-present. She missed Sophie's lightness, her energy, her laughter.

Rafael called, and they fixed a date for the weekend. 'I'm taking you somewhere special,' he promised. It was enough to lift her spirits. She hadn't spoken to him about the scans, and part of her didn't want to. She wanted to keep a small space in her life that could remain happy and light, where thoughts of her health weren't the dominant ones.

She knew she couldn't keep it from her mum, though. She called her and told her about the fall and the scan she was booked in for. She'd kept the call short and to the point. Her mum's voice wobbled a little. Isla told her not to worry – that she herself wasn't worried. The doctors were just making sure. Covering themselves. Medical care was good here.

That night she woke at three, when the night was dark and too quiet, and errant thoughts crept in. From nowhere an adrenalin rush flooded her system. She sat bolt upright, restless, her heart racing. They'd seen something, on her brain, she thought. Something was wrong with her. Her catastrophic thoughts gathered energy, skipping ahead of anything rational. It could be anything – she panicked – a tumour? She could be dying. She wished Sophie were still there, wished she could go into the next room and wake her friend, just to hear the comforting sound of her voice. She needed someone to help her make these thoughts go away.

She lifted her phone – she couldn't call Sophie, not now. Rafael? He wouldn't mind the late-night call – but, no. How could she tell him now, in the middle of the night, that something might be wrong? That instead of sending her home with the all-clear, the doctors were still investigating?

That she was possibly somehow damaged, broken. She didn't even know how. This wasn't how she wanted to be with him – anxious and panicked and with nothing concrete to say about what was wrong.

She texted her mum, instead. **I hope I didn't worry you. I'm sure it's nothing.**

She got a reply a few minutes later, even though it was the middle of the night.

> **OK, sweetie. Let me know when you know more. I love you.**

I love you too, she wrote, and sent the message.

She hesitated, then typed again. **Mum, I'm scared.**

She deleted the message without sending it. Then she put her phone down.

Don't be. That's what her mum would have said. And it was all she wanted to hear.

Rafael picked her up at the flat. 'It's good to see you,' he said, kissing her.

'You too.' She looked down at her outfit – black skinny jeans and boots, a turquoise top with silver jewellery. 'Am I OK like this?'

'Yes, you're absolutely right like that. I thought we could go to Rosa's tonight.'

Isla brightened instantly. It was a cocktail bar she'd been longing to visit ever since she arrived, but which was way out of her price range. 'Excellent.'

They got a taxi over, and Rafael ordered margaritas for them.

'Almost as good as they make them in Mexico,' he said, taking a sip.

'I hope one day I get to try the ones there too.'

'I hope so too,' he said. There was a slightly distant look in his eyes.

'You didn't have to do this, you know,' Isla said. 'I'd be happy eating a Big Mac in the station with you.' It was true. It was the normal things they'd done together – bike rides or tea in bed – that made her the happiest.

'I know that,' he smiled. 'But I think you deserve a bit more than that at the moment. All that stuff in the hospital – I'm so glad it's over.'

She forced a smile. 'Yes. What a relief.'

'It's not long till you go away, either. Let me spoil you a bit.'

'Worried I won't come back?' she said, relieved about the change of subject.

'Maybe a little,' Rafael said. 'It's going to go well for you out there. I know it. You're ready to make a mark.'

Her thoughts were in conflict with each other. Was she fooling herself, and the man she loved, by continuing to dream this dream? Or was keeping hold of it the only way of giving it a chance to happen?

'Rafael—' she started. It wasn't too late to backtrack. Tell him about the MRI scan, at least. Let him know that her plan for the autumn might have to change. 'The thing is, I don't know ... there's a chance things might not work out, with the play, with going away.'

'Come on,' he said kindly, misinterpreting her. 'You're always doubting yourself. Don't. It's happening. You're going to be great. We all know that. Trust in yourself.'

If only it were that straightforward, she thought. Nothing was that straightforward any more.

On Monday night, Isla poured all the energy and emotion she had been keeping inside into her performance. Backstage, when the curtains had closed, the other actors gathered around her.

'You killed it!' Alec said. 'The audience adored you.'

'It's great to see you back on form,' Greta said. 'That was fantastic.'

'I could never have done that,' said Annabel, a younger member of the cast who was also her understudy. 'All I can do is watch and learn.' Her eyes shone with admiration.

'Thank you,' Isla said, politely.

'Let's go for a drink – celebrate,' Alec said. The others agreed, and talked about where to go.

'I've got a couple of phone calls to make,' she said. It wasn't true, but she couldn't quite face the pub. 'I might catch you later on.'

A few minutes later, the others left. She went over to the mirror and began wiping off her stage make-up. Bit by bit the person she'd been out there in front of the audience was disappearing. She felt like a complete fraud.

Wednesday came around and she went back to the hospital for the MRI scan. She just had to play the game and get out of the system here, she told herself. A nurse led her over to the scanning tunnel. She lay down and it moved slowly, a noisy cocoon. She fought back the sensation of claustrophobia, and wished that Sophie were there. Inside the tunnel she could feel her heart thudding in her chest.

Afterwards, she sat down in the consultant's office, and waited for her details to come up on his screen. *Just play the game, get out, get to New York*, she reminded herself.

'We've got a bit more to go on now,' he said. 'The scan is showing some lesions.'

His words took the air right out of the room.

'What?' She forced the word out, needing to hear something more. Something that would help all of this to make sense.

'There are some lesions.'

'Lesions?' she repeated, her voice barely audible. 'What are those, exactly?'

'They're areas of damage on the nerves in the brain,' the consultant said, matter-of-factly.

The explanation hadn't shed much light for Isla. 'I'm confused,' she said, her heart racing. 'Are there – what – tumours?'

'No.' He turned the screen towards her and pointed at the small areas on the scan that he was talking about. 'Lesions are different. They can come about for various reasons. They might have been there since you were born, or they could be new. They can sometimes indicate certain chronic conditions.'

The words slipped past Isla, none of them catching.

'I wish I could tell you more now,' he said gently. 'I'd like to look at these with a colleague of mine, and then come back to you.'

'Right,' Isla said, numbly. 'But it's not cancer?' That was the thought that had come to her, in the darkest parts of the night.

'Nothing here indicates that, no.'

Isla tried to make sense of what he'd just said. Not cancer.

Beyond that she was lost. Sophie might have understood some of what the doctor was saying, from her time at medical school, and the reading that she still did – but Isla felt completely out of her depth.

'I'd like to get a little bit of background, if I may. You've had a certain amount of unsteadiness on your feet,' he said. 'Is that right?'

'Yes,' she said. 'Following the fall.'

Her heart was thudding harder now.

'Any numbness, tingling in your hands and feet?'

Her chest felt tight. She wanted to get out of the room, wanted to be able to breathe again. What was the right answer. Was there a right answer?

'Miss Rafferty?' he prompted her.

'Yes,' she said, finally. 'I've been experiencing that.'

Isla walked out of the hospital, hoping the fresh air would clear her head, but as she set out towards her home she felt more confused and dizzy. She didn't know any more what she could or should do for the best. The enormity of what could be going on with her, the unknowability of it, threatened to overwhelm her.

Her phone rang in her pocket. A Belle and Sebastian tune. The ringtone she'd allocated to Rafael.

She checked the time – damn. She was supposed to be meeting him in half an hour. She felt numb and tired. She couldn't face seeing him. How could she explain what was going on with her right now when she didn't know herself? She'd get her head together, then she'd call him back.

*

Sophie drove to work, humming along to the radio. Things felt different to her since talking to Liam about trying for a baby. The friction in the household with Rebecca had slipped into the background for a while, and they'd had space to think of their future.

When they were ready, it would be a new adventure for both of them. Sophie hadn't longed to be a mother, far from it – nothing had been missing. And she'd had her own reasons for holding back. Her parents weren't the role models she'd have liked them to be – her mum had always been cold, and quick to blame others for her own unhappiness. But she knew good mums – like Hattie, Isla's mother – and through that she understood some of what it took. If Sophie was going to be a good mother, she'd have to find the strength to do it her own way. The thought was daunting.

The morning at the hospital was even busier than usual, and she worked quickly to get the details of new patients coming in. Rob, who'd been on all night, rushed in to see a patient, a young girl with a fever, leaving behind some of the paperwork that he needed.

She left Karen in charge of the main desk and caught up with him, handing him the papers discreetly.

He was addressing the parents as he took the girl's temperature. 'When did the fever start?'

'She's been unwell since last night. It seemed to come on all of a sudden. We got her checked at A&E and they thought it was probably fine, but sent us up here just in case.'

'Any other symptoms that you've noticed?'

They shook their heads.

Sophie saw the exhaustion in Rob's eyes. It was clear that he was struggling. He lifted the girl's T-shirt up to glance at her chest quickly, then continued on with his other checks.

'Dr Hamilton,' Sophie said, quietly. She'd seen something – just for a second, but it was enough to alarm her.

'Yes,' Rob said, turning towards Sophie.

'You might want to check the skin on her chest again. The rash – I think it would be worth you giving it a second look.'

A quarter of an hour later, Rob came over to the main desk, catching Sophie on her own.

'Sophie,' he said. 'I nearly missed that. A non-blanching rash ... together with the fever ... I nearly missed it.'

'So you're treating her?'

'Yes. I got the consultant to look too, and she was concerned enough to feel we should act. We've put her on an antibiotic drip for suspected meningitis.'

He leaned against the counter, rubbed his forehead. 'I should have noticed that rash.'

'It was just a few dots ...'

He looked at her, and she saw the deep strain in his eyes. 'It was enough that I should have noticed it. But you did. I'm glad you were there. Thank you.'

'You think she'll be OK?'

'Gut feeling? Probably, yes.'

'But you want to be sure,' Sophie said.

'This is the right course of action to take. No one wants to see what happened last year—'

Sophie shook her head, and her eyes filled with tears.

'It mustn't happen again.'

In the silence of the moment that followed Rob's words, there was a connection. An experience that bound the two of them. They had all met the girl and her parents; they had all been there. Sophie and Rob were for ever joined by a memory they both wished they didn't have.

'You feel it too, don't you,' Sophie said, softly.

'Of course I do,' Rob said. 'I know I didn't treat her. But we lost that girl on this ward due to human error, and I think of it all the time. I don't ever want to see a child lost that way again.'

When her shift was over, Sophie headed straight home. In Bennett Street, children were playing out in the street on skateboards and with skipping ropes, their parents watching on from open doorways, one of the summer's purest joys. Maybe one day she'd be able to look out at her own child, laughing on the pavement with their friends. For the first time she could really picture it – how she would do her best to be loving, and accepting and kind. How she could, and would, do it differently from how her own parents had. Perhaps, she thought hopefully, if you saw history for what it was – acknowledged that there were lessons there you could learn from – you weren't destined to repeat it.

Sophie parked and went inside her house, then put down her handbag on the counter. She could do this. She felt ready. She took her birth control pills out of her bag and threw them into the bin.

Later that evening, in Amsterdam, Isla looked at her phone: SOPHIE.

The only person she felt like talking to right now. She'd spent the afternoon at home with the doctor's words

82

whirring in her mind. They didn't make any more sense to her now. She'd eventually called Rafael and cancelled their date, made an excuse about having to rehearse. He hadn't asked too many questions, which made it easier, but she still felt bad about lying to him. The alternative, though – meeting up with him and having to pretend that nothing was wrong – was too much to contemplate.

'Hi, Soph,' Isla said, summoning up some brightness.

'Hey, love. How are things going?'

'Not bad,' she said. She didn't want to talk about herself, what had happened that afternoon. 'You?'

'Good, thanks. I've just thrown out my pills. So I guess this marks the start of something.'

'Wow,' Isla said. 'That's exciting.'

'Have you heard anything,' Sophie enquired carefully, 'from the hospital?'

Isla felt slightly shaky. She knew she couldn't ignore Sophie's question. 'Actually I met with the consultant again this afternoon.'

'You did? And what did he say?'

She didn't want to say it out loud. Those words that felt alien and threatening to her. Words with implications she couldn't understand. 'They found lesions, he said.'

'Lesions?'

Hearing it back – hearing Sophie say it – made it worse. Made it sound even more like something that shouldn't be there.

'Yes. On my brain.'

'Right,' Sophie said. Isla could hear her breath catch. 'Did they tell you anything more than that?'

'He's not sure what they indicate – whether they are

new or have been there a while. Soph, I really didn't understand what he was saying. Do you know what they could be?'

'I know some things it could indicate,' Sophie said, her tone measured. 'And I can talk you through them if you want – but there's no saying it would be any of those things, so I don't want to worry you. I think you'd be better to wait and see what they come up with.'

Tears filled Isla's eyes – tears of fear, uncertainty, confusion. She knew if she spoke again all the emotion would come spilling out.

'I don't even know if I want to know, Soph.'

'You can do this,' Sophie said. 'Just take it a day at a time.'

'I don't know . . . I feel out of my depth,' Isla said, starting to cry. 'I never thought I'd have to deal with anything like this. I don't know what I'll do if they find something bad.'

'You'll find a way,' Sophie said calmly. 'I'm there with you, Isla. I'm always with you.'

The next day, Isla got up, made a strong coffee. She tried not to think about the previous night, but it came back to her in flashes. After talking to Sophie, and taking an hour to rest, she'd gone to the theatre to perform. She'd thought she could carry on as usual, but it turned out she couldn't. At one point she'd gone blank on stage and lost her way completely – the memory taunted her. Thankfully Alec had stepped in to get her back on track. Part of her wanted to stay in bed, and pretend it had all been a bad dream, the doctor's appointment and the performance, both of them. But if she wanted to feel in control again, she knew she couldn't do that. For now, regaining control meant carrying on as normal. She went downstairs, unlocked her bike, and cycled over to the theatre.

When she arrived, the other actors were already assembled on stage, talking to each other, and there was a buzz of activity and excitement.

'OK, people, let's get started,' Greta shouted, calling them to order. 'Only three weeks till we're doing this in the States, our flights are booked, the marketing's starting up and we need to be ready.'

Greta was sitting in one of the chairs at the front of the auditorium, sipping from a takeaway cup of coffee, a note-book on the seat next to her.

'Isla, can I have a quick word with you, please?'

Isla made her way over, with a sinking feeling. This wasn't going to be good, she knew that much.

'Talk to me, Isla,' Greta said, lowering her voice. 'Because we both know last night was far from your best night. You seems distracted, you dropped that line – thank God nobody seemed to notice – and you seemed kind of . . . well, the emotion was all wrong. Numb, I guess – which is not what we're looking for here. Whatever's going on with you, Rafael, whatever it is – I don't need to know – but tell me you're going to pull it together in time for New York.'

Isla swallowed back her pride. Greta had a point. She'd stalled last night. She'd tried to carry on as normal, but then that moment at the hospital would drift back to her. A dark, formless threat that was undermining her confidence.

'You're right – last night was a mess, and I'm sorry. I had a migraine,' Isla lied. 'I should have said – but I thought I could push on through it. I'm fine today.'

'OK,' Greta said, visibly relieved. 'I'm glad you're feeling better.'

Isla would have preferred to be honest. She hated lying to her friends – to Rafael – even if it was merely a sin of omission. But aside from Sophie and her mum she couldn't face telling anyone about the tests. There was nothing to say other than that things weren't clear.

Isla looked around at the rest of the troupe, who were talking to one another by the side of the stage. Alec had picked up on her distraction. Had they all noticed? Doubts crept in. Had any of the other actors questioned whether she was on good enough form to continue playing the female lead?

'I'll be ready,' Isla said. 'All of us want this just as much as you do, Greta.'

In three weeks' time, they'd be there. They'd be starting up a run of performances in New York – they'd wouldn't be here in this community theatre, with its cheaply constructed sets and unreliable lighting. They'd be on Broadway, playing to new audiences, with the potential to be watched, and spotted, by professionals who could transform their careers. Isla had met with a bump in the road, that was all, and now she was determined to work past that rough spot and keep on going. She would keep acting, get stronger and better. Nothing was going to derail her.

Sophie stirred her tea in the hospital staff room and took another biscuit from the tin. That morning at work had been fine, but she only felt half there. Thoughts of Isla had been with her ever since their phone call. She was too far away. She wanted to be with her friend, offer her some proper comfort.

She knew how painful the not-knowing could be. That torture of being in limbo. She saw it on parents' faces every day, while they awaited the results of their children's tests. Now Isla was in that non-place, and Sophie was powerless to do anything about it. She couldn't deliver the results into the right hands, or speed up the process, as she tried to at the hospital. Isla would have to wait.

Chapter 6

Isla looked at the small parcel on her coffee table. She didn't have long before she had to leave for her appointment, but she couldn't resist opening it. She held it for a moment, running a hand over the silver ribbon. Rafael had dropped it around the previous night – for your travels, he'd said. He'd stayed a while, long enough to kiss and hold her in the way she'd been missing, but had left it with her, told her to open it after he had gone.

She unwrapped it carefully. Inside, she found a small book, a guide to underground New York that led a trail through the Harlem jazz bars and Brooklyn coffee houses – the sort of urban secrets she loved discovering. Underneath that was a package of her favourite tea, some pistachio macaroons, and a necklace – a silver chain with an elephant charm. Rafael had managed to box up some of her favourite things, and in spite of him not being there, she felt the strength of their connection more than ever. He knew her.

As she put the empty lid to one side, she spotted a brown luggage label attached to it. On the underside was a note: For Isla. Who loves adventure. And who – here goes – I love. Rafa x

Her breath caught. The word. The word she'd wanted so much to hear. In the midst of all the stress that had come into her life uninvited, it felt for a moment like the only word that mattered.

The hospital – it was the same place, but it all felt colder now. Harsher. More empty. The smell of bleach filled her nostrils as she walked through the corridors. She sat with the consultant, listened to him. Wished she weren't alone.

It was another of those days. The ones you don't see coming, but when they've arrived everything is different. Nothing familiar remains. The word you want to mean everything gets rendered almost meaningless by two new ones. Everything is cast in a different light. None of what now gives your life its shape can be undone.

The diagnosis. *Multiple sclerosis.*

Isla sat opposite the doctor, dazed. She had a label now. And every part of her wished that she didn't.

She'd heard of it. One of those things that happened to other people. Older people, she'd always thought. She pictured a cane, a wheelchair, someone who couldn't do much for themselves.

She didn't know much, but she knew this could not be happening to her. It would not happen to her.

The doctor was still talking. Isla felt as if she had drifted outside her body. As if she were sitting beside herself, hearing the diagnosis that was about to destroy someone else's life. Because that was what this would do, if it was true. Isla was only thirty. She had plans. Getting a disease like MS was definitely not among them.

'I don't have one hundred per cent certainty, but it looks very likely,' the doctor said.

Isla felt dazed.

'I'm sorry,' he continued. 'I know this news will have come as a shock. I have some leaflets . . . '

'I don't want leaflets,' Isla said, flatly. She didn't need leaflets, because this wasn't really happening to her. 'All I've had is the tingling and numbness, some fatigue, now that I think back . . . there must be other things it could be.'

'As I said, Isla, we can't be certain at this stage, but the way the scans look, together with the symptoms you've been experiencing, would seem to point to this diagnosis.'

'I don't think it can be that,' she said. 'I've always looked after myself. I'm only thirty.'

'I'm afraid it's one of those things – it can affect you even if you've always been fit and healthy. Many people are diagnosed in their twenties and thirties. So you're in good company, for what that's worth. Do you have any family here who can support you?'

She shook her head. If her mum were here she would hold her. Hug her until the news sank in. If Rafael were here . . . she didn't want that. Didn't want him to see her like this, a mess.

Isla left the room and took those two words with her. An addendum to her identity she longed to shake off. She wanted to be herself again, the woman she had been before her future had changed overnight.

At home, she put the box from Rafael away in a cupboard. Tried to forget the words he'd written.

She opened her laptop, and found a forum. She hesitated before she clicked on the link. A little knowledge could tip her either way.

She scanned the posts. Unfamiliar acronyms and drug names, descriptions of symptoms and chronic pain.

I used to run marathons . . . now I'm housebound. Confined to two rooms . . .

. . . awful side-effects, the nausea is debilitating . . .

I try not to ask too much of my partner, but there's more and more I can't do myself . . .

She wasn't ready to step into that world yet. She closed her computer.

Multiple sclerosis. The words seemed hostile. Her symptoms might come and go, the doctor had explained. They'd monitor her over time, see which form of the disease she had. She might have long periods without a relapse, where she had few or no symptoms at all. He'd said that as if he was gifting her something. That had made her angry. She didn't feel as if she'd been gifted anything at all.

Her mind felt as if it had been flooded with new information. Information she didn't want, and she didn't want to ever need. She wanted things to be quiet again. There was only one thing she could think of that would mute those words and let her reclaim some peace for a short while. She got a bottle of wine from the fridge, poured herself a glass, and began to drink.

*

The next morning, Isla woke, still dressed in the clothes she'd been wearing the previous day. She couldn't remember falling asleep. Perhaps the empty bottle of wine on the floor by her bed had something to do with that. Her head throbbed and when she shifted position, a wave of nausea hit her.

She looked around her apartment. Sunshine filtered in through the windows and fell in squares on the wooden floorboards. It was peaceful, and beautiful. These four walls had become home.

But what good would the third-floor flat be if, or when, she started to have difficulty walking? Planning for that seemed as pointless as planning for anything else. It might be her legs that let her down, but equally it could be that her eyesight started to fail, stealing a different aspect of life from her. The disease followed no set pattern.

She wanted to hide away. To put on music so loud she couldn't hear her own thoughts.

Her phone, on silent, blinked with a call. SOPHIE.

'Christ, there you are,' Sophie said. 'I was calling last night and—'

'I fell asleep early.'

'Right. OK. Fair enough. Sorry, not sure why I worried, but you had another appointment yesterday, right?'

'Yes,' Isla said. 'I did.' She felt sick as memories of the previous day flooded back to her.

'And?'

'They know what it is.'

Sophie waited, silently, for Isla to say more. Isla forced herself to speak.

'Well, I'm not dying,' she said. 'Which is something.'

'Thank God for that,' Sophie said.

Isla steeled herself. 'But it's not good news either. Maybe I should have picked up on it earlier – I've had symptoms: tingling, numbness. I've been feeling weird for a few months. Maybe a year.'

'Isla, I wish you'd said something,' Sophie said softly.

'I didn't think it was worth going to the doctor about.' Isla paused. She felt raw, scared. She didn't want to say it all out loud. Once she'd said it, it could never be undone. They would be no denying what the doctor had said, no way she could insist to herself that he'd made a mistake, got the diagnosis wrong. 'It turns out I probably should have.'

'What is it, Isla?' Sophie asked.

Isla's throat seemed to close over. She felt as if she wouldn't be able to say the words. Those two words that were so final, and yet offered no closure, no answers really at all. She could sense Sophie on the other end of the line, waiting for her to answer. That was the only reason she felt able to say them – to put Sophie out of her misery.

'I've got multiple sclerosis, Soph.'

The line went quiet.

'Right,' Sophie said.

'You'll probably know more about it than I do, at this stage. I couldn't understand everything the doctor was saying. Scratch that, I could barely understand *anything* he was saying.'

'You know there are things—'

'Please don't,' Isla said, tears coming to her eyes. She wasn't ready to hear how her life might turn out. What disabilities she might have to come to terms with. She wasn't ready to be positive.

'Sorry?' Sophie said.

'Please don't tell me about medical advances, treatments, developments.'

'I won't.'

'Please don't tell me it could be worse.' Isla knew it could be – of course it could be. She wasn't facing the end of life, just, potentially, her life as she knew it. 'Don't tell me about other people who have climbed Everest with it.' Her tears were coming through in her voice now. 'Don't tell me it's all OK.'

'I won't,' Sophie said.

'Thank you.'

Sophie paused. 'I won't. I can't. I haven't got any answers for you at all.'

When Sophie said that, Isla felt safer. Now she knew she didn't have to be positive, didn't have to be brave. She started to let go.

'But I can listen, Isla. And I want to listen.'

When they'd finished talking, Sophie put down the phone, feeling numb. She hadn't wanted to mention it earlier, but she'd suspected ever since the lesions had been discovered that MS was probably what the doctors were looking for. Somehow that didn't make the diagnosis any less of a shock.

The disease was one of many she'd studied and read about. The long list of potential symptoms came back to her. Isla might eventually have many of them, or barely any, such was the unpredictability of the disease. The list had once seemed abstract, no more than facts to learn. Now, with Isla in mind, the words and phrases had become brutal, devastating.

The diagnosis had forced its way into Isla's life, completely uninvited – and now it was also part of hers.

Isla had still sounded the same – almost. But the doctors had confirmed that she wasn't, that inside her brain things had started to change. Her nerves were being damaged bit by bit. Slowly, if she was lucky. More rapidly, if she wasn't.

Sophie couldn't get past the injustice of it. Why now, why Isla?

Not Isla.

Liam put his head around the door. 'You OK?' he asked, seeing her there, still sitting on the edge of the bed, mobile cradled in her hands.

'Yes,' she said, automatically.

He raised an eyebrow. 'Really?'

'Actually no. I'm not OK at all. I just heard some bad news.'

He came over to sit beside her, putting an arm around her shoulders. 'What is it?'

'I just spoke to Isla.' Tears came to her eyes as she recalled her friend's distress on the phone. She'd felt so helpless – wanting to reach out and hold Isla but only being able to offer words of comfort from a distance.

'She's got a diagnosis,' Sophie said. It all still felt raw. Too new. Unwelcome. 'It's multiple sclerosis.'

'Oh, that's awful,' Liam said, shaking his head. 'Poor Isla. But she's—'

'—too young? Nope. Turns out she's not.'

'I'm sorry,' Liam said. 'How's she feeling now? Do they know yet how it will affect her?'

'It's too early to tell. And it's a notoriously hard disease to pin down. Her symptoms aren't severe; I get the impression they come and go. Each day could be different for her – and the disease progresses differently in different people.'

'So she doesn't know how long she'll be healthy for?'

'Exactly. What she's got is more uncertainty,' Sophie said.

'I'm sorry. How difficult it must be for her. How did she seem?'

'I don't think she's really taken it in yet.'

'She'll have to live differently,' Liam said.

'What do you mean?'

'You know – she's only ever thought about the present, hasn't she? Travelling, acting … That'll all have to change.'

'I suppose so.' It seemed a strange way of looking at it.

'No one can live like that for ever, Sophie. Perhaps this will be a wake-up call for her.'

Isla sat back on the sofa. The phone call with Sophie hadn't changed anything. But saying the words out loud, sharing the diagnosis, had made her feel a little less alone. One thing was becoming clear. She looked at the empty wine bottle, recalled the way she'd felt as she'd tried to process the diagnosis the night before. How she'd resorted to the only thing she could trust to block her feelings out completely. She didn't want to be in that place again. But she couldn't do this alone.

She called her mum.

'Hi, it's me,' she said.

'Hi,' Hattie said. 'I was just thinking about you. I was finishing up at the shop and I—'

'They've found out what it is.'

'They have?'

She had to do it again. She was going to have to keep on doing it. Telling people the news she had barely taken in herself. Letting people know was the only way to be sure that she would have support, that there were people who would make sure she didn't self-destruct, couldn't disappear without a trace.

'I'll tell you what I know so far.'

That evening she met Rafael at the boat, and they walked together to a Thai restaurant hidden away in the back streets. Isla thought of her mum, and hoped that she had someone to talk to that night. She'd tried to hide her worry, but it had been clear to Isla that she was shocked and deeply upset. Isla hadn't foreseen this – that managing other people's responses would be as hard as living through her own.

Rafael held her hand and she wanted them to stay like that, safe, warm, in a bubble together where nothing bad could touch them.

The afternoon's rehearsals had taken it out of Isla. She pushed herself delivering each line, muting out the voices in her mind that reminded her of her diagnosis and focusing only on what it would take to keep everything going as normal and get them out to New York.

She'd realised something, though – and that was that she couldn't go on pretending. Her symptoms, the mild numbness and tingling in her hands and feet, didn't affect her badly. The fatigue – which she could trace back a few months, now that she thought about it – was harder to conquer. But she didn't have that now. Her symptoms weren't affecting her performance – it was only the pretending that was wearing her down.

She would tell Greta about the diagnosis tomorrow, be honest about what had been going on. No big deal, no drama. Just the two words she'd been told herself, and an assurance to Greta that for now everything would carry on as normal.

She looked up at Rafael. He pushed open the door to the restaurant and then turned to smile at her, his handsome features softening, her heart doing the same. Once she'd told Greta, she'd tell him. She wanted to buy them just a little more time, to be like this. She wanted them to be able to be at ease – together, with nothing to think about but the moment – for a while longer.

The next morning Isla walked from Rafael's apartment over to the theatre. Spending the night with Rafael she'd felt suspended, away from the news, the shifts and changes that had come into her life uninvited – existing alongside him in a place that was calm and happy.

It had strengthened her. She was ready to make the first step towards taking back control. She pushed open the doors to the theatre, and waved hello to Greta.

'Hey, mate,' Greta said, pushing aside boxes so that the two of them would have space to sit down and talk. 'My God, it's crazy in here right now. There's so much to get ready, and two weeks now until we leave ... But we'll get there.' She smiled. 'Won't we? We'll pull it together as we always have.'

'Sure,' Isla said, taking a seat. She was aware, more so

than usual at least, of her heart beating in her chest, of the sound of her breathing, of the very fact that she was taking in air, and needed to let it out again. But if she focused, she could steady it. Greta was her friend; the theatre group was practically family to her. All she had to do was relay a little relevant information, and carry on as before.

'Actually, Greta, there's something I wanted to talk to you about.' It took a little forcing to get the words out, but they came.

'There is?' Greta said. She seemed to have only half of her attention on the conversation, the rest mentally reorganising the room into shipping boxes.

'Yes,' Isla said. 'It's not a big deal. Well, it is a big deal. But I can handle it.'

'OK, you're making me a little nervous now.'

'There's no need to be. I've had to go to a few hospital appointments recently, after I fell and hit my head. I was pretty sure it was nothing.'

'You should have mentioned it,' Greta said, sympathetically. 'Well, that explains a thing or two.'

'Yes. I know I haven't been as focused as usual lately, and this is why. I had a CT scan that first night, which led to me missing the performance. Then an MRI.'

'But it was all fine, right?' Greta said.

'No. The MRI showed something that they hadn't expected to find.'

'Oh, crap, really? What?'

It wasn't life-limiting, Isla thought, preparing herself to tell Greta, to repeat those two words that had destabilised her. It was life-changing. Only life-changing. The strangest kind of downgrade.

'I have multiple sclerosis.' There, the words were out. 'Early stages.'

Greta wrinkled her brow. 'Is that serious? It sounds serious.'

'It's a chronic condition,' Isla started. 'I'm not going to get better, but I might have long episodes of feeling well, as I do now. Due to the fall, and the scans, they were able to diagnose me more quickly than they probably would have done otherwise.'

'You didn't have symptoms?'

'I've had some, yes. But I didn't take them seriously.'

'God,' Greta said. 'This isn't the one, is it, where you could end up not being able to walk?'

Isla pushed past her irritation. Greta just wanted to understand it, that was all. She couldn't be blamed for trying to make a connection.

'That can happen, yes.'

'I'm so sorry.'

'Nothing's changed,' Isla said.

'Of course not.' Greta seemed unconvinced.

'I want to go on performing. I just wanted it to be out in the open, with you and Alec anyway. But I'm the same person I was yesterday.'

'I can see that,' Greta said. 'And sorry, that was a bit tactless. What I just said. I'm a bit shocked, that's all. It's just . . . What if something were to happen on stage? Or just before a performance?'

'We deal with that if it happens, I guess,' Isla said. 'But there's no reason it should. Not at this point.'

'Right. Well, that's fine, then. Nothing's changed.'

But when Isla looked into Greta's eyes, she saw that

something had already changed. The theatre group, they were supposed to be a family. At the very least they needed to be a team.

'Are you sure?'

'Sorry,' Greta said. 'I believe you, I do. I don't want to seem selfish, it's just we've waited years for this opportunity. For New York. I want it to work.'

'And you're not sure it's going to work with me,' Isla said.

It was sinking in. They'd all waited years, worked and rehearsed all the hours they could in the hope of a break like this. And now Isla might jeopardise it all. Greta hadn't said that in so many words, but Isla had heard it just the same.

Isla had made her excuses and left the theatre after her conversation with Greta. As she walked back through the city she wondered how it was that it felt as if her working life had fallen apart in the matter of a few hours. It had all been set – and now? It might be that Alec reacted better, if and when she told him – but her confidence had taken a serious knock. One of the younger members of the group, Annabel, was her understudy. She would be able to play Isla's role. It wouldn't be that difficult for them to manage without her. If she wanted to stay on board, she was going to need to convince Greta she could do it. But that thought filled her with humiliation. She'd proved herself already, hadn't she? She'd been one of the most consistently solid performers, and had often been name-checked in reviews. She wasn't even sure if she had the fight in her.

She walked past an elderly woman in the street, who was smiling at her. Isla didn't register until she'd passed her – it was Berenice. She'd been so caught up in her thoughts she hadn't even noticed. When she turned around, Berenice had gone.

Getting out to New York no longer felt like a dream come true, but a way of opting out. Would leaving be brave, or would she just be running away?

Chapter 7

Sophie and Liam were standing in their spare bedroom, looking around it. 'This would be big enough, right? Definitely for a nursery, and I'd have thought till he or she is about four.'

'Yes – and we barely use it, do we? For guests we always have the sofa bed downstairs, or Rebecca's room during the week. When the baby gets older and outgrows it we could probably convert the attic.'

Sophie smiled. 'This is weird, isn't it? Talking about a baby that doesn't actually exist yet.'

'I know. But it's nice too,' Liam said, putting an arm around her waist. 'We can make this work, I know we can.'

'Hopefully it'll all go smoothly,' Sophie said. 'Because I'm getting quite attached to the idea.'

'Let's hope,' Liam said. 'Right – I've got to go, I'm afraid. I have to give a lecture in an hour. I made some dinner earlier though, and left it in the fridge for you.'

'Thanks,' Sophie said. 'It's been a long day. That's music to my ears.'

Liam went downstairs and Sophie went into the bedroom. She took off her shirt and shift dress, and put on her pyjama trousers and one of Liam's sweaters. She opened her make-up bag, searching for a hairband. Inside, she found her packet of contraceptive pills. The last in the box – the very same ones she'd thrown away.

She flipped them over in her hand, confused. On the back was a Post-It with a note handwritten in capitals.

I THINK YOU MISLAID THESE. I WOULD HANG ON TO THEM, IF I WERE YOU.

The words sent a chill through her.

Later that evening, Sophie's brother Daniel called. She answered, grateful for the distraction. She'd felt unsettled – there in the empty house, after the note that she'd found. Knowing who, almost certainly, wrote it didn't make it easier to deal with; if anything it made it worse.

'How are you, stranger?' Daniel asked.

'Good, good. Are you guys ready for Christmas?' Daniel's wife was a great planner-ahead, and Sophie always teased him about it.

'Just like always! You know how organised we always are. Actually, since you mention it – why don't you come back this year? We're all going, the kids'll be there ...'

Sophie thought of the family home. The country mansion didn't even really exist on her mental map any more, it had been out of bounds to her for so long.

Now, in her heart, there was a bud of hope. Had her parents said something – had they said they might like to see her?

'Someone's got to make the first move,' Daniel said.

So no, Sophie realised, a sinking feeling dislodging the bud that wouldn't bloom. Nothing had changed.

'What makes you think they'd even want me to?' she said. 'I opened that door to them once, you know that.'

'You invited them to the wedding, I know – but that was very soon after everything happened—'

'You think that can just be forgotten?' Sophie couldn't keep the emotion from her voice any longer. 'I've tried to be the bigger person – believe me I have. But I'm not going to be a mug about it. I'm not going to turn up at their house for Christmas expecting to be welcomed with open arms, when all they've done the past few years is show me how glad they were to shut the door after me when I left.'

'Time's passed. I can talk to them. Let me talk to them.'

She might have a child soon. A baby who would – at this rate – not know one set of its grandparents. Maybe this was bigger than her now.

'OK,' she said to Daniel, her heart thudding at the thought. 'Talk to them.'

That weekend, Liam drove out to a Chinese restaurant to pick up their takeaway. She went upstairs – she knew she had to grasp the opportunity to talk to Rebecca. She stood outside her stepdaughter's bedroom door, building up courage. Music was playing inside. Rebecca had barely spoken a word to her that evening; she'd gone upstairs the moment she arrived and hadn't been down since.

Sophie mentally rehearsed what she was going to say, her heart thudding in her chest. In her jeans pocket were the pills and note that she'd found in her make-up bag.

As she readied herself to knock, the handle on the door began turning. The door opened to reveal Rebecca, in a sweatshirt and leggings, her dark hair up in a ponytail.

'Have you been waiting outside my door, you weirdo?' she asked, only half-joking.

'I was about to knock. Listen, there's something I wanted to talk to you about.'

'OK,' Rebecca said. 'What?'

'Can I come in?' Sophie asked gently.

'I guess.' Rebecca shrugged.

She went in and sat on the chair at Rebecca's desk, feeling slightly awkward. Rebecca was on the bed beside her.

Sophie had prepared herself to confront a bully, but instead she was faced with a vulnerable-looking teenager, barely more than a child.

'You said you had something to say,' Rebecca prompted her.

Sophie had planned to confront her with the note, but it didn't seem right now.

'I wanted to say, if there's anything on your mind – I'm here. I know that we haven't been getting on that well lately. But nothing's changed, not for me. I don't want you feeling unhappy. You're important to me, Rebecca.' Sophie thought of the pills again, the threat her stepdaughter might be feeling if she'd overheard something about a new baby coming along. 'You always will be.'

'Thanks, I guess,' Rebecca said, scuffing at her carpet with her toe.

'Is anything going on that you'd like to talk about?' she enquired.

Sophie thought for a moment that she might let her guard down. 'Nothing that you can do anything about,' Rebecca said.

'You could try telling me, you never know.'

'I do know,' Rebecca snapped. Her eyes flashed, but they were shiny wet. Sophie saw in that moment that there was deep hurt harboured there – then all emotion seemed to shut down.

'You're not the person I want to talk to,' Rebecca said, coldly. 'You're pretty much nothing to me.'

A wave of disappointment passed over Sophie. She'd felt for a moment as if she were getting somewhere.

'You may be right, that I am nothing to you,' Sophie said, hurt rising in her. 'But you'll always be something to me, Rebecca. I care about you. That's why I'm here. That's why I came to talk to you.'

'This is my room, Sophie. And I want to be on my own. When Dad comes back with the Chinese, you can tell him to come and get me.'

'Fine,' Sophie said, exasperated. 'All I can do is try.'

She left the room and went over to her bedroom, sat for a moment there on the edge of her bed. A message buzzed through on her phone.

It was from Daniel. Her brother. Her parents. She checked it.

I'm really sorry, Soph. I thought maybe Mum and Dad were ready – but they're not. Maybe next year. Daniel x

She wasn't alone. She wasn't totally alone, she knew that. But right then it definitely felt like it.

Isla went along to rehearsals on Sunday, but she couldn't really put the conversation she'd had with Greta out of her mind. There was an atmosphere between the two of them, Greta wouldn't quite meet her eye. It was all the confirmation Isla needed that they couldn't just slip back into behaving as if nothing had happened.

Alec caught them at their tea break, and led her over to the dressing room so that they could be alone. They'd spent a lot of time together, over the past three years, most of it playing opposite each other on stage, and in spite of his penchant for the occasional diva outburst, she'd become really fond of him.

'Greta told me,' he said. 'I'm really sorry to hear about what's going on with you, your diagnosis. That sucks.'

'Thanks,' Isla said. 'That pretty much sums it up, yes.'

'You should still come. To New York. I mean *obviously* you should still come,' he said. 'You're fine, right?'

Isla shrugged. 'Mostly, yes.'

She didn't feel it right now, though. It wasn't physical. It was something deeper inside her that had changed. A drive and confidence to get up on stage and make other people feel things that they hadn't felt before – that was what had gone.

'You're the strongest actor of all of us,' he went on, 'and believe it or not I include myself in that.'

'I'm not sure Greta is entirely behind my coming.'

'You know what she's like. She just wants everything to be controlled. Safe. She's obsessed with every last detail being perfect for the New York performances.'

'And that makes me . . . what? A potential spanner in the works, I guess.'

Alec glanced around, to check no one could overhear them. 'She's being a little over-cautious, I think. It's just because she's so on edge with this whole trip.'

'What has she said?'

'She's just worried, that's all. About you having to pull out, or getting distracted. I've told her if anything it's down to us now, to go the extra mile to let you know this is fine. You're an asset,' Alec said. 'You always will be. You founded this group, and you're one of the best things about it. I know that. The other actors know that.'

Isla wanted to believe Alec, but it was Greta's doubt that chimed best with her own thoughts. With the way she'd started to see herself.

She couldn't do this. She couldn't go to the States knowing that her group weren't a team, and not trusting herself to be able to give the play everything it deserved.

'Annabel knows my part,' Isla said.

'Who cares – she's not half the performer you are. I need you up there, Isla.'

Isla shook her head. 'I can't do it, Alec. I'm sorry. I can't go.'

A week after she left the theatre group and pulled out of the trip to the States, Amsterdam felt different to Isla. There were no rehearsals to attend, no evening shows for her to perform in – she seemed to have no purpose or direction in the city any more. It was as if her role had been edited out, with no new one written in. She didn't know how to write a new one for herself. Her acting career was over. How could she come back from this?

Her body, something she'd always taken for granted, could no longer be counted on to behave predictably. She'd almost stopped seeing it as part of her, and instead looked on it as an adversary, biding its time, preparing to trip her up.

She'd seen Alec and some of the other actors out in the centre of town. They hadn't told her in so many words, but it looked as if Annabel had taken her place, and would play the lead for the Broadway shows.

New York – so close to becoming reality – was now no more than a dream again. Isla dismantled the vision she'd had as carefully as she'd constructed it in the first place – walked down from the stage where she'd pictured herself. If you treasure something enough, she thought, you should take care even when you have to take it apart. She just felt numb, not sad. Not yet.

At home in the apartment, Isla scrolled through an employment website. If she wanted to stay in the apartment, she'd have to find new work, and soon. But, almost as soon as she'd started, she stalled. How could she commit to something new, not knowing when the disease might start to affect her more profoundly, and how?

The home she'd built for herself in the Netherlands had felt solid just a few months ago – but it now seemed like a flimsy, temporary structure. How would she be able to sustain herself here, and how would she navigate the system if she started to need more support? The medical process had been confusing enough, but she didn't know a thing about what benefits, if any, she might be entitled to.

She knew that Rafael, if he knew, would offer her his help – but that wasn't what she wanted. She hadn't intended to keep the truth from him, she'd just wanted to preserve the perfect thing they had for a while longer. She'd only had to lie once – to say she'd been given the all-clear. It hadn't felt good, but she reasoned it was better than the alternative. He'd looked so happy, his eyes bright, his smile immediate. How could she possibly not want him to feel that way? Why would she drag him down with her, when she didn't really have to? It turned out that she was better at pretending to be OK than she'd imagined she'd be. She wanted so much to be happy and well with him that she found she was almost able to fool the both of them. There were moments, of course, when Rafael caught her gazing out of the window, or noticed she was in some way distracted – and there were other times when he asked her straight out if something was on her mind – but she'd managed to gloss over them, citing the play. It hadn't taken much to convince him.

The longer she'd held back, the harder it had got – telling him the truth about her diagnosis didn't really seem like an option any more. She didn't want him to know she'd lied to him, and more than that she didn't want to tell him that the future they'd pictured was already fractured and bound to break. She couldn't bear to have him know that she could end up needing, not just his love, but his practical care. She didn't want to skew the dynamic in their relationship by having him imagine her as the sick person, and him her nurse.

Over the past few days, she'd been thinking of England. Her mum still lived in the cottage she'd grown up in, and Sophie would only be a short drive away. Isla knew she would be welcomed back by both of them if she chose to go. It was starting to dawn on her – all logic pointing in just one direction. She couldn't take her next step here in Amsterdam. Home, however imperfect the option, was starting to exert a strong pull.

She needed something familiar right now, to hear a voice she knew, and one she knew would understand her.

Isla looked around at her room and felt a tug at her heart.

The life she'd created here – it was already half gone. She didn't have Rafael, not really. She had him under false pretences. If he knew what was wrong with her, it would simply be the start of their relationship ending.

It was either hand back the keys to her life, or have it taken from her, slowly, when she got more ill. She wanted to leave this place with dignity, and good memories. Leaving now was the only way she could be in control.

The next day, Isla went to meet Rafael. She sat at a table indoors at the café on the square where she and Rafael had gone for their first breakfast together. She touched the elephant necklace he'd given her, and thought of the note that had come with it: *For Isla who loves adventure. And who . . . I love.* She wanted to say it back to him – let him know that she loved him too, more completely than she'd loved anyone before. But she couldn't now. If she told him she loved him, he'd feel obliged to stay with her. He'd feel he had to, even when he found out she was sick. She didn't want to trap him – that was the last thing she wanted.

Everything felt different. Back in May when they'd first met, the whole summer stretching out in front of her, Isla had been open to anything. There was something about Rafael that just invited a yes. Now, as August drew to a close, she was conscious only that her options were shutting down, one by one.

She gazed out at the square. The tourist crowds were starting to thin, and locals in shorts and T-shirts cycled through the throng or walked to their work. Children played on the cobbled square, making the most of their last few days of freedom before school started again. Isla welcomed the distraction of their shouts and laughter. Welcomed the chance to think about anything else other than what she was about to do.

Nine days ago, she'd been so sure she could face it – telling him the truth. That was, right up till the moment she'd told Greta. When Greta had hesitated, silently questioning her capability, Isla had witnessed her dream dissolving into nothing. It had been humiliating, and the shame had remained with her. She hadn't dared to tell Rafael and risk the same thing happening again. But she couldn't hide from the situation any more.

Rafael was approaching. He smiled and waved as he saw her. Her heart would normally have lifted at seeing him, but not today. It felt heavier.

'Hey there,' Rafael said, kissing her.

'Hey,' she said, as calmly as she could.

'How are things? All set for New York?' he said.

It was a plan that belonged to someone else now. She wasn't that woman any more: the one who was successful, happy and had a bright future ahead of her. She was fit for nothing more than curling back in on herself, retreating, going home. She wasn't proud of that.

'Is everything OK?' he asked, taking her hand. His touch sent a flutter of excitement through her. She loved him. She wanted to be with him. And yet she also felt pulled in the opposite direction.

He deserved better than being lied to. But he also deserved better than what she had to give right now, and what she would have to give in the future. In a way, she was setting him free.

She hesitated. She wanted to be here, in the time *before*, for just a little longer. Because being here – with his warm hand on hers – it was sweet and safe and warm. That bitter taste in her mouth, the flavour of fear that had become her companion, wasn't there when she was with him. Looking into his brown eyes, she felt vibrant and well. She could believe for a moment that the doctors had got it wrong. That nothing was the matter with her after all.

But it had to be done. And Rafael's life wouldn't have to change much, she told herself. He had built his contentment up over the years. She knew his routine – he opened the shop, he cycled, he saw his friends – she'd simply added to his happiness, not created it. The rest would remain. He would be able to move on.

'Look, Rafael,' she said, 'there's something I need to talk to you about.'

This was it. She'd set the wheels in motion.

'Yes?' he said.

Telling him the truth would mean pity, and she didn't want that – not from him. She wanted to walk away with dignity. She wanted him to remember her exactly as she had been.

Clean, Isla thought to herself. No ambiguity. That was the best way.

'I've been thinking.'

'Yes?' Rafael said, his eyebrows rising.

'This. Us.' She paused. Doubting whether she had it in her to do it. 'Look, I like you. A lot.'

She just had to keep going. That was all. If she stopped for one second and looked at him, she would stall.

'But I get the feeling that our lives are going in different directions,' she said. It came out more bluntly than she'd intended.

'Are you talking about the trip?' he said, confused. 'Because I thought we'd agreed that the distance was something we could manage—'

'I've changed my mind, Rafa,' she said, firmly. 'I need to make a proper go of this. And, to do that, I need to be free of commitment. I need a clean break.'

It was done. She'd said it. It had been done in all but words even before she arrived – notice given on her apartment. Flights booked to England. It couldn't be undone.

He looked shocked and hurt. 'What? Where has this come from? I thought we had plans, you said—'

'I wasn't thinking straight,' she said. Her voice was so cold. She could barely hear it as being her own. 'I was being idealistic. Long-distance isn't easy. I should have thought it through better.'

'Just like that? You've changed your mind?' he asked, disbelieving. He leaned back in his chair, shaking his head. 'This is crazy, Isla.'

'I'm sorry,' she said. Damn the tears that were pricking at her eyes. Damn how this all hurt. Just make it be over, she thought. Please don't fight me on it. Because I'm not strong enough to keep on convincing you.

'I guess that's it, then.' He was giving up. This was nearly over. 'It doesn't seem like there's much I can do to change your mind.'

This was it, her last chance. She forced herself to stay strong. 'I'm not going to change my mind. I'm sorry.'

'Then I guess this is goodbye,' Rafael said. He looked hurt, but in a distant way she could no longer soothe. As if he was shutting his own emotions down, protecting himself.

'Yes. It is,' she said, fighting back the tears.

She had taken Rafael's heart, and the love he had offered her, and handed it right back. Because he would need it. He would need it for someone else.

She looked away. This was it. Time to go.

Chapter 8

Sophie and Liam were settling down to dinner and she found her thoughts drifting to Isla. She'd spoken to her earlier in the week, and the conversation had left her feeling concerned. Isla had talked about going home to her mum's, but she'd sounded depressed about the whole idea. Much as she would be happy to see more of her friend, it saddened her that Isla seemed to see coming home as some kind of failure.

'You know how I mentioned that Isla's coming home?' Sophie said.

'Mm-hmm.'

'It's all right if she comes to stay for a night or two, isn't it?'

'Sure,' he said. He was eating and only seemed to be half-concentrating on what she was saying. She noticed his gaze resting on his phone, which was on a side table nearby. 'No problem.'

'I thought it might help ease her back into living in the

UK. I think she's feeling weird about going back to living at her mum's house.'

'I can see that. Must be hard giving up her independence, even if it's only a temporary thing.'

'Yes, I think it is. She's never liked relying on other people.'

It upset Sophie to think that Isla wasn't just giving up her independence, but almost certainly also her relationship with Rafael. At least that was how it had sounded. Sophie knew better than to interfere, but it had been difficult to hold back from saying anything.

'I don't think she's going to tell Rafael the truth,' Sophie said.

'Oh, really? Well,' Liam said. 'Right.'

'About the diagnosis, I mean.'

'Uh-huh.' He finished what was on his plate, and seemed anxious to get up.

'Liam – are you listening to me?'

'Of course I am,' he said.

'What did I just say?' she asked, unconvinced.

'Something about Isla. Rafael,' he said, sensing he'd been caught out. 'Sorry. Bit distracted – forgive me. I've got some course documents to write for the seminar tomorrow. I've been snowed under recently, and haven't had time to do them.'

Sophie shook her head, but smiled. 'All right, then, you're off the hook. Go and get your laptop. I'll do the washing up.'

When she'd finished washing the pans, Sophie took the bins out to the front garden.

A young woman approached her and smiled in greeting.

'Hi,' Sophie replied. She saw now that it was Kate, one of the students from across the road. She was dressed in running gear. 'How are you?'

'Good, thanks. Just getting a bit of fresh air and exercise – or avoiding my essay, depending how you look at it.' She smiled.

'How did your party go?' Over a month had passed since then, but she hadn't seen Kate since the invitation to come.

'It was great. Kept going till dawn. How come you couldn't make it?'

'Oh – I was away,' Sophie said. 'And while I have very happy memories of the heady days of student partying, I think I might be a bit past it now.'

'There's no reason they have to end just yet, is there? Liam certainly seemed to be enjoying himself.'

'Sorry?'

'Your husband. On the dance floor, letting it all hang out ... ' She mimicked his dance moves.

Sophie wrinkled her brow. 'That must have been someone else, I think.'

'I don't think so. Liam – the lecturer, right? Cracked us up that he was the one lining up the shots.'

'You're sure?' Sophie couldn't make sense of the story. She remembered the date – when she was in Amsterdam with Isla. Liam had definitely told her he and Rebecca stayed in that night. That they'd watched a DVD together.

'Completely. He didn't mention it?'

'No,' Sophie said. 'He didn't.'

Isla was at the departure gate in Amsterdam, waiting for her flight to be called. It had been twelve days since she said goodbye to Rafael. She didn't need to look at a calendar to know that – she'd felt every minute of those empty hours dragging by. She'd left the apartment early that morning. She'd spent the previous day cleaning it until every surface was spotless. She couldn't afford to lose her deposit – she was going to need every penny she had over the coming months, that was one of the only things she really knew for sure.

She wasn't expecting to find answers back in England. It wasn't answers she was going for. She just wanted somewhere she could get her strength back. It had been a long time since she'd felt this alone. She was letting her dreams go, all by herself. She had wanted to make her family proud, to return home with tales of everything she'd achieved – but instead she felt like a failure.

Leaving the theatre group, and the people she'd thought were friends, had been hard. But leaving Rafael – her eyes filled with tears at the memory of their last meeting. It had been awful. Horrible. But since leaving him she hadn't wavered in her conviction; she felt sure that she was doing the right thing – she was being unselfish, however it might have seemed to him.

She'd just have to carve something new out when she got back to the UK. She'd done it before – starting anew; she could do it again. She tried to stay positive even though her gut kept reminding her that things were different now, there was an invisible network of constraints around her physical self that would potentially limit everything – every single thing – that she wanted to do. She'd brought her list with her – she couldn't leave it – but instead of the usual lift it gave her to think of it in her handbag, the inspiration each line revived in her, she now felt taunted by it.

120

'Last call for Bristol.' The call came over the tannoy, and jolted Isla back to the moment. For once she wasn't dashing over from the bar or from duty free, where she would usually be getting one last drink or a gift for a friend. Today she'd got to the departure gate in good time, because life wasn't predictable right now. Nothing was predictable right now.

A message buzzed through on her phone.

See you at the airport in a couple of hours. Can't wait to see you. Mum x

She could adjust. She would have to learn to adjust.

Sophie came back inside and found Liam at the kitchen table at his laptop, a ringbinder of course notes open by his side. He was squinting slightly at the screen as he worked. He was the same Liam, her Liam – charming, but socially awkward. Which was another reason why what Kate said had made no sense at all.

'Close that a minute, will you?' Sophie said.

'Right now?' He glanced up, his brow furrowed. 'I've got to finish this for the seminar tomorrow.'

'Yes, now, if you could,' she said, taking a seat next to him. 'I've just heard something really weird, and I'm hoping you can shed some light on it.'

He closed the computer and put his things to one side. 'Sure. What is it you wanted to talk about?'

'Liam – were you at the party, while I was away in Amsterdam?'

'Which party?' he asked, looking blank.

'Don't,' Sophie said. 'I'm really not in the mood.

Kate – one of the students – just spoke with me. Said you were there, in their house, right to the end.'

Liam glanced down at the table, then back at Sophie. 'I'm sorry.'

'Why on earth did you lie to me?'

'I should have told you. I'm an idiot.'

'That part I figured out for myself,' Sophie said. 'So what happened?'

'I took Rebecca over – she was bored here, and I thought it might do her good to make a few friends in the street. Then somehow I ended up staying and got far too drunk. I brought Rebecca home and then went back. It's all a bit embarrassing really.' The colour in his cheeks lent his story credibility.

'Why did you keep it from me?'

'I didn't want you to think of me that way. You know how nervous I've been about meeting the new students, and it felt good, in the moment, that they were all chatting to me. I shouldn't have left Rebecca – or let her see me in a state in the first place. It was stupid—'

'Liam, come on.' Sophie shook her head. 'You're a grown man.'

'You're right, Soph, completely. I've been anxious about teaching and it made me feel a little better for a few hours that my students and their friends wanted to talk to me.'

Sophie felt a rush of warmth towards him. This was the Liam she knew.

'I missed you,' he went on. 'I guess it was one way to distract myself.'

'You should've just been honest with me,' Sophie said,

softly. 'It's not even that big a deal; it was the lying that freaked me out.'

'I know. And it won't happen again.'

'And if it were to?'

'I'd tell you.'

'Right. Now we're getting somewhere.'

'Can you forgive me?'

'Yes, of course,' Sophie said, kissing him gently. 'They must have had a right laugh at you afterwards.'

He wrinkled his nose. 'God. They probably did, didn't they?'

Isla walked out into the arrivals lounge, past the families reuniting and happy couples kissing. She saw her mum through the crowd – her curly brown hair under a purple beret, her eyes darting from person to person, seeking Isla out. Isla weaved her way over to her, and her mum gave her a big hug. Isla held her closely, and let herself feel safe there for a moment. She was home. She wished she was there for any other reason than the one that had brought her, but she was home.

They drove back to the outskirts of Bristol in Hattie's old Mini, and pulled up at the cottage. Isla looked up at the familiar grey brick. It was the house she'd grown up in – bright with lilac in the spring, freezing throughout in the winter. She'd played French elastic on the front lawn, hide and seek in the attic, made jam in the kitchen. In thirty years it had barely changed.

'The evenings are starting to get chilly,' Hattie said. 'I hope you brought some jumpers back with you.'

'Yes, Mum, I brought some jumpers.' Isla smiled politely,

but inside her emotions were mixed. Here she was, talking about the weather with her mum. It was as if she'd never left. She felt – young. Too young.

'It's just, you don't seem to have much,' Hattie said, looking at the suitcase they'd unloaded.

'I'm having the rest shipped over next week.' Then everything she owned would be back here, severing the last of her connections to Amsterdam. Her belongings were the easy part, though. She still felt torn and empty thinking of how she'd let Rafael go.

Isla and her mum went inside, and Hattie brought tea through to the living room.

'I'm glad you came home, love,' Hattie said, kindly. 'It can't have been an easy decision. I know how much you were enjoying it out there.'

'It wasn't an easy decision, no.' She wasn't thinking of the culture, or the bars, or the restaurants. Not even of the theatre group that had once meant so much to her. She was just thinking about Rafael. Rafael, who had filled in the colour of her life there. 'But I needed to be home. I need to work things out.'

Isla looked around the living room: the laden bookshelves, the vintage lamps and picture frames. The photos of her grandparents – her grandmother Sadie was still alive and living locally; her grandfather had died a couple of years back. Some subtle changes had occurred since she was last home – there was now a small desk in the corner, with a sewing machine on it.

'You're crafting more now?' Isla asked.

'Well, I had to do something to keep myself busy when you left.' Hattie smiled.

Isla nodded, feeling numb. She was back. But this was only the beginning. She didn't have any idea what she was going to do next.

'Come over here,' Hattie said kindly. She opened her arms and beckoned her daughter to join her on the sofa. Isla hesitated for a moment, then went over and sank into the comforting warmth of her mother's embrace.

'You don't have to have a plan, you know,' Hattie said. 'No one expects you to. This is your home, Isla. It's somewhere you can just *be*.'

Isla appreciated her mum's kindness, but it wasn't that simple. Without a plan, she barely knew who she was. She wanted her mum's words to be true – and believed them to a point. She believed that her mother would never judge her on what she had or hadn't achieved. But inside, she felt as if her control was slipping; she was becoming a child again, and getting further from who she'd wanted to be.

That night, when Isla was deeply asleep – not in that no-man's-land of pre-dawn insomnia she'd been stuck in lately, where anxiety flourished, but in the thick dark velvet of REM sleep – she dreamed she was on stage. Her body was agile and light; she glided. She was back on stage, perform-ing. She was treading the boards on Broadway, inhabiting the role she'd been cast in, and taking the audience on a journey, bringing typed words to life in the viewers' laughter and tears.

She looked out, and saw Rafael there. He was watching her intently, his dark eyes focused entirely on her face and body – willing her on, encouraging her to be her very best. Not smiling – it was all too important for him to be smiling.

That would come later, backstage, when they went for a glass of wine afterwards – then there would be the relief, and the smiles and the ease of being together.

When Isla woke up the next morning, in her teenage bedroom, for a moment the picture of him was with her, imprinted on her mind. She focused on it and focused on it, willing it to stay with her just a little while longer. But the more she tried to keep it there, the more it slipped away. It was happening too quickly, she thought, the end of them, her leaving him. It was all too quick.

Chapter 9

When the shop was quiet, Rafael would sit and read a book himself. If it was a good one, he'd lose himself in the lives of the characters and the way that their stories played out. Sometimes he would forget all about the real world. But this morning all he could think about was Isla. He wanted to feel angry, let down, betrayed, anything other than just empty like this.

Since she'd left, each time the shop door opened and the bell rang – each time, without fail – he would picture Isla coming through it. A whirlwind of energy in denim dungarees and untidy hair, one dangly earring. She'd be carrying a basket full of fresh flowers or some antique she'd picked up at the market. She had brought the colour into his life. That colour, that was the thing that was gone now: it had faded all the way out.

When the shop bell rang that day, he knew not to raise his hopes. It was Berenice, and that was enough to make the day a bit better, at least. So far, the morning had brought only a string of demands, deliveries and enquiries, and he welcomed the opportunity to put the kettle on and sit down for a few minutes.

'Hello, my dear,' Berenice said, pulling up her usual chair and taking a seat. 'I brought you a little something.'

She put a book out on the counter. Leather-bound, gold-embossed, like most of the ones that she brought.

Each week she'd bring one. He knew what it meant, and it didn't faze him. Berenice said it wasn't about being morbid – but she knew she was entering life's final act, and she'd prefer to give away her possessions now and be able to witness how they brought pleasure to people. With Rafael it was always books – a lifelong passion for Berenice and the thing that had brought the two of them together.

'Thank you,' he said, turning around to acknowledge the newest gift as he poured their tea.

'You're very welcome. Now come and tell me how you are.'

He pushed her teacup towards her, and tried his best to smile. She saw right through him. 'Have you heard from Isla?'

He shook his head. 'No.' Nothing. Nothing at all. From sharing their hopes and dreams to nothing, only silence. 'It's easier this way.'

'You don't look like you find it easier.' Berenice said, concerned.

'The truth? I hate not hearing from her – I miss her,' Rafael said. 'I'm upset with her, I'm confused by her, but I also miss her. I can't seem to get around that.'

'It's understandable that you feel upset. You'd have a right to be angry.'

'I don't know – I don't think I've got it in me to be angry with her. But I really thought we had something special. Now I just feel like a fool. If it was special, she wouldn't have been able to end it like she did. If she was the woman I thought she was, she wouldn't have put her trip – her career, whatever it was – ahead of our relationship. Maybe I was imagining that it was serious. Perhaps for her it never was.'

'You weren't imagining it. It was real. She was in love with you,' Berenice said, 'of that I'm entirely certain.'

'I thought I felt it,' Rafael said. 'And I want to believe you, but I'm starting to think I never really knew her at all.'

'You knew her,' Berenice said, 'don't doubt that. She was a good woman – genuine.'

Rafael felt more confused now than he had before. 'Then what happened? What changed?'

'I don't know. But something did. After the fall – she seemed different.'

'Different how?' He'd felt it too, but hadn't been able to pin down when it had happened, or why.

'I can't really say. But it was as if a light went out in her eyes. I think she might have fallen out of love with herself, Rafael. But not with you.'

Isla ate breakfast downstairs in the cottage. Her mum had already left for work. She thought about the day and how she might fill it, but drew a blank. A month ago, her life had been straining at the seams – she'd had so many things to do that the available hours had seemed meagre and inadequate.

Now, she was living that in reverse – the minutes and hours stretching out with nothing to fill them.

As she finished her toast, she saw that her mum had left a scribbled note on the table for her. *GP?* it said. The phone number of the local doctor's surgery was written underneath.

There was no point hiding from it, Isla realised. She had come home so that she could start to move on, and this would be her first step. She took a deep breath, then got out her phone and called.

An hour later, Isla was in the doctor's surgery.

'It's good to see you again, Isla.' Her local GP, Dr Graham, had made time to see her that morning. She had treated her since she was a child. 'I got your notes from the hospital in the Netherlands last week. They've filled me in on what happened over there.'

Isla wished there were some way to fast-forward through the details. She didn't want to have to think about it all again.

'It sounds as though they've done quite thorough investigations. We can do our own, too – but, on the basis of what I've heard, I'm satisfied that the diagnosis is probably correct.'

Isla nodded. Her last shred of hope – that that there might have been some mistake, something lost in translation – was gone now.

'I'm sorry, Isla. This must have come as a real shock to you. I see that they scanned you after a fall. Had you been having symptoms before that?'

'Minor ones. Tingling, numbness. I hadn't really given

them much thought, to be honest. Now it's mainly the fatigue.'

'Did they talk to you about medication? We've been seeing very encouraging results from patients using disease-modifying treatment.'

Isla shook her head. 'I'm not ready for that. I don't want to be taking medication every day when I feel fine most of the time.'

'I can understand that,' Dr Graham said. 'But if you agree, I'd like to refer you to a specialist at the hospital, to give you a further opportunity to discuss all those options.'

Isla felt as if the room was spinning. This – doctors and hospitals and treatments and medications – it was all going to be at the centre of her life now.

'I don't know how I came to be here,' she said. 'I feel like this is all a horrible dream, Dr Graham, and I just have to find a way to wake up.'

'I know,' Dr Graham said kindly. 'It's an awful lot to take in. And I know how active and healthy you've always been. But you're not alone, Isla. There are many women and men just like you who are coming to terms with or living with this disease – and the vast majority of them are able to continue leading full lives, doing many of the things they love.'

'I've seen a few forums on the internet. But some of the stories there scared me even more.'

'Perhaps avoid those for a little while, then. Perhaps we could get you meeting some people in real life instead.'

'I don't know,' Isla said. 'I don't think I'm—'

'There's a local support group.'

For people who were sick. Disabled. She wasn't either of those things.

The doctor picked up on her hesitation. 'I'll give you the details just in case.'

Isla folded the piece of paper and put it away. She didn't want to look at it. She didn't even want to have it there in her bag, where she might catch sight of it again.

After the appointment Isla went home via the shops. The little high street was ten minutes' walk away and she decided to go to a local café. She queued to order a coffee, and saw Laura in the line ahead of her. Laura Groves. The most popular girl in her class at school. Her instinct was to duck and hide, leave the café, but Laura spotted her before she could do that.

'Isla Rafferty,' she called out. 'Hi!'

She came up to Isla's side and gave her a hug and a kiss, as if they'd always been friends. Which, aside from Facebook, they hadn't. They'd moved in different circles, and Isla had never felt good in Laura's company: she had a condescending manner that was as evident now as it had been back then.

'I heard you were back.'

'For a while,' Isla said. She wanted not to be here. Wished she'd never come out.

'You were going to go to New York, weren't you? Something about a play.'

'Not any more,' Isla said, feeling a little stab at her heart. 'Didn't work out.'

'Yes,' Laura said, lowered her voice to a whisper. 'I *heard*.'

'You did?'

'Yes. And I'm so sorry. You – I mean, you're so *young*. I guess it could have happened to any of us.'

Isla fell mute.

'I feel terrible for you,' Laura went on. 'My auntie Cath told me. She spoke to your mum, I think.'

'Right,' Isla said, bristling with quiet fury.

Isla saw that her eyes were shining with unshed tears but her sympathy seemed thin. 'Awful. Absolutely awful. You must be devastated. I mean, this disease, it's crippling, isn't it?' she said, her voice lowered. 'Tragic. It's tragic. My mum's got all of the ladies at the church praying for you.'

Isla stayed quiet, but inside she was seething with fury.

'My great-uncle Kenneth has it. And he has awful trouble getting about. I'm not sure if you realise ...'

Isla could feel her blood pressure rising.

'Anyway, you must let me buy you a coffee, Isla. And a pastry. Anything really – a Danish, or a cinnamon swirl ...'

Isla shook her head. 'I should be going. I forgot I have somewhere to be ...' She stepped away from Laura.

'Oh, right,' Laura said, sounding almost disappointed. 'Yes, of course.'

Isla turned and left, hoping that Laura couldn't see that her cheeks were burning with humiliation.

Hattie was making tea when Isla got home. 'Nice trip out?' she asked.

'No. Not really,' Isla said. 'Mum – who have you been telling, about me being ill?'

'Oh, just a couple of people – friends who asked after you.' She seemed to notice the hurt in her daughter's expression.

'I'm sorry, love – I wouldn't have done it if I thought it would upset you. But people care, that's all.'

'Couldn't you let me tell people in my own time, and my own way? And I really would rather Laura Groves didn't know, full stop.'

'I thought you two were friends.'

'No. We're not friends. We never were – and we're not now.'

'It's difficult to keep track sometimes.'

'I don't want people to see me as this disease and nothing else – do you understand that? I'm still me. My health is the same this month as it was last month; I just have a diagnosis. That's the only difference.'

'I'm sorry,' Hattie said, glancing down. 'I didn't realise you felt that way.'

'Well, I do – I do,' Isla said.

She went upstairs to her room. She knew her mum had only acted with kind intentions. She knew the way she was feeling now wasn't her mum's fault – it wasn't anywhere near that simple.

She closed the door to her room – the teenage bedroom that hadn't changed at all in the time she'd been gone – went over to her bed and sat down. The weekend, and her planned visit to Sophie seemed a lifetime away, and right now she felt desperately alone. She picked up her phone, and checked Facebook. She needed something to distract her. Some view into another person's life that was rosier than the mess she was in.

A wedding, a new baby, a hen night. A friend who 'felt blessed'. And then Greta. She hadn't unfriended Greta – it seemed a childish thing to do, even after the way they'd

134

fallen out. So now she saw Greta – a selfie with Tiffany's in the background. A photo with Alec, the two of them on stage. And then a link – to a review.

She shouldn't click on it. She knew she shouldn't click on it.

She clicked through.

'British theatre group making waves on Broadway. *In the Hands of Strangers* is a heartbreaking and stunningly well-acted play from this talented . . .'

Isla felt her throat tighten. She'd help devise the play, she'd worked hard to make it what it was, she'd . . . But it didn't matter. None of it mattered now. None of it belonged to her. It was half a world away now, too far for her to touch any of it.

Chapter 10

That Friday afternoon, Sophie picked Isla up from the cottage. On the drive back to Bennett Street, Isla was quiet. She'd been back in Bristol a week, and already it felt as if Amsterdam, the happiness she'd had there, the sense of well-being, the joy of being with Rafael, had all been in her head. She looked out of the window at the grey, rain-spattered cityscape, and her usual smile was gone. Sophie took it as her cue to lighten things, so she attempted to bring back some cheer by pointing out the landmarks of their student days. Isla didn't respond, though, so she was more direct.

'How are things? You look . . . ' She paused, searching for the most tactful word.

'You want to tell me I'm looking better,' Isla said, bristling a little, 'but you can't, because I'm not. It's all right.'

'You do look tired. Anyone would.'

'I feel exhausted, Soph. I don't know if it's the illness, or just the total weirdness of being back here again.'

'It'll take time,' Sophie said gently. 'Settling back in after your time away.'

They drove through a part of town that was familiar to both of them.

'Hey,' Sophie said, pointing. 'The boat club we used to go to – remember? We should go there again. Now that you're going to be in Bristol for a while.'

'You're not serious?' Isla said.

'Why not?'

'Come on, Sophie. I just said how knackered I've been feeling.'

'Well, maybe I didn't hear that part,' Sophie said.

Isla looked back towards her friend. The ghost of a smile flickered across Sophie's lips. It triggered the same in Isla, and soon the two of them were smiling, then laughing.

'Oh, Christ,' Isla said. 'You're going to try and make me happy, aren't you?'

'Absolutely. I'm going to give it my very best shot,' Sophie said.

At Sophie's house that evening the atmosphere at dinner was lighter than usual.

'Good to have you here, Isla,' Liam said. 'I hope you know you're welcome to stay whenever you like.'

His eyes met Sophie's and she smiled. It meant a lot to her, him saying that.

'It must be cool, being an actress,' Rebecca said. She looked at Isla with admiration. 'I'd love to do something like that.'

'It's great,' Isla said. 'I'm not going to promise you it'll

137

make you rich, but I think it's the best job in the world.' She smiled. 'You're doing performing arts, right?'

'Yes,' Rebecca said. 'One of the only things I like about school at the moment.'

Liam gave her a look.

'What, Dad? I'm just being honest.'

'It's not a very positive attitude to take when you have exams coming up.'

Rebecca turned back to Isla. 'I am positive, just not about the things he wants me to care about. He doesn't want me to study drama, or anything like it, at uni. Says they're not proper subjects.'

'That right, Liam?' Isla said, raising an eyebrow playfully.

'Rebecca,' he whispered, reprimanding her.

'You said it, not me.' She held her hands up in a gesture of innocence.

'She's right, you did,' Sophie said. 'No ducking now, just because Isla's here.'

'I'm an academic, you know that, Isla. It's a different world. You can call me ignorant, if you like.'

She smiled. 'You're ignorant. Culture's important, Liam. Creative expression is what this country's famed for.'

'I wouldn't mind too much if she went into theatre, I suppose ... I just don't want her ending up on reality TV or something.'

Rebecca and Isla's eyes met, and Rebecca rolled hers. 'You see what I mean?' Rebecca said.

'It's pretty different,' Isla said to Liam.

'Totally different,' Rebecca added.

Sophie watched on as her stepdaughter seemed to relax, soften – turn back into the girl she had once been. Sophie

wished that she could join in, that she could open the door Isla
had been able to – but for now it was enough just to see that
the girl she cared about was still there, underneath. Hopefully
one day soon, Sophie would be able to reach her again.

After dinner, Sophie and Isla sat together in the living room,
in large armchairs by the bay window.

'How are you feeling?' Sophie asked gently. 'About leaving Rafael, I mean?'

Isla took a sip of wine. 'I miss him.' She sat back into the
soft velvet cushions. 'I miss him really badly.'

'You could still change your mind, you know. Tell him the
truth, give him the chance to—'

'No.' Isla shook her head. 'I made the decision for a
reason. I need space to get my head around all this, and my
life may well have to be different. I don't want to drag him
down into all that.'

'I don't think you're giving him the credit he deserves,'
Sophie said. 'From what I saw of him, I think he would have
been more than willing to support you.'

'But that's just it,' Isla said. 'I don't want him to support
me. I wanted him to love me, respect me, admire me. It
would have changed.'

'It seems a shame,' Sophie said. 'He's a good guy. And you
two had something.'

'I know. It makes me sad that we didn't even have a
chance to get started.'

'He must be finding it tough without you,' Sophie said.

'Who knows. He might have moved on already.' Isla
imagined it – Rafael with someone new. 'I hope he has.' It
wasn't quite true, but saying it made her feel better.

'I don't believe you.'

Isla smiled. 'I don't believe me either. But I do want him to find someone else, in time. Because I'm not an option any more. I'm not the woman he fell in love with.'

'Of course you are,' Sophie said gently.

'I don't think I am. The adventure has gone out of me.'

'For now.'

'Maybe for ever. I mean, I'm grateful I've got Mum's house to go back to, of course I am. I know there are lots of people out there who have nowhere to go back to at times like this. I'm grateful that I'll get the medical advice I need. I'll go to appointments, and do whatever it is I need to do to make this . . . this *thing* easier to deal with.'

'All positive.'

'But at the same time I feel like I'm rolling over and giving up – and it's hard to feel proud of that. I was going to go out to perform in New York – and instead I'm back at the house I grew up in.'

'You aren't giving up on anything,' Sophie reassured her. 'So much is still possible for you. You just have to work out what comes next.'

Sophie and Isla talked until around midnight. As Isla went upstairs, she instinctively gave her phone a glance. No messages from Rafael. Of course not. She was only looking out of habit. She'd deleted him from her social media, trying to avoid the torture of those glimpses of his life as he lived it without her.

She put on her pyjamas and picked up her toothbrush. When she got to the bathroom door, Rebecca came out, her eyes red.

'Are you OK, Rebecca?' she asked.

Rebecca looked dazed, then shook her head.

Isla took a breath. God, she really shouldn't be walking into this, not now. She barely had the motivation or energy to sort her own life out, let alone help someone else. But she couldn't ignore it, either. She couldn't turn her back now that she'd seen there was something wrong.

'Why don't you come into my room, and we can have a chat.'

Rebecca seemed reluctant, shy.

'I've got chocolate,' Isla said.

'OK, then.' Rebecca came into her room, and Isla offered her a chunk of Whole Nut.

'What's up?' Isla asked.

Rebecca stayed silent, nibbling at a square of chocolate.

'You don't have to tell me anything. You can just take the chocolate and run. But I get the sense there's something on your mind.'

'Sophie thinks I hate her. And I understand why.'

'Do you?'

She shook her head. 'No. I wish it was that easy.'

'So something is wrong?'

'Yes. But it's complicated.' Rebecca shook her head, making it clear she wasn't going to elaborate. 'I can't sleep with all this whirring around in my brain at the moment. That's why I'm so ratty in the day. It's not just me being grumpy, or difficult, or a teenager, like Sophie thinks. Something's changed and I can't make it go back to normal.'

Instinctively, Isla reached out and drew the girl in towards her for a hug. Rebecca hugged her back, and they stayed like that for a while. 'I'm not going to say it'll be OK, because I don't know that,' Isla said. 'But you're not alone.'

'Thank you,' Rebecca said, through tears.

Isla held her carefully. Rebecca was dealing with the way her world had shifted on its axis, just as Isla herself was. Isla didn't know why – but she knew just how that felt.

The next morning, in Sophie's spare bedroom, Isla woke up slowly, taking a moment to get her bearings. She recalled the previous night and how Rebecca had opened up to her as they'd talked together. If only she'd said just a little more – something that Isla could tell Sophie that could help her friend build a bridge. *It's complicated . . . Something's changed.* Rebecca hadn't said anything more than that, and Isla hadn't wanted to force it.

Isla picked up her phone to check the time and saw that Facebook was showing a new notification. Laura Groves, who she'd bumped into the other day, had posted on her page.

> SO great to see you, Isla. And you look amazing. Honestly, if I didn't know you were ill, I would never have guessed. Keep smiling ☺

Underneath was a string of comments from other friends below Laura's post. *You OK? What's up, Isla? . . .* She didn't pause to read them all. Panicking, she deleted Laura's post and put the phone down.

Bloody Laura, she thought. Hadn't she already said enough? The last thing Isla needed right now was five hundred well-meaning friends and acquaintances checking in with her.

She got out of bed and went downstairs to find Sophie. She found her in the kitchen, loading the dishwasher.

'Let's go out tonight,' Isla said.

'I thought you were determined to be a hermit,' Sophie said, with a smile.

'Well, I've changed my mind,' Isla said, resolutely. 'I want to go out.'

'OK,' Sophie said, seeming surprised at the turnaround, but pleasantly so. 'I'll book us a table somewhere nice in town, there's a great Thai—'

'Not a restaurant,' Isla said, shaking her head.

'Where then?'

'I want to go clubbing.'

Sophie smiled. 'Right! You're sure?'

'Completely.'

Sophie and Isla were getting ready in Sophie's bedroom, and Liam was working downstairs in the kitchen. He'd looked at them as if they were joking when they'd told him they were going out clubbing for the evening – but that made it more fun, Sophie thought. It was about time she left him at home for once.

Upstairs, Sophie lent Isla a dress to wear, and they sipped prosecco, listening to music, as they got ready.

'It's been far too long since we did this,' Sophie said.

'It has, hasn't it?' Isla adjusted the dress in Sophie's full-length mirror and tidied her hair, then turned towards her friend. 'We scrub up OK, don't we?'

'Beautifully,' Sophie said. She looked at Isla and felt a pang of nostalgia for the times when they'd done this a few times a week. 'It's good, having you here again,' she said. 'I wish you'd had different reasons for coming back. But it's good having you here all the same.'

'Agreed,' Isla said. She said it without emotion, but Sophie could tell she meant it.

A horn honked outside in the road. 'That'll be our cab,' Sophie said. They went outside to the taxi, and drove towards the pink and orange streaked sunset.

The cab dropped them in town, outside a bar on White Ladies Road that the driver had recommended. 'Full of lovely ladies like you,' he'd said. Sophie and Isla had seen what he meant almost immediately – it was crammed with women, yes, but most of them on hen nights, dressed in veils and L-plates, shouting at each other over the music. After a couple of cocktails they decided to move on. They made their way over to the boat club, walking slowly through the Bristol streets and reminiscing a little along the way.

In the queue for the club, Sophie sensed Isla hesitate.

'Maybe this was a dumb idea,' Isla said.

'There's no backing out now, you know,' Sophie said, firmly. 'We've come this far.'

'I know,' Isla said. 'You're right. I just – I feel weird.'

'Unwell weird?' Sophie asked, concerned.

'No, nothing like that,' Isla said, quickly. 'It just feels strange being back here.'

'This is where you brought me, do you remember?' Sophie said. 'After the stories came out, about the affair. Came here and bought me WKDs or whatever grim drink it was, until we were dancing and laughing so much that I'd completely stopped caring.'

Isla smiled. 'I remember that. You were worried you might get spotted – there you were, famous for five minutes – but no one knew who you were at all.'

'It was good to get out and realise that,' Sophie said. After that night she'd resolved not to care what people thought, and afterwards, when she did get the occasional sly comment from someone who'd heard about the scandal, she'd brushed it off easily.

'Maybe you owe me, then,' Isla said.

'You're right,' Sophie said. 'I think I do.'

Once inside, they ordered drinks, and sat at a booth by the side of the dance floor, watching the crowd, UV lights travelling over their figures. The bass throbbed, and Sophie felt it in her chest. A tune came on that she recognised from their student days.

'Remember this?' she said, excited. Isla nodded. It was Fatboy Slim's 'Praise You'. She grabbed Isla by the hand and motioned towards the dance floor.

'No, I feel ridiculous,' Isla said, laughing. 'Everyone else here must be, what, twenty?'

'Oh, who cares? We don't look much older than them. Look, those guys are even checking us out.' She pointed to a couple of younger guys propping up the bar.

'They're not looking at us.'

'They *are*,' Sophie insisted.

Isla glanced back, then started to laugh. 'You're right.'

Isla seemed to relax a little then, and start to let go. Sophie watched her dancing, in the haze of the lights and dry ice, and remembered the carefree student her friend had once been. There was nothing about her that suggested she wasn't well, that she had left the man she loved, that she was carrying a burden of uncertainty about her future. She looked happy and free.

Sophie wanted to bottle that moment, and keep it for ever.

It was Saturday night, and Rafael was out with friends at a bar in the centre of town. As he waited for the round of drinks he'd ordered to arrive at the bar, he glanced around the room. A group of women were sitting in a booth by the waterside window. One – petite with a black bob – caught his eye. She smiled.

He turned back to the bar, feeling slightly awkward about the way he'd flirted without meaning to, and paid for the drinks. He took them over to where his friends were sitting. It wasn't as if he was starting from scratch. He was simply going back to the life he'd had – before Isla came into it. Before that sunny day when she'd walked into the book-shop. The day he'd seen her dark red-brown hair glinting in the light and then locked eyes with her, known in that moment: *There you are.*

His heart felt heavy thinking of it. Christ, it hurt every damn time he picked his phone up. The way she'd just undone him from her life. Put up a wall on social network-ing, as if him no longer seeing her online could unpick the feelings they'd had for one another. The feelings he still had for her every minute of the day. The way he missed her jokes, her smile, the softness of the skin on the nape of her neck and her shoulder blades, when she'd lain next to him at night.

It had been almost three weeks. It had started to sink in, what she'd said. It wasn't as if there was any ambiguity in her words. He couldn't force her to be with him. But it hurt – there was no way around that. He'd been in this city for over ten years and never met anyone like Isla. He'd come to make a new start. He hadn't chosen his path, it had been the only one available to him. A way out.

He gave the drinks to his friends, sat down with them, and listened to their stories. But he missed her. Every day he missed her.

He felt a tap on his shoulder, and turned around to see a woman with long blonde hair, smiling at him. 'Hi,' she said. That British accent. For a moment, if he'd pressed his eyes shut, it could almost have been her. 'Me and my friend over there—' she pointed at the girl with the dark bob, who nodded in greeting '—we were wondering if you guys might like to join us.'

What was Rafael going to do – stay living in the past, give up? He looked around at his friends, who were waiting for him to reply. There was no hesitation from them, and there shouldn't be from him. He needed to move on.

'Sure,' Rafael said, with a smile. 'Of course.'

Isla and Sophie stayed in the club until it was almost dawn.

'Let's walk home, the long way,' Isla said. 'Past the suspension bridge. I haven't been there in ages.'

'It's so late,' Sophie said.

'Late, early, whatever,' Isla said. 'Tomorrow's Sunday. We haven't got anything to be getting back for.'

The streets were quiet, and they found an all-night café. They stopped for breakfast and got take-out coffee – by the time they reached the suspension bridge the sun was colouring the sky with streaks of pink and orange.

'Like the old days,' Sophie said, taking a seat on a rock, and leaning back a little to take in the spectacular view of the Avon Gorge. Clifton was more than just a bridge, it was a sign of what you could make possible if you were determined enough – a feat of engineering that she found dizzying, however many times she saw it.

'Yes, it is. And look – the sun's coming up,' Isla said, pointing over at the shy golden slice making its presence known on the horizon.

'This was on your list,' Sophie reminded her. '"See sunset and sunrise". We've done one of the items without even planning it.'

Isla smiled. 'You're right. It feels good.'

'Things might be different,' Sophie said, 'now that you have the diagnosis. But you're still you. You know that, right?'

Isla nodded, but didn't reply. The night had reawakened energy and hope in her, and she didn't want to ruin that all now with thoughts of her illness and what her future might hold. 'I guess you won't be having too many more nights out like this soon,' she said instead. 'If you and Liam have a baby, I mean.'

'Who knows,' Sophie said. 'I'm pretty certain I'm not pregnant yet. And while we're trying, we're not *trying* trying. Just letting nature take its course.'

'A lot of good babies get made that way. My mum still says she wasn't *trying* trying when she had a one-night stand that resulted in me.'

Sophie laughed. 'Maybe you're right. Maybe now's the time, for things like this. A time we won't have for ever. A time we need to take hold of.'

'You're right,' Isla said, determined. 'I'm not giving up, Sophie. There's too much I still want to do.'

'Good,' Sophie said. 'That's the Isla I know and love.'

Sophie put her arm around her friend, and they sat there for a while, just looking out at the sunrise. Isla knew then that if she was going to continue living in a way that made her happy, she was going to have to keep on being part of the world, part of nature, pushing boundaries, as she always had.

Rafael woke in the half-light of dawn. Opening his eyes more than a crack felt like an effort. When he did, he felt an emptiness that filled the room. No life in it without her.

He pictured the woman who might have been there, beside him, her sleek black hair mussed now. Niamh, that was her name. They'd talked until three. He'd liked her. He'd liked being with her, hearing her stories, feeling that she wanted to be with him. He'd even liked kissing her, when he'd got used to the way it was different. She was a tattoo artist. In the bar, he'd seen the elaborate artwork that was her shoulders and arms. She never inked herself; her ex had done most of it. That was something they had in common – the marks left on them by their past.

Niamh was here in Amsterdam for a few months, maybe longer, depending on how her studio went. She liked it here. People laughed more, she'd said. He'd tried his best to be one of those people.

She had almost been here, in his flat, had even asked to be – but she wasn't. His bed was empty, as it had been for weeks now. His life since Isla had left it had been a half-life, of sunsets on days that had been filled but not full. He didn't want to be that man, who tried to fill the gap with women he didn't really care about. He'd never been that man before, and now didn't feel like the time to start. Instead he was on his own with memories of Isla, because even memories of her were better than being without her, completely. When he'd looked at Niamh, the curve of her neck, her smile, all he'd seen was what was missing. It wasn't fair on her, this beautiful woman who would make someone else very happy. But there was only one person he wanted her, or any other woman, to be, and that was Isla.

Liam brought Sophie coffee in bed the next morning. 'Freshly brewed. I thought you could probably do with some this morning.'

'Thanks,' Sophie said, taking the cup gratefully. She propped herself up on pillows in bed. Her head felt a little sore and her ears were still buzzing, but, rather than blunting her joy, they were pleasant reminders of a great night.

'What time did you guys crawl in last night? I didn't hear you get back.'

'After dawn. Can you believe it?' Sophie said, with a smile. 'We've still got it, Liam. Still got it.'

'Yeah,' he said. 'Good for you.'

The note of sarcasm wasn't lost on Sophie. 'Did it bother you?'

'It just seems a little hypocritical, that's all. The way you judged me for staying out at the party over the road – acted as if I was making a fool of myself – but it's fine for you to do the same thing.'

'It's not quite the same, Liam,' Sophie said. 'Isla's my best friend, and we haven't been out together like that in years. Plus I didn't try and hide it from you – I thought I'd made it clear that it was that, not your going out, that bothered me.'

'I don't really see the difference. And yes, you might have been annoyed about me keeping it from you but you also did act as if I was too old to be out enjoying myself like that.'

'No . . . ' Sophie said, putting her coffee down. The shine was starting to come off her night out. Liam seemed to want to use it as ammunition. 'I just thought it wasn't the best way of bonding with your students. I guess you could call me a hypocrite for that too – given how the two of us got together, but we're older and wiser now, right?'

'Yes.' Liam's expression seemed to soften then. 'Sorry – I shouldn't have had a go.'

'Thanks. And we are only thirty, you know. It's not like we're past it.'

'That's right, bring that up again, the fact that you're younger than me.'

'That isn't what I meant and you know it.' Sophie sighed, sensing that this morning's battle was one she wasn't going to win.

Liam got to his feet. 'I'm going out for a jog, then taking Rebecca shopping today,' he said. There was an edge to his voice that suggested she had hit a raw nerve. 'So you guys will have the place to yourselves.'

After her and Sophie's night out, Isla was sleeping late. When she woke, she felt a wave of positivity – spending the time with Sophie had reminded her just how much was still possible. That some of the new limits on her life were real – but far more were in her mind.

That morning, over brunch, she put her proposal to Sophie.

'We're going on an adventure today.'

'What, now?' Sophie said, laughing. 'I haven't even finished what's on my plate.'

'Well, get on with it, because I've had an idea.'

'Yes?'

'Wild swimming. I want to do that. Today,' Isla said. She felt a rush of adrenalin as she said it. 'It's on my list. I just haven't found the right place – but now I've had a brilliant idea. We could drive over the border to Wales – there's a pool with a waterfall I've heard about, in Brecon Beacons . . . '

'Isla, you're insane! I'm hungover, you must be tired – Liam already thinks we're mad for getting back so late last night. Well, this morning. Plus it's going to be freezing. You should check the medical advice, at least, I'm pretty sure that extreme temperatures . . . '

'I've got *the rest of my life* to check medical advice, Sophie. Let me live in blissful ignorance just a few days longer.'

'I really don't think this is a good idea.'

'It may well not be. But you can't say no to me. Not right now,' Isla said, with the ghost of a smile.

'Oh, God,' Sophie said, 'you're not really going to pull the sickness card, are you?'

'Just this once,' Isla said. 'Yes, I am.'

They drove to the Brecon Beacons National Park, singing their hearts out to the songs on the radio. Here, in each other's company, they both felt safe. It might have been a bubble, but the sense of security was real.

When they arrived the cloudy sky had cleared, and autumn sun dappled the water with pale gold, and the damp day they had woken up to seemed as if it had belonged to a different season altogether. They could just see the waterfall and pool below it through the gap in the trees.

Sophie, standing beside the open car door, stripped down to her swimsuit, then wrapped a towel around herself. 'Come on, then,' she said, leaning down towards the car where Isla was still sitting in the passenger seat.

She could do it. She should do it. Isla tried to summon up the courage that had once been something she didn't need to seek, simply a part of her.

'I'll follow you in,' Isla said. 'Just give me a minute.'

'OK,' Sophie said, more gently. 'You wait here. Crank the radio up. My Kindle's in my bag if you want to read something. I'm going in.'

She gave her friend a kiss and headed off towards the water.

Isla kept the radio off, and watched Sophie's retreating form, reducing in size as she headed towards the water. She was tying her long hair up into a top-knot as she walked.

Isla sat there for a moment, frozen. She didn't even know what she was scared of. She thought of the list – the things she'd always wanted to do, one of them here for the taking. She got out of the car, stripped off down to her borrowed swimsuit and grabbed her towel. She ran towards the water, and Sophie. She was going in.

'Come in, it's lovely,' Sophie said, delighted to see her friend, and dipping just below the surface of the clear water.

'Liar,' Isla yelled good-naturedly as the icy temperatures

met her skin, sending a ripple of goosebumps over the surface. 'You are a complete liar.'

Sophie wrinkled her nose and laughed. 'I'd never have got you in otherwise,' she smiled. 'And it feels good, doesn't it?'

Isla leaned back and let the cold water cradle her body. Her body that in recent weeks had felt like a burden to her – weightier, somehow. Unreliable, unpredictable with the potential to trip her up. Here, supported by the water, cold as it was, her body felt perfect. The way it used to feel before she'd lost faith in it – sleek, its movements fluid. The shock of the chill sent the energy of adrenalin through her.

Sophie was swimming over to the waterfall, and Isla followed her. She watched the flow of her friend's swimming – Sophie had always been an excellent swimmer – and found that her body followed the movements without her commanding it to. Here in the pool there was no one else, not a sign of human life even on the horizon. Just birdsong, the sound of the breeze through the leaves and of the waterfall.

After a short swim, they got out, wrapped themselves in towels and dashed back to the car to get changed. Sophie brought out a thermos of hot chocolate and they took it in turns to sip from the small plastic lid. The swim had brought a smile to both of their faces. Isla wanted that feeling to last, and last, and last.

Chapter 11

Isla hadn't wanted to leave Sophie's. The weekend had lit a spark in her, and as she hugged her friend goodbye on the Sunday night, after their trip swimming, and travelled back to the cottage, she knew it was down to her now to keep it lit. OK, so going swimming in a freezing pool probably hadn't been the most sensible thing to do, and that night she had experienced a flutter of panic that it might bring on a relapse. She knew she was driving in the dark, not knowing enough about her health condition – and that she couldn't go on that way – but the moment of risk-taking had been a small slice of freedom. And that had meant a lot.

Plus, the feeling of drawing a line through two items on her list was hard to beat: *See sunset and sunrise the same night. Wild swimming.* Both done. The list was going to be her guide, she vowed, now more than it ever had been before. She wasn't going to give in to this disease. She was not going to roll over and let it take all of her dreams from her.

On Monday, back at the cottage, Isla took her tea out into the garden. It was a cool morning, crisp and sunny. When she'd emptied her cup, she picked up a bag and started to tidy up the branches and twigs that cluttered the lawn. The garden, which had always been her grandad's job – more than that, his hobby, one of his favourite things – was these days largely neglected. She picked her way through the brambles at the back, then got out some tools from the shed, pruning and cutting back the plants that were overgrown. Buried beneath some of the thicker brambles was the herb garden her grandfather had once tended so carefully. She saw the handwritten labels on the plants, and a lump came to her throat. She missed him. They all missed him.

At around eleven, the hazy sun higher in the sky now, Hattie came out and joined her.

'Your granny's going to pop round this afternoon,' Hattie said. 'She's longing to see you.'

Isla thought of Sadie. Her wild grandma. The circus performer. The traveller. The dreamer. The pensioner with more points on her driving licence than any boy racer. Sadie was her vision of a life well lived, and had always been a cheerleader when it came to Isla's own ambitions. 'Great,' Isla said. 'It'll be good to see her again.'

'No one else quite like your grandmother,' Hattie said, with a smile. 'Maddeningly stubborn, exhausting, and . . . '

'Amazing,' Isla said.

'Yes,' Hattie said, with a smile. 'That too.'

They sat there for a moment, in the calmness of the garden, just quietly being together.

That morning they worked alongside each other, chatting and laughing, unwinding tangled branches from the old wooden fences, sweeping up leaves and remnants of broken plant pots. Nothing would grow for months yet – not till March at least, when the first of the buried bulbs would start to show their colours. But when those shoots did start to show, when the first buds appeared on branches and twigs, it would be beautiful. Once there had been no more than a green and brown mess, a clouded memory of what the garden had once been. Next spring, they would both see something more.

Yes, Isla had once yearned for bigger things than this – of New York. Of Paris. Now it was the tiny green shoots or the promise of a spring bloom that elevated her spirits. To wake in the morning and to feel clear-headed and calm – that was what she aimed for now. That was what it took to have a good day.

Dreams were supposed to lift you up, not bring you down, weren't they? Perhaps it was time to adapt and change. Perhaps it was time to let some of her old dreams go.

Isla watched out of the window as her grandmother attempted to reverse-park her Morris Minor. On the third attempt she got it in, ramming the car behind her hard on the bumper. Isla ran out on to the front step to welcome her.

'Hi, Granny,' she said, greeting her with a hug.

'Hello, darling,' Sadie said, getting out of the car. 'Welcome home.' She pulled back to look at her granddaughter, their eyes meeting. 'You look pretty good to me,' she said. 'Now how are you at getting the kettle on these days?'

Hattie brought through tea and Isla and Sadie settled back on to the sofa. 'I meant what I said. You wouldn't know a thing to look at you,' Sadie said to Isla. 'But I'm sorry to hear about your illness, Isla.'

'Thanks,' Isla said. 'You get the hand you're dealt, I guess.'

'You do. And that can be tough. But you never know which card will be next in the pack.' Sadie smiled.

'I suppose,' Isla said.

'I mean, look at when your mother met the sperm donor.'

'What?' Isla said, laughing.

'Oh, you didn't know we called him that?' Sadie said.

Hattie flushed pink. 'Oh, c'mon, Mum. It wasn't quite like that.'

'A one-night stand, a trip to the sperm bank – there's not too much difference, is there?'

'I didn't see the point in being careful,' Hattie explained to her daughter, 'when really all I wanted was a baby. And that baby turned out better than I ever could have expected.' She smiled proudly at her daughter. 'But I should really have got his name,' she said. 'I mean, it makes you think, doesn't it? You getting ill. You should know about your genes . . . '

'Don't worry,' Isla said. 'I've never wanted to find out who he is, and I don't want to now. I'm sure he's a lovely guy, but he's probably got his own life and family now, and I've got no wish to go charging into that. Anyway, as far as my health's concerned, there's very little evidence to suggest a genetic link. It just seems to be one of those things. Some people might want to make sense of it, find a reason, but I just want to get on with life and deal with how things are going to be now.'

'OK,' Hattie said. 'Well, I'm glad to hear you've not been longing to meet him.'

'I'm surprised you ever thought that. I would've told you, Mum.'

The three women fell quiet for a moment, Sadie sipping her tea and her mother satisfied that she had the answers she needed for now.

'Can I ask you two something different, though?' Isla asked.

'Sure, anything,' Hattie said at once.

'My list. You know, the one with the things I really want to do in life.'

'Yes, love,' Sadie said. 'What about it?'

'You know that one day I'd really love to learn to fly a trapeze. Just like you did,' Isla said.

'Well then, you should,' Sadie said. 'Of course you should. I've yet to find a greater pleasure.'

'But for starters, what I'd like you to help me with isn't too wild – no circus equipment needed,' Isla said.

'Yes?' Hattie said, curious.

'I'd like to make a quilt. One with our family's stories in it. Taking the fabrics and materials that we have and making something new.'

'That's a lovely idea,' Hattie said. 'You have lots of material, don't you, Mum? In that old chest at your house.'

'Haven't looked in that for years,' Sadie said hesitantly. 'Perhaps all I've needed is a reason.'

*

That weekend, Sadie brought a bag over to the cottage in the boot of her car, and showed Hattie and Isla the fabrics. They were a wild mix of seventies prints, bold colours and delicate florals. Hattie supplied the tea, and Isla brought out a hazelnut and chocolate loaf, fresh from the oven. They laid the textiles out on the floor and took a good look over them all, choosing the best ones for the quilt.

'I haven't looked in that chest for a good long while, you know,' Sadie said. 'Probably not since before your grandfather passed away.'

Five years. Sadie's eyes, and the way she rested her hand on Hattie's, silently seeking understanding, revealed her lingering pain.

'After you'd decided on what you wanted to keep, Hattie, I put the rest of his belongings in the study, you see. Then I shut the door. Easier that way. Only trouble is, there were things in there already, you see. Like the chest. And so I ended up not looking at those either.'

'How did it feel,' Isla asked, gently, 'going back in there after so long?'

'You know what? I think it was good for me,' Sadie said. She sat up a little straighter as she said it. 'And, while some of the things were hard to see again – his wedding suit, his ring, that awful Christmas jumper he used to love wearing ...' She paused for a moment after saying that. Isla noticed her mother grip Sadie's hand more tightly. 'Well, some of the others brought a smile to my face. A snow globe from our honeymoon in Scotland, photos from the trips we took with you and your sister when you were young, Hattie.' Sadie touched a yellow blanket as she spoke. 'Your baby blanket. Should've passed it down to you with the rest of

160

the things, when Isla was born, but, perhaps unconsciously, I couldn't really bring myself to part with it. I still remember your father holding you wrapped up in it, as we left the hospital. Proudest man in the West Country, he was, that day.'

Isla thought fondly of her grandfather, remembering his strong arms, kind eyes, the way he'd read to her on the sofa at her grandparents' house. OK, so the questions at school hadn't always been easy to answer, but she hadn't felt the absence of a father as keenly as people presumed she did. She'd had her grandfather, and he'd been the only man she'd needed when she was growing up.

'We're obviously not cutting this one up,' Hattie said, touching the fabric of her own baby blanket and then gently folding it. Isla saw then that her mother had been holding a lot inside. She had been hurt by her father's death but hadn't always shown it; she'd just shut the door to her own private room, and it hadn't been clear from the outside.

Isla had often longed to be able to share memories of her grandfather with her mum, but it hadn't happened. Now she saw that some things only came with time.

Isla, Hattie and Sadie sat up together till midnight, cutting and sewing, some sections by hand and others on Hattie's old Singer. By the time they all said goodnight, they had pieced and pinned half of the quilt.

With each square that they chose, they talked through a memory. Sadie recalled how it had been raising Hattie and her brother in the fifties. Hattie talked about how she'd given birth to Isla, not in a cabin in the woods as she'd planned, but in a supermarket car park, with a parking attendant assisting her. How scared she'd been when she was able to take Isla home, and realised that this was it – the immense responsibility of single motherhood dawning on her.

Isla went upstairs to bed feeling that, in piecing together those sections of fabric, she was doing so much more than crossing something off her list. She was back in the loving intimacy of her family, and she'd always be the same Isla there. Nothing could take her identity away.

Chapter 12

Rafael opened a new delivery that had come into the Floating Bookshop that morning – a shipment of Scandinavian crime thrillers tipped by the publishers to be the next big thing. He put them out on the central table, then went back to the counter. A customer, a young man who hadn't been in the shop before, went over and picked one up, reading the back. Sales had been slow lately – the city was always quieter as winter approached – and Rafael hoped that things might pick up with the new stock.

Behind the counter, he got out a second box of books. These were different – these ones wouldn't be going on display. He'd gone to the antiques fair the previous afternoon and found some beautifully bound titles he couldn't resist buying. There were days that he had his business head firmly on – and others when he let the passion for reading that had led him to open the shop in the first place take over. He took out the hardbacks and handled them gently.

P.G. Wodehouse. Back home in Mexico, as a teenager, he'd found one of the novels online and ordered a copy. It had opened a window on to a world of English eccentricity that surprised and delighted him. He'd told Isla that, before meeting Berenice and other English friends in Amsterdam, it had given him his first ideas about England. She had laughed, and said they were books that she had adored too.

Picturing her face, remembering her joy in that moment, was bittersweet.

He understood that it was over, that they weren't getting back together – he didn't even know for sure what country she was in right now, that was how disconnected they'd become. But he still felt bound to her, somehow.

It didn't have to mean anything, he told himself. Only that, for a moment, he'd thought of her. That however painful and difficult their last conversation had been, he didn't bear her any ill will.

He put the books back in the box and packaged it up, adding a label. He didn't know Isla's address in New York, if that was where she still was – but presumably her mum would. Isla had written down the address for him, in the shop address book – 'For when you come at Christmas,' she'd said. He tried not to linger on how it felt, knowing that moment would now never come. He copied out the details.

Berenice came in, waving over in greeting, and Rafael instinctively put the box back below the counter. His pride cut in. Perhaps sending it wasn't the right thing to do, after all.

'Hello, Bea,' he said, cheerily. 'How are you today?'

'Well, thank you,' she said. 'Bakewell tarts today.' She put the tin on the counter.

'Perfect. And I know that's my cue.' He went over to the coffee machine and made two cups, then brought them over with an empty plate.

Berenice laid out the handmade treats. 'Has it been busy this morning?'

'So-so,' Rafael said. 'Those new thrillers should help, with any luck.' He pointed to them, over on the table. The customer Rafael had hoped might be interested had left empty-handed. 'You know how it is over winter.'

'Does get rather quiet round here, doesn't it?' she said. 'But look, I've got a nice order for you.'

'Yes?' he said, brightening.

'Yes – my book group have made up their mind on this month's title.' She passed him a piece of paper. 'We'll need them by Friday. You can do that, can't you?'

'It would be my pleasure,' he said. He brought his laptop over and entered the details, scanning the list of titles at the warehouse so he could make sure he chose the right edition.

As he was typing, he caught sight of his phone on the counter, flashing with a call. Berenice also glanced over at it.

'"Patricia",' she read out.

Patricia, Rafael thought. It had been a while since he'd heard from her. She usually had a reason for calling.

'I'll ring her back later,' Rafael said.

'Sorry,' Berenice said. 'I shouldn't have looked.'

'It doesn't matter,' Rafael said. He knew what she was wondering – Berenice was hopeless at hiding her curiosity. It might have bothered someone else, but not him. It didn't mean he had to tell her everything, though – and he didn't know if he was ready to tell her this.

'It's none of my business,' she said.

'Agreed,' he said, with a smile to show he didn't mind.

'You really are a mystery, aren't you?'

'I'm far less interesting than you might think I am,' he said.

'I'll keep asking, and one day I'll get somewhere. Tell me, what brought you here, to Amsterdam, in the first place?'

'It's not a secret. Just not the happiest of stories, Berenice.'

'You think I got to this age only hearing the good things?' she said, raising an eyebrow. 'I think you'd be surprised.'

'Another day,' he said. 'That's a promise.'

At six, Rafael closed the shop and walked back along the canal, pushing his bike. He paused at a bench and got out his mobile phone. He hesitated briefly, then dialled through to Patricia.

'*Hola*,' Rafael said, when she picked up.

'*Rafael*.' It was his name, the same one he heard every day, but with the Spanish pronunciation he felt transported home. He felt again like the young man he'd been there. Patricia's voice – it was coming from thousands of miles away but sounded so very close. Hearing it took him right back to the town where he'd grown up, and where she still lived.

'*¿Estás bien?*' he asked.

There was a pause. He wasn't sure if there was a delay on the line, or if she didn't want to reply.

'What's up, Patricia?'

'I'm in trouble, Rafael,' she said, tears in her voice. 'I've got no money. None at all.'

He felt for her – he heard her desperation, and thought of the basics she might be facing doing without. But he struggled to comprehend how it had happened – he'd sent her money barely a fortnight ago. How could it have gone already?

'What is it that you need?'

'Food, money to pay the bills. Santiago needs new shoes, too. He hasn't got any that aren't worn through ... He also needs books for school, a bed that's not broken.' Her words came rapidly.

'But the money I sent through, P – I thought we agreed that it was for those things?' He felt bad, but he had to ask. This seemed to be happening more and more frequently. 'What's happened to that?'

'Something came up,' Patricia said, sounding embarrassed. 'Something urgent.'

'Right.' He paused. There was no point dragging through the detail of it all. As long as Santiago had the things he needed, nothing else really mattered.

'OK – I'll organise a transfer tomorrow.'

'Thank you.'

'You don't need to thank me – just ensure that Santi has the things he needs, OK?'

'I will, I promise. You know, I think sometimes that you have forgotten about us.'

His sympathy for her was becoming edged with frustration. She always did this. She didn't need to – he would help her, no matter what. But she always did. The nudge at his conscience, so that he felt bad for going.

'You know I haven't forgotten about you,' he said, calmly. 'I won't ever forget about you and Santiago. I may be here, but part of me will always be back there.'

'It's so hard,' Patricia said, through tears. 'It's all so hard.

Your mother helps when she can, but ... he needs a man here with him, Rafael. Santi needs his father.'

It didn't matter what he told himself, about his reasons for going. He couldn't shake his guilt – for leaving in the first place, and for not being a role model, when that was what Santiago needed most.

'It'll be OK, Patricia,' he said. The words were for him as much as her. 'I know how hard it is for you to wait. But there are better days to come. Please try and keep the faith. Try not to worry.'

Chapter 13

The next day, Hattie and Isla sat down to eat breakfast together in the cottage kitchen. It was crisp and cold, and pale morning light came in through the blinds.

'Raspberry jam?' Isla said, passing her mum the jar.

'Thanks.' Hattie looked at her daughter, as if seeing her anew. 'You seem different this morning. Brighter.'

'I guess I am a bit,' Isla said. 'Getting used to being home, I suppose.'

She still thought of Amsterdam, of Rafael – all the time. She still thought of what might have been, if life had played out differently for her. If she hadn't got ill. But she wasn't angry any more; she didn't have it in her. And it was easier, the two of them not being in touch – to hear his voice on the phone and see photos of him online would have been painful. This way, it was as if she'd never left England . . . almost as if the love they'd shared had never happened at all.

'It was good to see Granny yesterday, wasn't it?' Hattie said. 'I know it's cheered her up, having you home.'

'It was lovely. I'm glad she's starting to talk about Grandad a little more too.'

'She had to wait until she was ready, I suppose,' Hattie said. 'I did too. But it's the best way to keep him with us, talking about him, isn't it?'

'I think so. I feel close to him sometimes when I'm out in the garden, too.'

'He always loved it out there. Much more green-fingered than I'll ever be.' Hattie smiled. She seemed to catch herself, before the emotion could rise too close to the surface. 'So, today,' she said, matter-of-factly. 'Sophie's coming around later, isn't she?'

'Yes,' Isla said, glancing at the kitchen clock. 'She'll be here in an hour or so.'

'I'm looking forward to seeing her again. It's been a good couple of years. I expect she's changed a lot.'

Isla smiled. 'Not really. She's pretty much the same, actually. It's quite comforting.'

'She's still working at the hospital?'

Isla nodded. 'Yes, and still with Liam.'

'They made it against the odds, those two, didn't they?' Hattie said. 'Quite a story they have.'

'Yes. I suppose they did. It's been so long I can't imagine her with anyone else now.'

Hattie paused for a moment, curious. 'What do you think of him – Liam?'

'Really?' Isla said.

'Yes, of course.'

'He's fine.' Isla hadn't stopped to think about it for a while.

Sophie was with Liam – they were married, committed to one another. It didn't really feel like her place to judge – they'd had enough of that to deal with. 'He cares about her, looks after her.'

'But?'

Her mum's nudge prompted her to dwell on her gut feelings a little more. There was something. Something that didn't quite click. 'If I'm completely honest, I think she might have been happier with someone else. Been able to be herself more, with someone who was less set in their ways.'

'There was a certain dynamic from the start, I suppose,' Hattie said, 'with him being a tutor and her a student.'

The idea resonated with Isla. 'I'm not sure they've ever really changed that. Even now, with them thinking about starting a family – it's all been down to him making a decision, him changing his mind. I suppose there's part of me that, as a friend, is annoyed with him about that.'

'I can see where you're coming from,' Hattie said.

Isla felt bad for a moment, saying these things out loud. It seemed disloyal. 'But he's fine,' she repeated. 'He gives her security, and she's always said she needs that, what with her family being so distant.'

'She never made things up with her parents?'

'They've not forgiven her, no.' Isla was aware that it still hurt her friend deeply, the rejection. But from everything she'd heard about Sophie's mum and dad, she was inclined to think Sophie was much better off without them.

'Such a shame, that,' Hattie said. 'For them as much as her. You'd have to marry someone truly awful for me to disown you, Isla.' She smiled. 'Not that I'm suggesting you test me out.'

'I won't. But I'm very much single at the moment, anyway, so there's no need to worry.'

Hattie looked at her, her blue eyes kind and enquiring. 'I'll admit I was wondering. You mentioned that there was someone in Amsterdam. Rafael. I wondered—'

Isla thought of Rafael again, and her heart ached. An ache she hadn't really believed existed until she'd felt it for herself, conscious of a little piece of her that was missing. She was moving on, slowly, but it still plagued her – the knowledge that she'd hurt him. That in doing so she'd hurt herself, too.

'I thought it might be something serious. I cared about him, but it didn't work out.'

'I'm sorry.'

'Don't be,' Isla said, hoping that her sadness didn't show. 'It really was for the best.'

When Sophie arrived at the cottage, the two friends sat together in the living room, having tea. After saying hello, Hattie excused herself and went through to the kitchen to take a phone call.

'So how is it going?' Sophie asked, her voice lowered.

'Oh, you don't need to whisper,' Isla assured her. 'Mum won't hear a thing in there. It's not bad, actually. For the most part, Mum's been great.' Isla thought for a moment about the run-in with Laura Groves, and how annoyed she'd been about word getting around about her illness. Somehow, with the passing of time, it didn't seem to matter much any more what a girl she'd barely known at school had to say. 'It's been better than I expected, actually.'

'I'm pleased to hear that,' Sophie said.

172

'It's been great to catch up with Granny, too.' Seeing Sadie had really lifted Isla, and reminded her of some of the positives about being back home.

'She's a wonderful woman, Sadie,' Sophie said, echoing Isla's thoughts. 'You're really lucky to have her.'

'I know. Mum might need a little reminding of that from time to time, when Granny's showing her stubborn streak – but we all know it really.'

Sophie smiled. 'What about some of the things your doctor mentioned,' she asked gently. 'Have you gone along to the support group yet?'

Isla put her fingers in her ears and started to sing tunelessly. 'La la la.' Her feelings on that hadn't changed. The time wasn't right. It might not ever be right.

'OK, OK,' Sophie laughed. 'I get it.'

'Not ready.'

'And you haven't thought any more about the disease-modifying treatment—'

'Stop,' Isla said, firmly. This was not why she wanted to talk to Sophie. She wanted to relax, have a break from the medical stuff for a while. 'Everything in time.'

'Sorry,' Sophie said, sensing she had overstepped the mark. 'I don't mean to meddle. It's just that I want the best for you. I care.'

'I know that, Soph. But there are some things I'm going to need to do on my own.' She had to say it now – set up her new boundaries and ask those that she loved and cared about to stick to them. 'If it's any reassurance, I have realised I need to take things a little easier.'

'No more late-night clubbing and freezing swims?' Sophie asked with a smile.

'Perhaps not right now,' Isla said. It had been an unforgettable weekend, but she'd seen since then that she could do various things to make herself happy, some at a much slower pace. 'On that note,' she added, getting to her feet, 'let me show you something.'

Isla brought over the carefully pinned quilt. 'Look what we got up to with Granny last night.'

'That's beautiful,' Sophie said, touching the fabric. 'A family quilt. This was on your list too, wasn't it?'

'Yes, it was.' Isla felt a deep sense of achievement. It was a small step, but one that mattered.

'You're making progress,' Sophie said.

'It's keeping me out of trouble, for the time being.' It was also distracting her from her broken heart, Isla thought – an unexpected side-effect, and one she was grateful for.

'It's something you will always treasure,' Sophie said.

Isla folded the quilt carefully and put it back by Hattie's sewing machine. 'How's Liam doing, by the way?' she asked. 'I remember you said he wasn't thrilled about us staying out the other night.'

'He's all right,' Sophie said. 'He thinks we're both nuts – our trip out swimming the next day only confirmed that, of course. But I'm not going to pander to him. He can think what he likes.'

'That's the spirit,' Isla said, smiling.

Hattie came back into the room with a tray of biscuits and passed one to Sophie. 'Here you go, sweetheart.'

'Thanks, Hattie,' Sophie said.

'Sorry about dashing off just then – that was the shop calling about the rota for next week. Had to take it.'

'Don't worry. Isla's just been showing me the quilt you've been making. It's going to look gorgeous.'

'Isn't it?' she said proudly. 'Mum found some really nice fabric back at the bungalow. My old Singer sewing machine's seen more action since Isla got home than it has in months.'

'Isla's list is a powerful thing,' Sophie said.

'Isn't it just?' Hattie said. 'I was talking to Mum about it earlier today, as it happens.'

'You were?' Isla said.

'Yes. We put our heads together, talking about what we can do to help you.'

'Mum . . .' Isla said. 'Don't. You're already doing enough, letting me live here rent-free until I get back into work. Putting up with me moping around on my bad days.'

'Not things like that,' Hattie said. 'That's all part and parcel of being a parent. But Granny and I know you've had a hard time, and we want to do something a bit special. I know the list is important to you.'

Isla was quiet, but Sophie nodded. 'It is. It does matter to her a lot.'

'Granny and I were talking. Now, it won't be me swinging from a trapeze with you – or your granny getting back up there after all these years – we can't help with that part. But we've got a bit of money put aside – not lots, mind, but enough to make a difference, we hope. We'd like you to put it towards completing your list.'

Isla didn't know what to say. She knew that every penny her mum was talking about would have been saved carefully, over years, and earned by long hours on her feet in the shop. And she was willing to give it up – just like that.

'I can't, Mum,' Isla said, a lump coming to her throat. 'You might need it – and Granny's getting on—'

'I've been thinking about tomorrow for too long, Isla. Your grandmother feels the same way. What we both want, more than anything else, is to do what we can so that you can have the very best today.'

Isla felt overwhelmed by their generosity. But it wasn't charity, she could see that now – it was something they both really wanted. It would be churlish to reject it. 'Thank you,' she said. 'Thank you so much.'

When Hattie left the room, Isla brought over her laptop to where Sophie was sitting, and opened it.

'Your mum is so kind,' Sophie said.

'I know. She really shouldn't—'

'Let her,' Sophie said, putting a hand on her friend's arm. 'It's obvious that she wants to.'

'She's always been too nice for her own good. She'll probably be living off baked beans after this.'

'But she'll be doing so happily, in the knowledge that you're fulfilling your dreams.'

'So where are we going to start?' Isla said. She unfolded her copy of the list, the worn piece of notebook paper barely holding together at the folds, and they looked through it.

'I know what's tempting me,' Sophie said, almost immediately.

'Don't tell me. Paris,' Isla said. 'The chocolate-making.'

'You know I've always fancied that. Time together, a French adventure, shopping, art galleries . . . '

'Macaroons,' Isla said, smiling.

'Macaroons,' Sophie echoed. 'Yes, that too.'

'Could you afford to take the time off?'

'Yes – I've still got holiday days to use up at work. I'll need to check the dates, but I'm sure we can work something out.'

'Great. I've not got too much in my diary at the moment, as you might have noticed. Right then, let's see what Paris has to offer.' Isla went on to her laptop and scrolled through links to chocolate-making courses in the French capital.

'Look at this one . . . ' She showed Sophie the screen, with mouthwatering images of chocolates and truffles. 'Right by the Seine. A five-day course.'

'It's actually fairly reasonable,' Sophie said.

Isla clicked on a thumbnail and brought up a photo of the venue, an old-fashioned chocolate shop on a cobbled street. 'It looks perfect.'

'More than perfect.'

'Shall we book?' Isla said.

They looked at each other, barely able to contain their excitement.

'Let's do it.'

That night Isla lay in bed, dreaming about the trip to Paris. She and Sophie had reserved places on the course, and would book their flights as soon as Sophie had cleared the time off work. It all seemed frivolous, delicious, unnecessary – and yet it made more sense than anything else in Isla's life right now.

A gentle knock on her bedroom door roused her from her thoughts. She got up and found her mum was standing outside. 'I meant to tell you, a parcel came for you earlier. It was around at the neighbours' place.'

'For me? Intriguing.' She took the box, wondering who it might be from. 'Thanks, Mum.'

In her bedroom, Isla opened the parcel. Inside were four beautifully bound books. She took them out, one at a time – P.G. Wodehouse. The books that had always made her smile, however gloomy the day. She scanned the outside of the box for confirmation – the writing on the label, the Amsterdam postmark – but she already knew who they were from.

Rafael, she thought. Rafael. Her emotions came to the surface, delight mingling with sorrow. You're going to make this hard for me, aren't you?

Chapter 14

When Sophie got back to Bennett Street later that same evening, the house was empty. She allowed herself a little while on the sofa, browsing through accommodation options in Paris, from pretty guesthouses to cheap Airbnb apartments, narrowing her search down to those close to the chocolate-making course. An hour or so later she heard Liam's car pulled up outside.

'Hi,' he said, coming inside and giving her a hug. 'Sorry, bit later back than I planned. I just dropped Rebecca back at Véronique's and ended up staying for a drink.'

'Everything OK?' Sophie asked. He seemed a little flustered.

'Yes, fine, fine. Véronique had a guy over – Paul. He seemed like a nice enough bloke, and I got the sense she wanted me to meet him.'

'Sounds like it might be getting serious,' Sophie said. She couldn't recall Liam meeting any of Véronique's boyfriends before.

'I think it is. She seems happy. We didn't row about anything, which was refreshing.' He said it as a joke, but they both knew how the strained relations wore him down.

'How was Rebecca?' Sophie asked. 'Did she seem all right about the situation?'

'Yes – she didn't seem fazed. She said she's met him before, and they were laughing and chatting together.'

Sophie felt the tiniest bit of jealousy – this new man was clearly having an easier time of it with Rebecca than she was. But she stopped herself – what mattered was that Rebecca was happy, and that her mum was too, nothing else. They both deserved that.

They went through to the sitting room and sat together on the sofa.

'How was your day over at the cottage?' Liam asked. 'Is Isla getting along OK?'

'It was great, thanks.' Sophie thought back on the day and how nice it had been just to chat in a normal way with Isla – it felt good to have her so nearby. 'It was lovely to see Hattie again, and Isla seems much more positive about things.'

'What do you think's made the difference?' Liam asked. 'Has she started on medication yet?'

'No – she's not ready for that.' Sophie felt a little guilty for the way she'd pressured Isla to talk about it. She was an adult, and ultimately it had to be her call. 'It's something quite different, actually. Do you remember I told you about those lists we made at uni?'

'Vaguely, yes.' Liam said it without any particular interest.

'Mine's in a drawer somewhere, but Isla's always been keen to do everything on hers. Even more so now, given that she doesn't know how long she'll be active and healthy.'

'Fair enough,' Liam said. 'So what kind of things are on there?'

'Staying up to see sunrise was one; wild swimming was another—'

'Ahh,' Liam said, knowingly. 'This explains a few things.'

'Yes, that's why we went off the other day. I should've explained, really – I guess I just thought you might think it was—'

'A little bit childish?'

'I guess,' Sophie said. She waited for him to say that it wasn't, that he understood why these things mattered to Isla, to the two of them. He didn't.

'So what does she want you to do next?'

'Go to Paris,' Sophie said, with slight hesitation. 'We're going on a chocolate-making course, and we've found the loveliest little—'

Liam interrupted her. 'Wait. Let me get this right,' he said, flatly. 'I know this is going to sound horrible. But she's just been diagnosed with a serious illness, and this is her main priority? Learning to make chocolate?'

It sounded different when he put it like that. Trivial. Silly, even.

'You said she wasn't even acting on the doctor's advice and starting meds. Don't you think there are more important things that you could be helping her with right now?'

Sophie felt frustration rise in her. It wasn't as if she hadn't been trying to help Isla get on track with that too. 'Doing these things is what she wants, Liam. It's making her want to get out of bed in the morning. It's giving her hope. Surely you can see that's valuable? I have to respect that.'

'She's not dying, Soph. You don't have to do everything she wants. There's no reason you should feel guilty.'

'It's not like that,' she said, shaking her head. 'It's not like that at all. And anyway, I want to go.'

'This is because you want to go on holiday again? If so, just say it straight out.'

'So what if I do?' Sophie said. 'I haven't had a proper holiday in years – you never seem to want to go anywhere, and Amsterdam wasn't quite the break I was expecting, with everything that happened.'

'That's fine, really. Just don't hide behind her, when it's you who really wants to do these things. You who clearly wants to escape from this – from us.'

'What?' Sophie said. 'Isla's my best friend and I want to be there for her, it's as simple as that. Come on, Liam. Be fair. Whoever said anything about escape?'

'You didn't – explicitly. But I know you, Sophie.'

She picked up on a change in the atmosphere. Liam was holding something back.

'Is there something else you want to talk about?'

He sat down and she saw he was upset. His anger had gone, and he looked defeated. 'I just thought this mattered to you, Soph. Starting a family. But we've hardly been together long enough lately to start trying.'

Sophie thought about it – perhaps she had been putting Isla first too often lately. She had been so caught up in worrying about her friend's health, that she hadn't spent much time with Liam at all. The missed anniversary meal she'd planned to reschedule, to make special, had fallen by the wayside, forgotten.

'I want to get closer to being you and me again, and instead it feels as if we're getting further away from that. Shouldn't being together be what we're putting first at the moment?'

She put her hand on his, and their eyes met. As they fell silent, the tension eased.

'I can understand what you're saying,' she said. 'And perhaps you've got a point. I could have done more to be there for you recently. But it doesn't have to be a case of either/or. I want to be there for Isla. She needs someone right now. But I also want to be here for you, for us.'

'Thanks,' Liam said. 'I'm sorry. I didn't mean to make it seem as though you had to choose. I don't want that. I know Isla's important to you – I mean, damn, she was there before I was.' He smiled. 'But since we started talking about the baby, I suppose I've become a little impatient. I started picturing it, and now I want us to make it happen.'

'I get that,' Sophie said. 'I'm excited about it too, believe me. I really am.'

She squeezed his hand, and his expression softened.

'For what it's worth,' she said, 'I have no plans at all for tonight.'

Isla opened the first of the P.G. Wodehouse books in the morning with tea in bed. It was part of her wider plan to go a little easier on herself. She was tired that morning, a sweeping fatigue that made getting out of bed seem like climbing a mountain. Rather than force herself to be productive, she'd decided to give in to it. The books from Rafael gave her the perfect excuse.

As she read, duvet pulled up around her and a pile of cushions propping her up, she smiled, even laughed to herself a couple of times. Every three or four pages, she'd think of Rafael. Wonder if he had laughed in the same places. She told herself that there was no harm in it – she could remember him, miss him, and still be fine. She could think about him and still find a way to move on.

After finally getting up around lunchtime, Isla got the bus into town. As she walked down towards the back, she caught sight of the blue priority signs – the wheelchair symbol that reminded people to give up their seats if a disabled person needed them. She'd always got up, without even thinking about it – she hadn't needed a sign to remind her, so she'd barely noticed them before. Now they took on a new meaning. Now they nudged their way into her peripheral vision as she travelled. In a few years, they might remind some young kid in his school uniform to make way for her. The thought made her feel weak and vulnerable, invisible, even. Perhaps, sooner or later, she might need signs like that to help remind people that she existed at all.

In Bristol, she went into a clothes shop, and picked out a new top and some trousers to take to Paris. She couldn't splash out too much, but it felt good to have something new to take away with her. She'd started packing, and each time she looked at the suitcase in the corner of her bedroom, or added another item to it, she experienced that small thrill of anticipation that came before a holiday. The new things, in their crisp tissue paper packaging, held promise. As she held them in her lap on the journey home, she felt protected. They staved off the threat of the wheelchair signs; they reminded her that she was fine, now, and that there was every chance she might continue to be, for a long time.

Back at the cottage, she put on the radio and sat down

to check her email. There – among the new messages from Sophie, with subject headings relating to Paris – was his name: Rafael Rodriguez. Rafael. Her Rafael. She hesitated for a moment, her heart beating hard. She'd let that door open, just a crack, when she'd read one of the books he sent. She shouldn't open it further, she knew that. But she couldn't help herself. She clicked on the message.

To: Isla
From: Rafael

Dear Isla,
   You might think I've forgotten about you, but I haven't.

I don't think that – not really, she thought. Because I know you, and I know you are no more capable of undoing what you felt in a matter of weeks than I am. And I haven't forgotten, Rafael. I sometimes wish I could.

I've wanted to forget, sometimes. I've tried to work it out, why you left. Why, when for me everything felt right, for you it didn't, and it was better to walk away. I can't make sense of it. It's probably time to stop trying.

Please stop trying, she thought. Don't do this to yourself. You don't need to know why, only that something changed and I couldn't be the woman who would make you happy any more.

When you walked into the bookshop that day, I know there was something. There you were, pretty, and funny, and – I don't know – just ... right. You were looking at me, and there was something about your eyes, so wide and blue, that made it seem as if you'd never seen anything but the good things in the world.

That was never true, Isla thought. It was you who saw the world that way – that was what *I* saw in *you*.

There are things I didn't tell you, when we were together. I saw the light way that you looked at life and I wanted to join you in that place too. I wanted to share in the beauty of an early morning with you, to eat, to dance, feel your skin against mine. But I wasn't telling you the whole truth. Maybe I was a coward. Life can be complicated – but those complications don't make it any less worth living – in fact, sometimes they're the very things that make it worth living. Those little pieces are what make you, you, and me, me.

Tears came to Isla's eyes as she read, and the words resonated. She couldn't hide from him, even here. He seemed to know, inside and out, who she really was.

Maybe we missed our chance, Isla.
But I meant it when I said I loved you.
Rafael.

Isla read, and reread, his email. She wondered what it was he had never told her. She lingered over those final words.

Over the past weeks, she'd built a new beginning for herself – but it was fragile. Rafael's words threatened to undermine the progress she'd made, to render her list meaningless. That couldn't happen. The points on it had become her life-raft.

She had been wrong, she decided, to think she could read his books, hear his words and still keep going. It wasn't possible to live in limbo. She needed to let go.

She took a deep breath, deleted his email, and tried to forget that she'd ever read it.

Chapter 15

The Paris trip drew closer, and it became a welcome distraction for Isla – from the hospital appointments she'd been unable to avoid, and from thoughts of Rafael. She hadn't heard any more from him, and she was grateful for that. The words in his email had started to fade from her mind – all except the final ones. On Friday, Sophie called her.

'I've got most of my things packed already,' Sophie said, excitedly. 'A week to go, but I couldn't resist. You?'

'Same here. I haven't had a whole lot else to do, apart from go to the hospital, that is. And no – I don't want to talk about that. I've got the *Rough Guide* downloaded, so we'll have all the local info when we arrive. The woman running the course sent me through the recipe itinerary for each day, I'll forward it on to you. It will make your mouth water.'

'I can't wait,' Sophie said. 'In a week, we'll be sitting by the Seine, sipping wine, chilling out . . . bliss.'

'And we'll soon be master chocolatiers, too,' Isla said.

'See you then?' Sophie said.

'Yes. Let's have Bellinis at the airport.'

After she'd spoken to Isla, Sophie went downstairs to the living room. Rebecca was engrossed in watching something or other on her iPad. After the discussion she'd had with Liam the other night, about balancing her family life better, Sophie was determined to improve communication with Rebecca. They both deserved better than for the house to feel like a war zone.

It was going to start today.

'Rebecca,' she said, gently. She got no response.

'Rebecca,' Sophie repeated.

Nothing. Sophie's patience began to fade.

'I need to talk to you,' Sophie said, irritation creeping into her voice. 'Can you stop ignoring me, just for a minute?'

'I'm not ignoring you,' Rebecca said, barely looking up from the screen.

'Yes, you are. And it's really quite rude.'

Sophie positioned herself in front of her stepdaughter, and waited until the girl's eyes, finally, drifted to look at her. How had Isla done it – broken through to Rebecca, and helped her to talk? She wished she had just an ounce of whatever her friend had that had prompted Rebecca to open up. Since Isla had told her about her talk with Rebecca, Sophie had tried to be more patient with her – if there was something wrong, she wanted to be able to support her. Rebecca deserved kindness. But Sophie's approaches had been met with hostility and sarcasm, and resulted in nothing more than the usual stalemate.

'I'm watching a programme,' Rebecca said. 'Can it wait?'

'Not really, no,' Sophie said. 'I'm going away for a week, and I need to speak to you about a couple of things. Come on – you're not a kid any more.'

'Despite the way I get treated round here,' Rebecca said, bitterly. Reluctantly, she put the tablet down. She still wouldn't meet Sophie's eye.

'You're upset because you think your dad and I don't treat you like an adult?' Sophie asked.

'Sometimes.' She shrugged. Her gaze drifted to the window, and settled on the houses across the road. 'Sometimes the opposite.'

'Well, I'm going to talk to you like an adult now,' Sophie said. 'While I'm away, there are a couple of things around the house that'll need doing. Nothing big. I've written this list . . .'

'You're really sure you want to go away?' Rebecca asked.

'Yes,' Sophie said. 'Why wouldn't I be?'

'You think it's a good idea, to leave now?' Rebecca said, sceptically.

'What are you getting at?'

'Nothing,' Rebecca said, shaking her head.

'It's clearly not nothing, or you wouldn't have said it like that.'

It was happening again, Sophie thought. Rebecca was succeeding – she was getting the rise she wanted out of Sophie, Sophie was letting her get control.

'Leave the list and I'll do the things on it,' Rebecca said, simply. Then she picked up the tablet again, signalling that the conversation was over.

*

190

That evening, Sophie was getting ready to go out. She'd been looking forward to tonight. She and Liam hadn't been to a party together in a long time. It was a fortieth birthday celebration for Don, a neighbour of theirs. She picked out a necklace and laid it on her dressing table.

A few moments later, Liam came out of their en-suite bathroom in a cloud of steam, a white towel wrapped around his waist. His hair was wet, and he scrubbed it roughly. She was as attracted to him now as she'd been when they first met. It was only that life had come between them for a little while. Now, things were going to be different. They already were.

At the party, Liam chatted easily to all of their neighbours, asking the right questions about their children. Sophie loitered at the entrance to the kitchen with a glass of wine, and felt oddly out of place. She wanted to talk to people, she just couldn't think what to say. She sipped at her wine and hoped it would ease her into things.

'Hello, Sophie,' said a voice beside her. 'Now here's a surprise.'

'Hi, Rob!' she replied, with a smile. 'What are you doing here?'

'I'm here with Kate. My little sister.'

Kate smiled and said 'Hi again.'

'Do you two know each other?' Rob asked.

'Yes,' Sophie said. 'We've met. I didn't realise you guys were related.'

'Number twenty-seven, right?' Kate said.

Sophie nodded, feeling a little embarrassed. 'We spoke the other day, about my husband, and the party you had.'

'Yes, of course.' Kate laughed. 'Liam. The only tutor who's downed Jägerbombs with us so far.'

Rob raised an eyebrow, laughing. 'Really?'

'Yes. Don't ask,' Sophie said. 'I think we've agreed he won't be making a habit of that.'

'He's welcome any time. So Rob's been showing me the ropes in Bristol,' Kate said, 'and I wanted him to meet some of my housemates – Chiara, Freddie . . .' she pointed across the room, then looked around for someone else ' . . . and Melissa. I'm not sure where she's got to.'

'They seem like a pretty cool bunch,' Rob said. 'I promised I'd report back to our parents, let them know she's in safe hands. Nearly twenty but we all think of her as twelve and a half.'

Kate nudged him in the ribs. 'Shut up, Rob.'

'She'll be fine,' Sophie said. 'This is a nice street. Quiet, mostly. The occasional drunk tutor aside.'

The three of them talked for a while longer, then Sophie excused herself to go to the toilet before the toasts got under way. The guests were congregating in the living room, close to the grand piano. She glanced around, but couldn't see Liam.

Sophie listened politely to the toasts, but inside she felt numb. She wanted Liam back by her side. When he finally came back into the room, he didn't seem to be looking for her, and instead went over to the group of Kate's house-mates. They welcomed him with a cheer. Another girl with long dark hair joined the group a moment later. He hadn't even glanced in Sophie's direction. She felt as if she was invisible.

Liam was laughing with the dark-haired girl and Kate. Sophie thought about weaving her way through the crowd to join him, but something held her back. She finished her wine and put it down on the side, going out into the hall-way instead. Some fresh air, that was what she needed. She opened the stained-glass front door and stepped outside.

'You all right, Soph?' She turned to see that Rob had followed her outside.

'Yes, fine. Just needed a change of scene,' she said.

'Quite crowded in there, isn't it?'

'Yes – I'm not sure I'm in quite the right mood for a party after all.'

'Let me bring you another drink, at least,' he said. 'We can talk out here for a while.'

'Thanks,' she said. 'But I'm OK, really.'

'If you're sure,' he said, unconvinced.

'I'm sure.'

The front garden was dark apart from the pale glow of a streetlight. It was calm out here. She'd feel better in a few minutes. Perhaps even go back inside.

'Look, if you see Liam, tell him where I am, would you?'

'Of course.' Rob said goodbye, turned and went back inside.

She was fine. She and Liam were the same people they always had been, the same couple. Just on the cusp of something new, starting a family, and that was bound to be unsettling. She was dealing with it in her way, and he was dealing with it in his.

An hour later, Sophie was still standing outside, and the cold had started to creep inside her coat. He could have come to look for her – he hadn't. But then she hadn't been back inside to find him, either. Perhaps tonight was just one of those nights better spent apart. Sophie crossed the street, then typed out a text.

Hi, gone home, bad headache. See you later. x

Inside, the house felt empty and cold. Rebecca's room was quiet, and presumably she was asleep. She sat down in the kitchen, and thought through the evening's events. Nothing had happened, had it? She hadn't had Liam by her side all night, but she didn't usually feel the need for that – it was something about the way he'd acted, the way he'd seemed to come to life around people younger than her, that had made her need that additional reassurance. Her insecurities had been speaking, that was it – the little voice in her head that told her she wasn't as bright, or funny, or interesting as she might once have been. That was it. Though realising it didn't make her feel any better at all.

The next morning, Sophie looked over at Liam, still asleep on the other side of the bed. She'd heard him come back in the early hours of the morning, tiptoeing in the way only a drunk person could. He hadn't just stayed at the party a little longer, or for one more drink – he'd chosen to spend hours there. While she hadn't expected him to follow her, wouldn't have wanted him to, it still hurt that he had preferred to get drunk rather than make things right with her.

She thought of the day ahead – Liam had mentioned he had classes to prepare for, but Rebecca would need ferrying to her friend's, and later to a dance class. Sophie anticipated the stony silence that there would be between them on the car journey – or, worse still, the comments. She got out of bed, stood up, and looked at herself in the mirror. What was she – a doormat? Liam could do it. He could do it with a hangover. It wouldn't kill him.

She went out in the hallway and called Isla. 'Are you free today?'

'Yes,' Isla said. 'Come on over.'

'Great.'

Sophie arrived at the cottage half an hour later, feeling a little like she'd run away from home. She'd left Liam a note, explaining that she had gone out and that she'd let him know later that day when she'd be back. She'd left the details of Rebecca's commitments, so that even if his brain was fuzzy when he woke, he'd remember to take her.

Isla let her in, dressed in the same fluffy dressing gown she'd worn at university. It made Sophie smile to see it again. They went through to the kitchen and Isla made tea for them both.

'So tell me what's up,' Isla asked. 'Not that you need a reason to visit, but I get a sense there might be one.'

Isla looked tired, Sophie thought. She didn't want to mention it, though – Isla probably didn't appreciate the constant reminders that she wasn't well. Paris would bring some colour back into her cheeks, Sophie told herself.

'Something or nothing,' Sophie said. 'Liam and I went to a party last night, and it was a bit of a weird evening.'

'Weird how?'

'I don't know,' Sophie said. 'And the more I try to zero in on it, the more it slips away from me. It could have been nothing. He was hanging out with some of the students, from the house across the way – you know I mentioned them?'

'Yes, I remember. The party he went to.'

'That's it. So he was laughing and joking with these young women, and I don't know ... maybe I'm just jealous. It felt awkward. Different. I went home early, he came back late. It's no big deal – I know that. It's just not what normally happens. We always come home together.'

'How have things been otherwise?' Isla asked.

'Fine, I think. He wasn't thrilled about you and me going out clubbing the other weekend, as you know – and there's the tension with Rebecca that doesn't help.'

'But he hasn't given you any reason to think anything else might be going on?'

'No. Not really. But it does make me slightly paranoid, that he seems to want to spend time with other women, rather than with me. I swore I'd never let myself mistrust him, just because he once cheated on Véronique with me. But the other day I got in the passenger seat of his car and the seat was tilted back. I never have it like that. And it was pulled forward a little, so that I didn't have room for my legs like I usually do ... ' Sophie rubbed her forehead. 'You see what I mean? I'm doing it already. And I'm starting to sound totally nuts.'

'Maybe,' Isla said. She felt for Sophie, having these tiny details standing out and fuelling her suspicions. She had always trusted Liam completely, and for her to dissect their relationship like this, so forensically, was out of character. Isla wished she could tell her for sure that her fears were unfounded. There was the chance that Liam was straying, of course, or the possibility – and she felt disloyal even

196

thinking it – that the decision to have a family together was causing Sophie to find fault where there was none.

' . . . or maybe not,' Isla finished.

'I've lost perspective,' Sophie said.

'You could ask him,' Isla said.

'I don't know – I don't really even know what to ask. Nothing's happened.'

'You don't need a concrete reason – he's your husband. You're allowed to ask him questions.'

'I don't have the energy for an argument right now, and I have a feeling that's where this could all lead.'

'Well, in that case, just keep an eye on it for now. And in the meantime we have Paris. A break from all this.'

Sophie smiled, and Isla continued talking.

'It's not like you really had one when you came to visit me, after all, what with all the drama there ended up being there. Paris will be different. We won't talk about my illness, and we won't talk about your relationship. Nothing we can say can change either situation, anyway, so the way I see it we might as well relax and enjoy ourselves. *Que sera, sera* and all that.'

'Wrong language.'

'But the right sentiment.'

'Can I stay here tonight?' Sophie asked, hesitantly.

'Stay as long as you want.'

Isla couldn't give Sophie the answers she needed – but this she could do, offer a little space for her to start to look for them on her own.

That evening, after Sophie went to bed, Isla passed her mum another section of material for the quilt that she'd pinned, and Hattie deftly ran it through the sewing machine.

'It's coming together nicely, isn't it?' Hattie said, holding it up for the two of them to look at. 'We'll be able to finish it off when you get back from Paris, I think.'

'Yes, we're nearly there.'

'Paris,' Hattie said, staring dreamily into the corner of the room. 'I went there once, a long time ago now. It's such a beautiful city. You and Sophie are going to have a wonderful time.'

'Thank you – for giving me the chance,' Isla said. 'It's so nice to have something to look forward to. It's really generous of you and Granny. I know you've saved hard over the years, and I just want you to know that I really appreciate it.'

Hattie gave her a hug. 'You're welcome, sweetheart. Now go, and have a good time. That's all we ask.'

Isla smiled. 'I'll do that. And now I'm going to get up to bed. I'll see you in the morning.'

'See you then,' Hattie said.

Isla walked upstairs to her bedroom. She held on to the banister, and found herself leaning on it more than usual. Halfway up, her left leg gave way – just as it had back in the bookshop that first time – and she collapsed. She caught hold of the step above to stop herself from falling, but couldn't get back on to her feet. She scrabbled to reach for the banister again and slipped back. Tears sprang to her eyes. She couldn't do it on her own.

'Mum,' she said.

It had happened again.

Desperation welling in her, she called out again, louder this time. 'Mum! Can you help me?'

*

The next morning, Sophie picked up her phone and checked it. The bright light greeted her, and the news that there were three missed calls from Liam. She'd called him the night before and let him know she would be staying at Isla's, but they hadn't had a proper conversation. She'd stopped checking her phone after that.

The calls suggested he wanted to put things right. That he cared. That there was a good chance that she had left – stormed off, really – over nothing. Thinking about it now, her own behaviour had been little better than a teenage strop – the kind of thing she would have had words with Rebecca about doing.

She resisted the urge to call Liam back. It could wait until after breakfast – then she'd drive home and they could spend the day together, make things right again.

Hattie made breakfast and sat down beside Isla. Sophie thought she saw a look pass between them, but she couldn't be sure.

'Thanks for having me,' Sophie said.

'Any time, Sophie. You know that,' Hattie said kindly. 'You don't need a reason. This place will always be a home for you, if you need one.'

Sophie thought back to the wedding. The simple register office ceremony. And Hattie there, watching her and Liam commit to each other. There when her own family had chosen not to be. 'You've always been so good to me,' Sophie said.

'You're the daughter she always wished she had,' Isla said.

'She's made that sound all wrong,' Hattie said, nudging Isla in the ribs. 'The *other* daughter, is what she means. I always wanted to give Isla a sister or brother, but life didn't work out that way, did it? But she started at that posh old university and who would've known. She found you.'

Isla smiled, then fell quiet. Her skin paled.

'Isla,' Sophie said. 'Are you feeling OK?'

Isla's composure faltered, and her eyes welled up. 'I don't know what to say. I can't fake it, not with you. My legs – last night I almost fell down the stairs. I'm worried I'm having a relapse.'

'God. I'm sorry,' Sophie said, concerned. 'Did you hurt yourself, are you OK?'

'I'm fine. Mum came to help. We both knew this would happen at some point. It's going to be a new kind of normal, this, I guess.'

'But still,' Sophie said.

'The doctors told me I should probably expect it. But it's still gutting,' Isla said, tears starting to fall.

Sophie hugged her. 'Yes. Yes, it must be,' she said, softly. 'How do you feel this morning?'

Isla shook her head. 'Not great. Pretty dreadful actually.'

'I've been telling her she needs to go to the doctor,' Hattie said.

'She has,' Isla said to Sophie. 'I know I need to.'

'And we . . . ' It pained Sophie to say it, but she knew it was the only sensible option. 'We need to cancel the trip to Paris.'

'*I* do,' Isla said.

'What do you mean?' Sophie said. 'We both do.'

Isla shook her head.

'What – you think I should go anyway? On my own?'

'Yes. Go for me, Soph.'

'We can rearrange.'

'We could, or we might not be able to,' Isla said. 'I don't know.'

The words struck Sophie like tiny darts, and she longed to pick them out, dismiss Isla's fears. A look passed between Sophie and Hattie. There was a pleading look in Hattie's eyes that urged Sophie to do what her daughter wanted.

'I'm not giving up on the list,' Isla said. 'But I'm – let's say – adjusting my expectations.'

'What do you mean?'

'Help me do the things that I can't,' Isla said. 'Paris now, and the other things when you get back.'

'You'll be able to do these things,' Sophie said. 'Maybe not right now . . . '

'Maybe not ever, Sophie,' Isla said bluntly. 'My head isn't in the sand any more. I want to keep living. But right now I have to tread water, at least until I know what's going on. Help me keep living.'

'I can't – this was about the two of us together. Never about me—'

'If you go – and you tell me about it,' Isla encouraged her, 'then I will at least have come close.' She forced a smile. 'I will feel as if I've been there with you.'

'I don't know,' Sophie said. 'Are you really sure this is what you want?'

'Yes,' Isla urged her. 'Tell me you will?'

Sophie felt torn. What Isla wanted was the priority right now – but she felt so sad that they wouldn't be going on the trip together. She couldn't see how her going alone would help, but she had to respect her friend's decision.

'OK,' Sophie said. 'I'll go – and I'll bring a piece of Paris back with me for you.'

Sophie drove home, thinking about the trip. In the end it hadn't really felt like a choice – Isla wanted her to go on with their plan, alone, and had made it clear that it was important to her. It would have been impossible to say no.

She'd texted Liam to let him know she was on her way home, and that she'd be back for lunch.

Liam answered the door to her, and he hugged her – as if nothing had happened, as if she hadn't even been away. They sat down and ate lunch together. Sophie had prepared herself to talk, at least to explain why she'd left, and why she'd stayed the night at Isla's. But he didn't ask.

It didn't seem like the right time for her to ask questions, either. Not when they were questions like, *Do you still love me the way you used to?*

Instead, to fill the silence, she told Liam about Isla's relapse, and about Paris.

'So I'll still be going. It's what she wants.'

'On your own?' he said, eyes wide.

'Yes. I've booked the time off, so it makes sense anyway, I suppose.'

Liam seemed shocked. 'I thought the whole point was for you and Isla to spend some time together? I mean, wasn't this all about her being ill?'

'Yes, and in a way it still is,' Sophie said, trying to rationalise it.

'I'm not sure I really understand that.'

'She's worried she won't ever be able to get there,' Sophie said. 'She can't predict how the illness will affect her, no one can – and she's concerned that it'll all be out of her reach. I doubt it will be – I see no reason it should be – but that doesn't change the way she feels. She thinks if I'm there – to take photos, tell her about it, that'll be a close second to being there herself.'

Liam raised an eyebrow, but didn't dismiss the idea entirely. 'I'd have thought it would make it worse for her – seeing you enjoying yourself when she's at home unwell.'

'I know what you're saying, and that was my first reaction too. But it's what she says she wants. I can't really ignore that, can I? Would you?'

He shrugged. 'I'm not sure me and my friends are the same as you two. We've never needed to get under each other's skin like you two do in order to support each other. A pint and a chat normally does the trick – but who knows, perhaps I'm emotionally repressed.'

'It's only a week,' Sophie said.

'Of course,' Liam said, shaking his head. 'I didn't mean to suggest that you shouldn't go, only that I didn't quite get her logic on it. Go, have fun, bring back some chocolates like you promised. I've got no problem with it.'

'OK,' Sophie said. It dawned on her that he didn't mind that she was going to be away – not really. Not at all.

And the part that unsettled her was that she would have felt better if he had.

Chapter 16

Today Sophie would be flying out to Paris. Isla knew she should get up and out of bed; it must be nine, if not later. Outside, the sky was a dull white-grey and there was drizzle on the window. She watched the raindrops trace a path down, silently willing on the one that was trailing behind. It picked up pace and overtook the other.

Her limbs were leaden. It was one of those phrases she'd heard before, but never really appreciated. Even lifting her leg or arm felt like a Herculean effort. She'd gone to the doctor's yesterday, but there had been no miracle cure. Her GP said she could either wait it out, or take steroids if things got worse. For now, Isla was just seeing how things went.

She pictured Sophie in the departure lounge, sipping on a Bellini, reading her Kindle or just watching the world go by. For a moment, envy threatened to sneak in. But Isla pulled herself up on it. It was better that Sophie was there than neither of them. She would look forward to Sophie's first update – the first photo, or postcard – and that would enable her to be there a little too.

Sophie had packed light for the trip – her favourite clothes, toiletries and a few books for the journey. There was just one thing she'd hesitated over – the pregnancy test in her bathroom cupboard. She had been feeling different recently, different enough to wonder. Liam had already left for work, though, so she'd decided to wait – she and Liam would do the test together when she returned.

That evening, when she arrived in Paris, she caught a taxi to the guesthouse. Familiar landmarks caught her eye – the Eiffel Tower was silhouetted in the fading light. She felt a rush of excitement about being there at last. It was as if everywhere she looked stills from her favourite films were brought to life – elegant townhouses, sophisticated older women, adorable poodles. She snapped photos, and uploaded them for Isla. She typed her friend a personal message.

Dearest Isla. Here I am, in Paris – starting our adventure together. Really do wish you were here. It feels as if you are. x

The next day, Isla checked the photos from Sophie, and smiled as she saw the images from her friend's trip. She didn't know if it was Sophie's message, or the symptoms of her relapse fading, but she felt strong enough to leave the house that day.

She picked up the leaflet that the GP had handed her. A local support group for sufferers – why that word? – she wished there were another, better, one – that took place weekly in the local library. At the time, she had stuffed it into her bag, meaning to bin it. But today it didn't seem such a bad prospect. The library was only a short walk, and the leaflet promised tea and biscuits. It had to be better than sitting at home all afternoon.

The library was housed in a small building at the crossroads, a 1960s block. It was a place Isla knew well: she'd borrowed her first library books from here as a child, handing over her library pass excitedly as her mum held her up at the counter, and gleefully accepting the books in return – *Dr Seuss, Mog, The Tiger Who Came to Tea.*

This time Isla was walking through the automatic doors as an adult, and everything felt different. A sign directed her through to the meeting, in a quiet side room. A few chairs were set out in a circle, most of them filled. She went in, and stood by the door. She was used to being around people who were young and vibrant, but here were women and a handful of men, almost all middle-aged, a couple of canes propped up against their chairs. She couldn't see herself or her experience reflected in any of them. They chatted to one another cheerfully enough, but they couldn't be happy, not really. She saw a wheelchair in the corner and her heart sank low in her chest. She didn't know who it belonged to, but someone here must have to use it. There was nothing – nothing – to say she was going to be one of the lucky ones. Years down the line she might be any one of these people; years down the line, she might be in that chair. Her face felt hot and her eyes pricked with tears. It wasn't that she thought those lives weren't worth living. It wasn't a judgement of those who were already there. It was just – that wasn't her life. She didn't want that to be her life.

She thought about turning around, sneaking out again – perhaps nobody would even notice. Then she felt a hand touch her shoulder.

'Hi. I'm Andy. You're new here, I think?' Andy must have been around her age, with glasses and a beige jumper that made him look a little older. 'Welcome,' he said, his smile warm.

'Hi,' she said, embarrassed that she'd been about to run out. 'I'm Isla.'

'Come and sit down,' Andy said, pointing to an empty chair. 'Everyone, this is Isla.' She was welcomed kindly by the other members of the group.

'So, let's start with a little catch-up,' Andy said. 'Marjorie. How have you been feeling this week?'

Marjorie was in her fifties, with short, spiky red hair and long beaded earrings. 'It's been a difficult week. Me and my husband have been arguing a lot. It's hard enough getting about, but then he leaves things lying around that I could trip over, and when my balance is bad that's easy to do . . . '

Isla nodded, but started to tune out. Even though she wanted to care, she found she couldn't hear it – she didn't want to hear it. How life might get. If she didn't listen, perhaps it would never happen to her.

There was a creak as the door to the room opened, and Isla was conscious of a presence at her side. A woman, in her late twenties. Glossy, waist-length black hair and winged eyeliner with red lipstick. Skinny jeans and biker boots. She sat in silence for a minute, then caught Isla's eye.

'Pretty intense the first time, isn't it?' she said, in a whisper.

Isla nodded.

'Just let it wash over you, and think of the Jammie Dodgers.'

At break time, after each of the members had talked about their week, their current symptoms and challenges, Isla went over to the tea table. She'd kept quiet, and Andy seemed to understand that she wasn't ready to talk yet.

'New diagnosis?' It was the young woman who'd been sitting beside her.

'Yes. I guess it must be obvious.'

'A bit,' she said, in a matter-of-fact tone. 'Same look of pure horror I had when I first came.' She smiled. 'I'm Jo.' She offered her hand and Isla shook it, introducing herself.

Isla smiled. Jo had none of the obvious signs – a cane, a chair, a hand put out to steady herself. There was nothing, in fact, to suggest Jo was remotely unwell.

'How long ago did you find out?' Isla asked.

'Five years.' Jo said it in a detached way, picking up the last Bourbon biscuit as she did. 'Five years since that bombshell.'

'How did you find out?'

'Oh, it took them months. Scans, then finally a lumbar puncture when they'd ruled everything else out. It was awful. I thought my life was over.'

The words chimed with how Isla had been feeling. How at some points she'd thought it might be easier for everyone if she just disappeared.

Jo took a bite of the biscuit, and shrugged her shoulders. 'Anyway, here I still am, so I guess I was wrong about that.'

'Are you in remission now?'

'Yes. Though I always find that word a little weird, don't you? Because people think of cancer, being better. But the next relapse is always coming. Two weeks, six months – it'll happen again.'

Isla braced herself to ask a question. 'How do you deal with it – that uncertainty? I think that's what I find hardest of all. Not knowing what's coming next.'

'Oh, that, yes. You have to roll with it, I guess. I've never really planned out that much in life so I suppose I didn't have much room for disappointment. And in my case, having a baby helped. It made things more scary, in a way, but a million times better in others. You never know what on earth a kid's going to throw at you next, and so your health becomes just one of a whole load of variables.'

A kid. Isla tried not to let it show, but the news surprised her. Jo looked young, although, when she thought about it, no younger than a lot of mothers.

'How old?' Isla asked.

'Four.' Jo smiled, and got out her phone, showing Isla a picture of her little girl. 'Ava. She's a gem. Aiden, her dad, was my take-home from a hen weekend in Dublin . . . Neither of us planned to end up living here, back in my home town. And neither of us imagined I might get a diagnosis like this, before my thirtieth birthday. But her? She was about the only thing we did plan.'

'That's lovely. About your family, I mean.'

Jo seemed to pick up on her mixed feelings, and she spoke again, her voice softer this time. 'The first few months are really bloody hard,' she said. 'There are no shortcuts. That's just the way it is. But it gets easier. It gets harder, and easier. If that makes any sense at all.'

It did, Isla thought. It was the first thing that she'd heard that had made much sense to her at all.

That evening, Isla got into bed, and felt more at peace in her own skin. The talk with Jo had given her fresh perspective on what was happening, and it had felt good to swap phone numbers after the meeting. Isla was starting to feel less like a list of symptoms and a diagnosis, and more like her old self. She was simply a human being, with complications, baggage and potential, just like any other. For the first time in a long time, she felt like she might be OK after all.

Chapter 17

Sophie woke up in Paris for the first time, and it took her a moment to get her bearings. She was lying in fresh white sheets in an attic room, sunshine streaming in through the window.

There was no alarm clock, no rhythmic snore from Liam at her side. No hospital ward and filing cabinets to hurry off to. Instead there was the sound of birds singing and gentle conversation in French drifting up from the street below.

The chocolate-making course started at nine. She dressed in a lilac top and black skinny jeans, with grey pumps, and headed downstairs to the small dining room on the ground floor of the townhouse. Her landlady, Michelle – a kind woman in her fifties whom Sophie had met briefly the night before – brought her hot chocolate in a bowl, and a breakfast of fresh croissants. She and Sophie exchanged a few words, Sophie dredging up what she could remember of her GCSE French, and then Michelle left her to eat. Sophie dunked a corner of the pastry in her hot chocolate and bit into it – she wasn't sure if that was correct etiquette or not, but it tasted exquisite.

After breakfast she went out into the street, loosely following the map in her Rough Guide. She had set out deliberately early, so that she could explore a little of the city before starting the course. She stopped for a *citron pressé* on the banks of the Seine, and watched the boats go by. She paused for a moment to take in the energy of the place and take some photos – the joggers, the tourists, the elegant locals – and posted them on Instagram. She was immediately nudged back by the glow of a red heart as Isla saw them.

It wasn't quite the same as having Isla there with her – but in a small way Sophie still felt her presence. She hoped that Isla was feeling better – it had been hard to see her so affected by the relapse. She didn't ask. Isla had insisted that the best possible medicine would simply be knowing that Sophie was enjoying the trip for her.

When Sophie finished her drink, she went over to the course venue – the old-fashioned chocolate shop overlooking the river was even more enticing than it had looked in the pictures. Sophie was the first to arrive, and the teacher – a dark-haired woman wearing a crisp white apron – greeted her warmly.

'I'm Amandine,' she said.

'Sophie.' Sophie held out her hand.

'Ah – the English woman, lovely. Welcome to the class. I'm so sorry your friend wasn't able to make it.'

'Thank you,' Sophie said. 'And yes, she was really looking forward to it. She's got a serious macaroon obsession.'

'A good focus for life,' Amandine said, with a smile. 'Day four, we'll be doing those.'

A couple of other students drifted in – a man in his twenties, handsome and coiffed, and a pretty young woman. They were chatting to one another in French, and seemed to know what they were doing. They went straight over to the equipment cupboard and got out bowls and spoons.

'I have to admit, this is all completely new to me,' Sophie confessed to the teacher.

'Don't worry,' Amandine said, kindly. 'Most of my students say that. By the end of the week you'll be ready to steal my job, I promise.'

Sophie arrived back at the guesthouse in the evening, pleasantly tired. She'd spent the afternoon at the Louvre, and walking around some private art galleries. Then she'd explored a local park, stopping for tea and cake in the now-bare rose gardens and writing out a postcard for Isla. The effect of being in Paris on her own was invigorating – she didn't feel like Sophie the ward clerk, Liam's wife Sophie, or Rebecca's stepmother Sophie. She felt like *Sophie*-Sophie – vibrant and alive, with no role to fill, no achievements to be measured by.

She had dinner with Michelle back at the guesthouse, then went up to bed. In the room upstairs, she stretched out in the double bed. She thought of how her legs would normally entangle with Liam's during the night. She'd wondered if she might miss that familiar feeling, one she'd experienced most nights for over ten years, but she didn't, not really. She found she enjoyed stretching out, the bed just hers tonight, the only touch on her skin that of the fresh white linen.

She thought of Liam – checked the time and decided to text rather than call. He'd probably be writing his lecture notes. **Hi love**, she wrote. **A fine day of chocolate-making and sightseeing, now bedtime.**

This was where she should write it. *I miss you.* It hadn't been long enough, she reasoned. It would sound silly. She'd say it next time.

Love, S x

She'd started to feel separate from him, the very opposite of how she'd expected to feel when they first spoke about having a baby together. Recently she'd begun to distance herself from him in small ways – nothing he'd notice, but she found she was reaching out to touch him less, she wouldn't always kiss him before she fell asleep. It wasn't conscious, but perhaps it was a small act of self-preservation.

She needed to be sure. She needed to be far more sure that they were still the couple that they'd been, that their foundations were still intact. She hadn't felt that certainty lately. Perhaps it had been the way he'd acted at Don's birthday party, the tension around Rebecca's behaviour, or the comments he'd made about her support of Isla – she couldn't be sure if it was all or none of those things. But recently she'd felt as if they weren't connecting, weren't functioning as a team any more. Whatever else had gone on around them, they'd always been that. Perhaps part of what she'd been nervous of, before she came out to Paris, was just this – having the space and time alone to see that her marriage wasn't what it had once been. She couldn't ignore it, now.

For years she'd relied on Liam in order to feel OK about herself. She'd been scared that if she wasn't with him, people would see her for what she really was. They'd see that she wasn't – whisper it – good enough. It had always been there, even when she was a child, that voice that told her she was somehow lacking. As she'd grown, she'd started to block it out – and moving away from her parents had helped. But the night that she and Liam were found out, it had started to creep back in.

She let herself remember it. The night, at university, when both her and Liam's lives had changed irrevocably. They'd been in a world of their own making that summer, filled with wine, books, and love – or lust – whatever it had been right at the start. A bubble without real time, or consequences, where they didn't have to answer to anybody. It had felt like blissful rebellion to Sophie, the first in her lifetime. He was an established tutor, a man she admired and who made her feel clever, funny and special – things she'd rarely felt at home. Above all, he'd made her feel wanted. She'd never had a proper relationship before, and this, in its own clandestine way, was starting to feel like one. She would have preferred for it not to be a secret, but she'd known from the start that those were the terms. She'd bent the rules a little and confided in Isla though; it was impossible to keep it entirely to herself.

It seemed at first as if it could go on for ever. There was no reason anyone else needed to know. Looking back on it now, Sophie couldn't believe how naïve she'd been. One night in early September, Liam had got complacent, and their luck ran out. They were staying in a hotel, and his mobile phone had rung, and rung. He'd ignored it, even when Sophie urged him not to. After a while he'd finally checked it, seen the name, and put it to silent.

Sophie had thought about Véronique then, and felt for her – pictured her, imagined how she might be feeling – confused, not knowing why her husband wasn't picking up the call. She'd wondered what Liam's wife was like ... whether, in other circumstances, they might even get on. Liam had fallen asleep there, which was never part of the plan. He always left, before midnight. They'd got too relaxed.

The next morning, he'd woken up, panicked, and listened to the messages Véronique had left. His face had paled. Sophie asked him what was wrong, and he explained. Véronique had been drunk – more drunk in each message, until in the one left at three a.m. he could barely work out what she was saying. It wasn't until he got home that he realised what had happened. His neighbour, Jon, explained that his wife had passed out cold in her daughter's bedroom. A terrified Rebecca, at only six years old, had woken to find her mum unconscious beside her. She'd run to the next door house to ask for help, and woken him – she'd stood beside him as he called for the ambulance that took Véronique away.

Even Liam, well-versed in excuses and alibis, had struggled to explain away the night out of contact. Véronique had seen through him, and she didn't hold back in letting people know. Rebecca had watched her family fall apart, and in public too. Very soon Sophie's name was known across campus, and then far more widely, for all the wrong reasons. Liam was the one who had broken the rules, but it was her name that people remembered. Mud sticks, that much she'd learned.

Every day of her life since then Sophie had, in her own

quiet way, tried to make amends. She'd tried to be a better person than the one who'd caused so much damage. The ongoing memory of that night, when so much fractured and broke, was why it was easier not to look at her own life too closely. It was why she had to make it worth it – she had to make the marriage she had worth the damage she had caused.

Chapter 18

Isla looked through Sophie's updates on Instagram. The sunny autumn streets of Paris, the chic private galleries, and the chocolate – oh, God, the chocolate. Sophie promised her that she'd be bringing back plenty of samples for her to try, and as far as Isla was concerned that time couldn't come around soon enough. There were a couple of selfies in there too, and she noticed that Sophie looked different. Her face was fresh and her skin bright, as if a weight had been lifted. Sophie's updates were like tiny vials of adventure and pleasure. They kept her going.

Wellness. It was a word they'd discussed at the support group. She'd been sceptical at first. Surely you couldn't think yourself into a better place, just by wanting to be there. It was difficult listening to Andy, someone who wasn't ill himself, offering advice. But as he had talked, some of it had started to make sense. Mind and body were closely interlinked, and MS was a condition that could flare up during periods of stress. She understood now that concentrating on what made her feel good wasn't an indulgence, it was a form of preventative treatment. Andy had encouraged her to focus on what she could do – which, for now, was almost everything.

Isla realised she could submit to the illness – roll over, give in – or she could change her own life to make it better. During a relapse, there were small things she could do to make her everyday activities easier, and Andy and the other members of the group had offered her some advice on those.

Isla had always imagined that at thirty she'd be taking great strides forward, and instead she was having to learn about some things from scratch. But she could do it. She was going to do it.

Isla and Jo arranged to go for dinner at a tapas bar in town. It felt good to meet up as just the two of them, outside the stuffy confines of the room in the library. Jo wasted no time ordering a few dishes for them, and herself a beer. 'I try not to drink too much these days,' she said. 'But I'm making an exception. New friend and all that.'

Isla smiled, raising her own drink. 'I'm glad you consider me that.'

'I get a good feeling from you,' Jo said.

'Feeling's mutual,' Isla said. 'I'll be honest, before you came into that meeting I was still half thinking about walking out. I felt like a fish out of water. I mean, they're all good people, but ... '

'I know what you mean. You don't have to explain. So, tell me more about you. You must have a man squirrelled away somewhere,' Jo asked. 'Am I right?'

'Oh, no.' Isla shook her head. 'I'm – er – well I'm living back with my mum, as it happens.'

'Ah, I see. You guys get on OK?'

'Yes, we're close.'

'Well, then, it sounds like a good place to be, for now. It's a journey, working out your treatment and so on. It's important to be with people who you're comfortable seeing you when you're not at your best.'

'I'm starting to realise that.'

'Have you been single for a while, or was it this – the diagnosis . . . ?'

'It was this. I was with someone, when I was living out in Amsterdam. But . . . it wouldn't have worked.'

'I'm sorry to hear that,' Jo said. 'But you know what: this stuff, it really sorts the wheat from the chaff. If someone isn't strong enough to handle it – then they're not worth your time.'

Isla nodded. What she said was true – of some people, Greta for one. But something nagged at her. A feeling that Rafael might have been strong enough to handle it. That perhaps she'd dismissed him too quickly. She hadn't even given him a chance.

That night, in bed, Isla thought about the evening with Jo. It had felt so normal – she had felt so normal – being out, making a new friend, chatting. But Jo's questions about Rafael had also stirred up her feelings. Perhaps she had been too quick to assume how Rafael would react to her illness. She had thought she knew what was best for him – but maybe she hadn't. She hadn't even allowed him to think about their life together, in these new circumstances, and perhaps she should have. Jo and Aiden had somehow made it through – but only because Jo had let him be part of her life as it changed.

The day after Isla's night out with Jo, a postcard fluttered down on to the Welcome mat at the cottage. Isla bent down to get it. Her symptoms had let up a little, and she was feeling close to normal today.

She smiled when she saw the photo on the front – two friends drinking coffee at a pavement café. Sophie had written their names in pen, drawn arrows pointing to each of the women.

Isla smiled, took a seat on the bottom stair and flipped the postcard over.

Dearest Isla,

So, here I am! Wow, Paris is everything I imagined and more. The course is a total treat – now, you know I've never really been in my element in the kitchen – but somehow here it feels like everything is possible. I promise to spoil you with plenty of chocolates when I get back. I've found a bookshop you'd love. It's a beautiful place, with a little café upstairs, and I spent a quiet afternoon there just watching the world go by.

OK, I think I've squeezed as much as I can on to this card. I'll instagram more pictures.

Love and hugs, Soph x

Isla held the card close to her chest. She could almost smell the bookshop Sophie was describing – the freshly brewed coffee, the mustiness of the antiquarian books. She thought for a moment of Rafael, and his bookshop, and pictured him there, behind the counter. She felt a pull towards it, but forced herself to dismiss the thought. It was nostalgia, nothing more.

'Beautiful day out there,' Hattie said, pausing in the hallway and standing beside her daughter.

'Yes,' Isla said. Sunlight was filtering through the stained glass on the front door, and falling in coloured patches on the black and white tiled floor. It was bright today.

'Perhaps a walk?' her mother ventured.

'I'll do some gardening, I think,' Isla said.

She put on her wellies and took a mug of tea out to the garden. In the peace of the increasingly green space, she became absorbed in her tasks – planting and weeding and tidying. Her mother's classical music drifted through from the kitchen, and the rich notes and dramatic crescendos nudged at her soul, reminding her what it was to feel. She had got in the habit of shutting down those corridors of emotion, the ones that led to highs as well as lows, but the soaring music forced them open again.

She brushed her hair back with a hand, probably getting more muck on her face. She didn't care. More than that, she relished it. There was no one here to see her, no one here to judge. The plants would grow, or not, whatever she looked like, and whether her balance occasionally wavered or not. Nature didn't care that her body was straying from perfect these days, and perhaps would continue further down that path. It was absorbed in the business of growing and changing seasons, and, when Isla let herself be, she was too. She thought of Rafael, from time to time, flashes of his smile, the tenderness of his touch, the rough stubble she didn't mind grazing her cheek, the expert way he kissed her. She thought of him, but she didn't let those thoughts torment her any more. He was there, woven into the tapestry of her past; those feelings, good and true, still made her feel alive when she thought them. She could revisit them now, whenever she liked: being kissed by him again, laughing with him. It didn't hurt anyone – not her, not him. Not everything needed a future.

Chapter 19

Berenice and Rafael sat down with coffee, and she looked at him with a no-nonsense expression.

'I think it's about time we talked about you,' Berenice said.

She continued, not leaving room for him to object this time.

'I usually find the beginning is as good a place as any,' she said. 'And I'm in no hurry at all.'

Rafael smiled. Maybe it was time, but where to start? He thought back to what had happened with David. It was only one of a hundred beginnings, but it would do.

'OK. If you insist. Let me tell you first about David.'

Rafael took a photo from his wallet, and showed it to Berenice. It had been hidden away for a long time, behind his driving licence and receipts.

David, his younger brother. There he was – there they were. Two boys together, dark-haired and their skin nut-brown from the sun. They must have been about four and ten when it was taken. Standing on the dusty road where they'd grown up, in a Mexican border town.

'I was quiet, bookish … I think that was probably my salvation. The gangs weren't interested in me. But David – we were always different.'

'Where is your brother now?'

'He's in prison.'

'Oh – I'm sorry.' Berenice's brow creased and she reached for Rafael's hand. He took it.

'It's OK. I mean – it's not, it never will be, but we've all accepted it now. We had to. David was only sixteen when it happened. He promised me he would stay in that night. We watched a movie together. Then, after I went to bed, the leader of one of the local gangs came by for him. He went out.' Rafael paused. It hurt him to remember the night, when everything had changed.

'David went out and ruined two lives that night. He shot a teenage man in a bar, left him in a wheelchair.'

'How terrible,' Berenice said, her voice trembling with emotion.

'Yes, it's that. I told you this wasn't a happy story,' he said, apologetically.

'Go on,' Berenice prompted him.

'He didn't even know the guy, or the reasons why he was pulling the trigger – it was an initiation. An initiation that damaged both of their futures. He pleaded self-defence, but I knew just looking in his eyes what the truth was, and when I confronted the man who sent him, he told me. Five years to go until David gets out. What can we do but wait? We talk. My mother visits. David says he prays a lot there, teaches the other inmates how to play chess. He was always good at chess.'

Rafael smiled at the memory. He and his brother used to sit on the veranda whiling away the hot afternoon after their siesta in games that would sometimes go on for hours.

'It must have been hard to leave,' Berenice said.

'Very hard. And yet easy too. I didn't want to stay, not after that. A friend offered me a job in Europe. I didn't know much at all about this place. Only what I'd learned from the pages of books, from snatches of TV dramas. But I had a feeling I could make a life for myself here. I wasn't far into my twenties, but I'd already seen enough of life, and death.

'I hugged my mother goodbye. I can still remember it now. She's strong to the core, always has been, but her body is just like a bird's, so fragile.

'I wish I could have taken David with me,' Rafael said. He paused, torn apart by the guilt.

'Tell me about Patricia,' Berenice said.

'Ah, you remember.' Rafael smiled. 'From my phone.'

'I don't forget a name.'

'My brother's girlfriend. This has taken a toll on them all, but Patricia more than anyone. She was pregnant when the police took him away.'

'Poor girl.' Berenice shook her head, saddened.

'Her family turned their backs. She was unmarried, still a teenager, and having a baby with a no-good *bandero*.'

'How unfair – people can be so cruel.'

'It was their loss,' he said. 'When my nephew Santiago was born – I was there, my mother too – and he opened his eyes, I knew how wrong they were to miss out on him. I knew it was down to me to help give him a chance. I didn't want to leave him, but I knew it was the only way.'

'And here – with your business – you're giving him that.'

'I send back money each month, I do a little to help with the other small things that he needs. My brother can't do anything from inside, and I know it's hard for him. In five years things will be different, but five years is a long time in a boy's life.'

'You're only partly here, aren't you?' Berenice said.

She saw it, Rafael realised. The way he felt – the way he was torn between there and here every day of his life. 'Yes.'

'We're all in pieces, really, aren't we? Our feet in one place, our heads in another. You can put down roots, Rafael, but that doesn't keep you in one place. Seeds will always get scattered by the wind.'

Chapter 20

Four days in and Sophie was really enjoying the course. She couldn't wait to get out of bed each morning, to get started on the stirring, and crafting and decorating – Amandine, as promised, had showed them how the delicate chocolates were actually surprisingly easy to make. The city seemed to welcome Sophie that morning, on the sunshine walk over to the chocolate shop.

'Today is the one I know some of you have been particularly looking forward to.' Amandine caught Sophie's eye across the room and smiled. 'Macaroon day.'

It wasn't just Sophie that had been waiting with anticipation, Isla had been texting asking when she'd get to see some pictures of Sophie's macaroon creations. They'd spoken yesterday on the phone, and Sophie felt reassured – Isla sounded as if she was making a good physical recovery from the relapse, and that the support group had been useful for her. She knew it wouldn't have been easy for Isla to go along – she'd resisted it quite fiercely at first – so it seemed like a positive sign that Isla was starting to come to terms with the disease, and its potential impact on her.

As the morning went on, following Amandine's expert guidance, Sophie made pistachio, rose and chocolate macaroons. The other students whirred and buzzed around her, crafting their edible masterpieces. She'd made friends with a few of them – Jean and Amélie, who were locals, and Liliana, who was visiting from Milan. Her French had come back to her slowly – particularly when she was chatting to Jean, an art student. While she might have misunderstood something in the translation, she'd started to wonder if he was flirting with her a little.

Sophie took a moment to breathe in the sweet aromas. Paris had brought it out in her, this new impulse to stop what she was doing, for just a second, to take in the details of it: the rustle of wind through the trees, the way shadows danced, even the hum of traffic.

It wasn't only the chocolate – that intoxicating smell and taste that made the rest of the world disappear when you took in the flavour – that had created an indelible impression on her. She had also learned about herself. She'd been genuinely scared of coming here on her own – nervous that people would judge her, that her French would be bad and her baking worse. Yet, when she'd actually done it, the very opposite had happened. Other people were warm and friendly towards her, and she was more capable than she'd given herself credit for. As others looked on her kindly, she found she was inclined to look more softly on herself, too. There had been nothing to fear. The world turned out to be a gentler, more forgiving and richer place than she'd ever imagined.

Chapter 21

Isla walked around to Jo's house. They'd arranged tea at hers when they'd parted on Sunday, but she hadn't called to confirm. Hopefully Jo remembered the plan, because the thought of this outing had really lifted Isla's spirits. The street was neat, the properties well-kept, but Jo's wasn't one of the semi-detached houses, with their gleaming Audis – she had told Isla that in advance. 'Keep going till you get to the 1960s eyesore of a block, the one the neighbours moan about,' Jo had said, but not without affection. 'We're on the second floor.'

The block was easy to spot at the end of the road, beyond the neatly trimmed hedges, a stocky five storeys of concrete, with an exterior stairwell. Isla climbed the stairs and knocked on the door, 34B.

Jo answered, with her little daughter huddling round her knees, giving a mischievous smile. 'Morning, Isla.'

'Hi,' Isla said. She bent down to the girl's level. 'And I'm guessing you're Ava,' she said.

'Yes. I am.' After a split-second of shyness, she took Isla by the hand. 'Come and see my toys,' she said brightly.

Isla was dragged into the front room, smiling, and introduced to Barney the bear, Snap the crocodile and a doll called Lily. Jo sat on the sofa, and asked Isla quietly, 'You couldn't make some tea, could you?'

'Sure,' Isla said. She got up and went to the kitchen, bringing back two cups of tea and a few Jammie Dodgers that she'd found in the biscuit tin.

'Here you go,' Isla said, passing her friend the cup.

Jo nodded, and Isla saw that her eyes had dark shadows beneath them.

'Are you OK?' she asked, lowering her voice to a whisper, as Ava dashed around the living room bringing them tomatoes, bananas and other pieces of plastic play food.

'I don't want her to realise,' Jo said, quietly, 'but I feel terrible today.' Her eyes filled with tears. 'I'm sorry, truth is I forgot you were even coming. Getting out of bed and getting Ava some breakfast was as much as I could focus on this morning.'

'I'm sorry,' Isla said.

'Don't be,' Jo said. 'I'm glad you're here. And look – she loves you already.' Jo motioned to her daughter, who was beaming with delight at the chance to show off some of her toys, her hair a mass of dark curls, and her cheeks still toddler-chubby.

'It hit me late last night,' Jo said. 'Stress of everything.'

'What's going on?' Isla said. 'It's not Aiden, is it . . . ?'

'Oh, no, he's still my good thing,' she said, brightening a little. 'He's at work today, doing a double shift, in case we need the money.'

'What then?'

'I've been called in for an assessment. I haven't worked in six months, since some of my symptoms worsened. I don't think I can do it – and I'm so scared, Isla, that they're going to take our allowance away.'

'But surely they can't – you have a diagnosis, you have . . .'

'It's not worth much,' she said. 'You know what it's like with this condition. One minute you feel fine, the next you're struggling. They could assess me one day and get a totally different impression the next. Since I got the letter it's all I can think about.'

Isla tried to think of some reassuring words for Jo, but didn't want to make light of something that seemed, really, to be fundamental to how Jo's family got on.

'I hope you're OK.' Isla's words sounded hollow, but it was all that she could think to say. She felt out of her depth. Any problems she'd thought she had seemed insignificant compared to what Jo was facing.

'I almost hope I'm not,' Jo said, with a wry laugh. 'How crazy does that sound? But at least if they see how ill I am, it would help. It's not just the money – though God knows we need that . . . it's not being believed.' Jo's eyes showed the strain. 'We go through all this, day in, day out, the dis-comfort, the pain, the unpredictability of it all. And I can handle it, I really can. I've found ways to manage, and we all muddle through. But having someone tell me I'm making it all up?' Her voice cracked. 'That – is pretty much the ultimate insult.'

'They'll believe you. They'll have to.'

'There are plenty of others they haven't,' Jo said. She put a hand to her forehead, as if she were trying to push the thoughts aside. 'Look, I don't want to saddle you with all this. I wanted to be, you know, positive for you – I know how the first year can be, and I wanted you to see, in me, that this doesn't need to change you.'

Isla touched Jo's shoulder. 'Jo. You don't need to be anything. Just be you. You're inspiration enough – it's not your job to make me feel OK about this.'

'I try to be strong, but sometimes, it's just too much.'

'Go back to bed,' Isla said. 'I'm serious. Take the morning off. Let me get to know this lovely daughter of yours.'

Jo opened her mouth to protest, but Isla shushed her. 'Ava,' Isla said. 'How about you show me how to make some cupcakes. They're my absolute favourite.'

'OK.' Ava walked over to her toy cooker. 'I use a digger,' she said, picking up a yellow JCB from the floor.

'Of course,' Isla said. 'Everyone needs a digger in their kitchen.'

Isla tied a knot in the long piece of string, and then wound it round her hands in the way she remembered from school. It had been years since she'd last played cat's cradle, and yet the motor memory kicked in and she found it came back to her naturally.

'Here, see this?' Isla said to Ava. 'A tiny bed for a cat. Do you want to try?'

Ava brought back a toy kitten and laid it in the cradle. She let out a gurgling laugh. 'Bed!'

It was almost midday. She'd been with Ava for a while now and yet the time had passed so quickly – minutes going by without Isla even noticing, as they played and laughed together. It was tiring – yes – she wondered how Jo coped, even when she was having a good day – but Isla enjoyed it. For the first time in months she hadn't had a chance to think about herself, her future, anything but being in the moment.

Jo came back into the living room, wearing leggings, a sweatshirt and giant tiger's feet slippers. 'I'm ready for action,' she said, her voice stronger now, though Isla could tell she was still trying to disguise her physical discomfort. 'And this little miss will be wanting some lunch.'

'Can I help?' Isla said.

'You already have. A lot,' Jo said. 'I really appreciate it.'

'Any time,' Isla said.

'Well, you have to look after yourself,' Jo said.

Isla realised she felt better than she had since she returned to the UK. 'I think this is looking after myself.'

Chapter 22

Isla met Sophie at the train station after her flight home, and they went to a café in town. 'So – how was it?' Isla asked, eager and curious.

'Amazing. No other word for it,' Sophie replied. She was still glowing from the success of the trip, and the beauty of everything she'd experienced in France. She'd got on well with her fellow students, and even made a few friends out there.

'I loved seeing the photos. And getting your messages and postcards. I genuinely felt as if I was there with you,' Isla said.

'Good – that was what I was hoping,' Sophie said. 'But that's only part of the story. Here's the best bit.'

She took a gold box out of her bag and handed it over.

Isla opened it – a line of perfectly crafted, delectable-looking macaroons, truffles and chocolates were laid out inside.

'You made these?' she said, incredulous.

'I did! Can you believe it? The teacher was so patient, and she gave us this little recipe book to take back,' Sophie held it up. 'So I'm all set to teach you what I learned.'

'Thanks,' Isla said. 'I'm glad you enjoyed it.'

'I'm glad you made me go,' Sophie said. 'It was just what I needed – gave me a good dose of perspective.'

'Great. Have you had a chance to talk to Liam yet? Get things straight?'

'Not yet.' The thought made her slightly anxious. 'Anyway, how are you? Are you feeling any better?'

'Yes. The relapse passed. I went back to the GP and spoke to her about starting on some new medication to slow the progress of the MS.'

'I thought you were dead against that?'

'I was. But I spoke to Jo about it, and she convinced me it was probably worth a go. She said it's a bit grim having to do the injections every day, but that you get used to it.'

'Who's Jo?'

'A friend,' Isla said. 'From the support group. She's a little ahead of me on this journey and a fount of knowledge.'

'That's good,' Sophie said. She felt the tiniest pang of jealousy, then berated herself for it.

'Don't worry,' Isla laughed, seeming to read her thoughts. 'She won't replace you, if that's what you're thinking. No one could ever replace you.'

Sophie smiled, reassured.

'You heading home now, then?' Isla asked.

'Yes.' Given that she was going back to her own house, Sophie had the strangest feeling of trepidation. This was more than going home – if she and Liam were going to move on, to a more honest and settled place, it would have to be. 'I'm going to confront him, Isla. I realised over there that I can't brush this under the carpet, I'd be doing us both, and our relationship, a disservice. I have to know for sure if anything is going on.'

'That's brave. You're doing the right thing,' Isla assured her. 'And with any luck he'll have a good explanation and you'll be able to forget all about it.'

'Yes,' Sophie said, buying into that hope. 'We have so much going for us already – and then there are the new plans too. I just want us to get back to normal.'

'Hopefully he'll tell you what you need to know to do that.'

Sophie felt nervous at the thought of talking to Liam, but saw even more clearly now that it was the only way for them to move forward. 'Wish me luck.'

'Good luck. But you won't need it. You know what you're doing,' Isla said.

'I'm glad I've convinced you,' Sophie said, smiling. 'But I'm not that sure at all. I just hope he doesn't think I'm paranoid, or that I'm creating problems where there are none.' She might have been caught up in doubts about her marriage recently, but it was still the most precious and valued thing in her life. She didn't want to do anything to jeopardise it unnecessarily, which was why she was finding this such a tough judgement call.

'I'm sure he'll want to know what your concerns are,' Isla said. 'He's your husband. You have the right to ask.'

'Yes,' Sophie said, taking a breath to steady her nerves. 'That's right.'

'Let me know how it goes,' Isla said, taking her hand and giving it a squeeze.

*

That night, back in the house, Sophie felt out of place, like a doll who had found herself in the wrong dolls' house. Liam was sitting opposite her at the kitchen table, and they were finishing dinner. It was all fine – and yet not.

'It hasn't felt like home without you,' he said.

'What, no one to do the laundry?' She said it to lighten the atmosphere, but it had the opposite effect.

'I'm serious,' Liam said, looking hurt. 'It's really made me realise how much I miss you when you're not around. How much you mean to me.'

Perhaps they didn't need to talk. Perhaps he'd been doing enough thinking when she was away for things to be OK now.

'I'll get us something to drink,' Liam said.

'Right,' Sophie said. Isla's voice crept into her head. *You know what you're doing*, she'd said. *Update me.* What would Sophie do – go back to her and tell her that she'd glossed over any of her concerns, and decided to take the easiest path available to her? She had to be strong – Paris had taught her that she was capable of doing things that were difficult – that was what she had to do now.

'Liam,' Sophie said, steeling herself. 'I need to ask you something.'

'You do?' He seemed surprised. 'Go ahead then.'

'It seemed weird between us. Before I left.'

'Did it?'

She knew it. She had been imagining things – and now she just sounded paranoid. She forced herself to keep on, though.

'Yes. The way you were at Don's birthday party – I got the feeling you were happier talking to those students than you would have been talking to me.'

'Oh, Soph,' he said gently.

'What?'

'I'm sorry you felt like that. That's not true at all. I was sad that you left. I didn't know what was going through your mind – and then when you went to Isla's . . . I felt even more confused. I started to think maybe you were having second thoughts.'

'About what – the baby?'

'Yes. I mean I wouldn't blame you if you were – I know I've done my fair share of going back and forth on the matter. But I worried that you were having doubts and keeping them inside.'

'Why didn't you say anything?' Sophie asked.

He smiled. 'Why didn't you?'

She put her hand on his, and felt a connection return. Liam kissed her, and in that kiss all the tenderness and intimacy that she'd been missing flooded back. It was as close a connection as they'd had when they first met, or on their wedding day. They went upstairs together, and Sophie felt herself become whole again.

She texted Isla just before she fell asleep.

Thanks for listening. It's all OK x

239

Chapter 23

Isla had been relieved to get Sophie's text and to know that she and Liam had made up. They'd been together too long to fall out over a misunderstanding, and it sounded like that was what it had been.

That morning she walked over to the support group meeting. She'd decided to go regularly. This time, she got a bit more out of it. In that hour and a half, Isla went from being acutely conscious of her own symptoms and likely future to almost forgetting about them altogether. She saw that she was lucky. And she also started to appreciate how precious this period of feeling well was.

Today they heard first from Errol, a man in his early sixties. He'd kept his diagnosis a secret from both his family and his employer for four years, until a severe episode had forced him to tell the truth.

'The freedom, being able to tell people what was really going on – not just the symptoms others might notice, but those that were less visible, were below the surface – that gave me another lease of life. My boss sorted out so much for me – he let me change my working schedule, and got me the equipment I needed. They've done so much more to make my working life possible than I ever thought they would.'

'And rightly so,' Andy said. 'It's their legal responsibility, after all.'

'Doesn't mean they always do,' Marjorie said. 'Some people really do have to fight to be treated as equals in the workplace; there's still a lot of prejudice.'

Isla thought of the theatre group. No one had tried to prevent her from being there. It was the subtlest of hints that she'd picked up on. She couldn't imagine how hard it would be to carry on working in a place where the prejudice was more obvious and explicit.

She looked around the room and noticed an empty chair. At break time, she went over to Andy.

'Where's Jo today?' she asked.

'She called this morning. She's not been feeling that well.'

'She always tries to make it, though, doesn't she?'

'I suppose it must be worse than usual today.'

She texted Jo after the meeting but didn't get a reply.

On Monday morning, early, her phone rang. JO.

'Isla. This is a tough one to ask,' Jo said. 'And just say no, really. But is there any way you could take Ava to school this morning? I know it's only Reception class but she loves it so much and I'm stuck. I can't do it, and Aiden's going to get the sack if he goes in late again.'

'Sure,' Isla said, sitting up in bed. 'That's no problem. I'll be there in fifteen.'

Jo answered the door to her, her tears red from crying. 'Thank you,' she whispered. 'I really feel dreadful this morning. Aiden and I will work something out – for the future – but this morning, I don't want Ava missing out – she loves school.'

'Don't worry about it. It's sorted.' Isla walked into the hallway and saw Ava picking up her school bag. Her cheeks were flushed with excitement, but she looked nervous – perhaps because she was picking up on some of her mother's anxiety.

'Will you come with me today?' Isla asked, bending to Ava's level. 'It would be such an honour to take you to school. What do you say?'

'Yes.' She beamed.

'We'd better get going, then,' Isla said, as brightly as she could.

Ava kissed her mother goodbye, and Jo hugged her really tightly. 'Mum's not very well today, but Isla will take care of you.'

Isla could see the emotional wrench as Jo handed her daughter over. 'Daddy will be there to pick you up later.'

'Thank you,' Jo said.

Isla did her best to hide her own emotion, and took Jo's daughter downstairs and out into the street. The reality of Jo's situation – the way she couldn't predict from one day to the next what she'd be able to do for her daughter – was really starting to sink in, and all Isla could think was how cruel it all was.

As they walked towards Ava's primary school, Ava looked up at Isla. 'I don't say it to her. I never say it. But I wish my mum was well.'

Isla felt a surge of sympathy for the little girl.

'I know, Ava,' Isla said, gently. 'There are some days, like today, when she can't play with you.'

'Yes. And some when she can't even come outside. She's not like the other mums.'

Isla remembered the way she'd once felt different herself, without a dad to go home to when it felt like all the other children at her school had one of those.

'She is different, in certain ways,' she said to Ava. 'But she's even more special in others, isn't she?'

'Yes,' Ava said, nodding. 'She's the best. It's just – I want her to be happy. Not sad.'

'She is happy, Ava. You make her very happy.'

'I hope so,' Ava said, scuffing the toe of her shoe on the pavement.

'Believe me,' Isla said, bending to her level. 'You do.'

Chapter 24

The weekend had brought Sophie and Liam closer together. Close enough for her to feel that now was the right time. She'd lost track of how many days late her period was, and the pregnancy test had been unopened in the cupboard for a while now.

After dinner, she led Liam by the hand up to their bedroom, to sit on the bed. 'You wait here for a minute,' she said. 'There's something we need to find out. I've bought a test.'

'Really?' His eyes glistened with hope. 'Do you think there's a chance . . . ?'

'Yes, there's a chance. A good chance, in fact,' Sophie said. 'But there's only one way we're going to know for sure.'

'Go on, then,' he said excitedly, suddenly impatient, like a child.

Sophie went into the bathroom and, after a moment of performance anxiety, managed to pee on the stick. She put the lid on the test, a tingle of anticipation running up her spine. She felt strangely alone, even with Liam in the next room. She wanted Isla there, to hold her hand through this minute that seemed to last for hours.

'Right,' Sophie said, putting her head around the door. 'Do you want to check it together?'

'Of course I do,' Liam said, smiling and motioning for her to join him on the bed.

She showed it to him, looking herself at the same time. 'That box has got a line in it too. What does that mean?'

'Oh – damn. You'll have to do another one. It means you peed on the wrong bit – the test hasn't worked properly.'

'Oh, God. Really?' She looked at it again. 'Are you sure, I mean in the first box ... that bit looks like a positive, right?'

'I'm sure,' he said. 'Same thing happened to Véronique.'

The simple comment needled her. He'd been here before. Seventeen years ago, he had been in the same situation, with Véronique. Waiting to find out if he'd be a father. And that time, not this, had been his first time. A memory that, even if it was darkened by the fog of animosity, he and Véronique would always share.

She pushed the thought aside. She was far past petty jealousies – this one had caught her at a weak moment, that was all.

So, here they were, without a yes or a no.

'Can you do the other one?' Liam said. 'There are usually two in a box, aren't there?'

'I got the most expensive one, to be sure.' Her heart sank with disappointment. 'There was only one test in there. How frustrating that I messed it up.'

Liam checked his phone. 'Don't worry. It's still early. I'll run up to the chemist now and get a new one. You wait here, don't move.' He smiled, then kissed her forehead. 'I'll be back in a minute.'

'Thanks. I'm dying to know now, whatever it is.'

'Me too.' He pulled on his running shoes. 'Look – I'm actually going to jog there. That's how keen I am.'

They laughed and he kissed her on the mouth.

This could be it. The moment they could start to look forward to becoming parents. And she didn't think she could wait another second to find out.

Ten minutes later, Liam wasn't back. Sophie looked out of the window to see if she could see him on the pavement below. She mentally calculated the distance to the Boots on the high street. Of course he wouldn't be back in ten minutes. More like twenty, even if he was running. She sat back on the bed and picked up her phone, trying to settle her nerves.

She texted Isla.

> **Hey. Waiting for some important news. Baby news. Distract me with something.**

Two minutes later, a reply buzzed through.

A photo message, with two dachshunds dressed up as pirates, carrying a treasure chest. It looked like an American Hallowe'en parade. Sophie smiled.

> **Hope that hits the spot. Best I could do at short notice. I have jokes, too. No end of them. All terrible. How long do you have? Two minutes?**

Jokes would be good. I've got a bit longer, Sophie wrote. **Liam's gone to get a new test.**

As Sophie waited for Isla's reply, there was a knock at the bedroom door.

Phone still in her hand, she got up to answer it. She opened it to see Rebecca standing there, her cheeks blotchy and her eyes ringed with red.

'Rebecca. What's happened? Are you OK? Come in.'

Rebecca started to sob, and Sophie led her through into the bedroom.

'Dad's gone out, hasn't he?'

'Yes – just up the road, he'll be back in a minute. We could call him if you want . . . ' Sophie fumbled to bring his number up on her phone.

'No.' Rebecca shook her head. 'It's you I wanted to talk to.'

'Oh.' The words startled Sophie, they were so unfamiliar. 'Hold on a sec, then.'

She quickly texted Isla, **Got to go, Rebecca here.** Then she put her phone down and turned towards her stepdaughter. 'Right, what was it you wanted to talk about?'

'Dad's not telling you the truth,' Rebecca said, looking Sophie in the eye.

Not this stirring again, Sophie thought. Not now. I thought we were past this.

'I don't really care if you believe me or not,' Rebecca said, through tears. 'I have to tell you what I saw that night.'

There was something in her tone that demanded Sophie's full attention. She was serious – this was serious.

'Dad was kissing her,' Rebecca said, haltingly. 'The girl

247

from the student house. Melissa. When I left the party it was because I saw him kissing her.'

When Liam got back from the shop, dropping the paper bag on to the bed beside Sophie, she was bristling with fury.

'Are you going to tell me what's really going on?' Sophie said.

'What?' he said. 'I've only been gone twenty minutes. You'll have to fill me in, Soph, because I don't know what you're talking about.'

She wasn't going to give in, go easy on him. Not this time. The truth was all that mattered right now. 'That night – at the student house.'

He glanced down.

He was going to make something up, she thought. The truth wouldn't require this much thought – it would come. A lie, on the other hand, required time to craft it.

'We've already talked about that.'

'I don't think we really got anywhere, though, do you? Let's try again. Maybe we could start with Melissa,' she said, stonily. 'Tell me a bit more about Melissa.'

Something flickered across Liam's face, leaving a trace of unease, but he didn't say a word.

His silence infuriated Sophie. 'You're not going to say anything?'

'What about her?' Liam said at last.

'Tell me about her.'

'What a strange thing to ask,' Liam said. 'But if you insist—'

'I insist.'

'She's a student, isn't she? Lives over the road. Studies psychology, I think.'

'And – tell me more,' Sophie said. He was holding back. She could see it. 'How do you know her?'

'I spoke to her at the party,' Liam said.

'Was she interesting, then?' Sophie asked.

'Yes, I suppose so,' Liam said, looking a little flustered. 'But anyone is after you've had a few too many glasses of wine, aren't they?'

'So you chatted, and you enjoyed that?'

'Yes, she is, if not quite intellectual . . . engaging. She had a positive outlook. A good view of the world,' he said. 'So yes, if you must know, I enjoyed talking to her.'

'I'm sure you did,' Sophie said.

'What is this?' Liam said. 'Why all the questions all of a sudden? Are you jealous? Because I thought we'd gone through this all. Yes – I should have told you about the party right away, but . . . '

She steeled herself. The only way out was through. 'I get the feeling you've not been telling me the whole truth, Liam.'

'I have,' he insisted.

'So you just talked, that was it.'

'Yes. We just talked. I talked to a lot of people that night.'

For a brief moment, Sophie doubted herself. Doubted what Rebecca had said. Perhaps there could still have been some misunderstanding, after all. But there was only one way to know, for sure. She forced herself to ask.

'You never kissed her, then.'

And there it was. The glance down. The flush in his cheeks. The answer she'd been pushing for.

'Oh, God, Liam. Tell me you didn't.'

Sophie saw it now – he wasn't strong. He was falling apart in front of her.

'I lost my way a bit that night,' he said, running a hand through the front of his hair awkwardly. 'Like I told you.'

'I don't care if you accidentally took the bloody high road to Scotland,' Sophie said, anger and distress welling up in her. 'Did something happen between you?'

In the seconds it took before he finally replied, she felt their once-solid marriage begin to crumble. The future, the things that they had talked about – the things that *he* had talked about. It all seemed a hazy sort of fiction now. Their house was no longer a home but an empty shell, rife with dishonesty.

'Yes – we kissed. I was drunk.'

Sophie felt winded, and she could barely bring herself to ask the question. 'And then – that was it?'

'Yes.'

'You're lying. You slept together, didn't you?' He was silent, and the fury rose in her. 'Talk to me, Liam. You owe me the truth, at the very least. You slept together, didn't you?'

'It was never about sex. Like I told you before, there was a connection.'

'Oh, spare me,' Sophie retorted. 'She must be, what, nineteen?'

'Yes, I suppose so.'

'That's not even that much older than Rebecca.' She shook her head, then it slowly dawned on her. How much of a horrible cliché the whole situation was turning out to be. Nineteen – the same age she had been.

'There was something about her, an energy—'

'Liam, the fact that you felt a special *connection* with a nineteen-year-old is really not something to be proud of. And the fact that your daughter had to witness you indulging your midlife crisis makes it all even worse.'

'It's not a midlife crisis,' Liam said. 'I just … I think it was all about you, really. About us, Sophie. I know it sounds strange, but I've been wanting us to get back to how we once were. That passion. I was looking for what it was that made me fall in love with you.'

So this was it – this was the crux. The man she had married had wanted to preserve her as she was then, a barely formed woman, still working out what she wanted from life. Now she'd grown up, he had looked for the same thing, the thing he wanted, elsewhere.

His words gave Sophie a sudden assurance. There was nothing left in her marriage that she wanted to salvage. Liam had once wished to capture her, like a butterfly on a summer's day. Now – as a confident, strong woman of thirty, who knew what she wanted – all she could offer him, in his eyes, was diminishing returns.

And, looking at him now, absorbed in his own emotions and entirely unrepentant, she realised he was no longer offering her anything at all.

'That's one of the most stupid things I've ever heard, Liam. But perhaps I should be grateful that you tried. Because I'm definitely not going to waste time looking for what made *me* fall in love with *you*. Whatever that was – it's gone.' She kept her voice steady and even. 'Long gone. And it's not coming back.'

*

Sophie slammed the door and went into the spare room. There was no way she could spend another night in their bed. She had no way of knowing what had gone on there, because she knew, without Liam even telling her, that it hadn't been a one-off. She might not have trusted her intuition up until this point, but she couldn't ignore it now.

She had no wish to know more about Melissa. *The other woman.* Those words. Those words that for years had been her own label. They had cut her off from her family, from friends, tarnished her reputation. Now there was another *other woman.* It wasn't for her to pass judgement on Melissa, only on Liam. She had chosen him, and she saw now that she had chosen badly.

She bit her lip, trying desperately not to cry. But she could only hold back the emotion for so long. Her body started to quake with dry, heaving sobs.

She heard a creak as the door opened, revealing a figure in silhouette.

Rebecca came over and sat beside Sophie on the bed. They sat for a moment in silence. No venom or vitriol this time, Sophie was relieved to note, just quiet.

Rebecca reached out her hand and touched Sophie's. 'I'm sorry,' Rebecca whispered.

'Don't be,' Sophie said. 'You did the right thing, telling me. And I should have listened to you more.'

'No – I mean I'm sorry Dad is the way that he is.'

Sophie put her arm around her stepdaughter's shoulders. An arm that had been shrugged away a dozen times. This time, Rebecca allowed it to rest there. She even moved closer.

'I'm sorry too,' Sophie said, fighting back tears. 'You shouldn't have been dragged into this.'

'I still love him,' Rebecca said. 'He's still my dad. But I hate him. I hate him so much right now.'

'I know,' Sophie said, gently. 'I hope that this will have made him realise he has to do better by you. Because he does care. He just doesn't always know how to show it.'

Sophie barely slept during the night. Instead, her thoughts whirred as she fruitlessly attempted to piece together fragments of her life and Liam's, of the relationship she'd believed they had. She pictured him beneath the duvet in the adjoining room, wondering if regret and self-loathing were creeping in, disturbing his rest, or if he was sleeping calmly, convinced by his own justifications for what he had done. The whole time Sophie kept thinking of Véronique – of how Liam's first wife must have felt when she realised what was going on all those years ago. She must have felt the same sense of betrayal, of her life turned upside down. Sophie had played her part in causing that grief.

When the sun finally peeped above the terraced houses opposite, after long hours of darkness, Sophie picked up her phone and called Isla. She knew her friend would be worried.

'What happened to you last night?' Isla said. 'You left me hanging—'

'Rebecca had something to tell me. Something important. It turns out my instincts were right in the first place,' Sophie said. 'About Liam. He's been having an affair.'

'I could kill him,' Isla said, her voice measured but the sentiment raging. 'Seriously, if I were there with you now—'

Isla was seething. How *could* he? How could Liam do this to Sophie, who had done everything for him, who had only ever tried to do the best for him and the family that had become hers. Isla could wring his neck right now. And all that – what was it, bullshit – about him wanting to have a baby with her? How twisted, to mess with her mind on that when all the time, he'd been with someone else.

'He's not worth your anger,' Sophie said. 'Or mine. It's pathetic, and that's all.'

'What – who – was it one of the students, like you thought?'

'Yes. But it wouldn't really have mattered who it was. It's the fact that he did it. That his vows – what we promised each other – clearly mean nothing to him. God, I sound like a fool, don't I? After what happened the first time around. Or worse still – a hypocrite. We did this to Véronique after all.'

'It doesn't mean that you deserved this,' Isla said. 'You never deserved this.'

'I don't know. Perhaps it really is karma.'

'It's not karma. It's your husband being a twat. I'm sorry, but it is. You can't stay there,' Isla said.

'No. I don't think I can. Not right now, anyway.'

A thought flicked across Isla's mind, and she silently prayed that it wouldn't turn out to be true – that Sophie wasn't already pregnant. That he hadn't already trapped her.

'Call in sick at work. Come here,' Isla said. 'There's cake, a comfy sofa and a full drinks cabinet.'

'Thank you,' Sophie said. 'I'm going to take you up on that. But, before I do, I need you to help me do something.'

She picked up the new test and took it with her into the bathroom. 'OK, don't listen to this bit,' she said.

254

They waited in silence, on the two ends of the phone, until the result showed. Sophie felt as if she had barely breathed.

'Thank God,' Sophie said, her voice a whisper.

'Negative?'

'Negative.'

Chapter 25

Sophie drove over to Isla's cottage later that day. On the journey, she thought about Liam, the truth she now had in her hands. Her marriage had been her one true anchor for ten years. She'd always feared that without it she would drift off into an ocean that was hostile and full of unknown dangers. But maybe she didn't need an anchor at all. Maybe that chunk of iron had merely served to tie her down – and here was her second chance, a chance to be free. She didn't quite believe it yet, but perhaps she could start to.

When she opened the door and saw her best friend there, the tears she'd been trying to hold in all flooded out at once. Isla took her into her arms, and Sophie sobbed on to her jumper. She sobbed until she had to catch her breath, and Isla didn't say a word, just held her there.

'Come inside,' Isla said, finally. 'Let me get you some tea. It's the English way.'

Sophie managed a smile, and sat down on the sofa.

Isla came back in with a teapot and a pretty set of 1920s teacups. 'I thought this called for the fine china.'

'Thanks,' Sophie said. Those pretty cups couldn't fix a thing. She knew that. And yet, the sight of them, and the fact that Isla had picked them out, made her feel a little stronger somehow.

'What a total, total, tosser,' Isla said.

'*Total* tosser,' Sophie repeated.

'*Massive* tosser,' Isla raised her.

'*Mega* tosser.' Sophie felt bolder for saying it out loud. He was. He really was. There was no ambiguity any more. No doubt. Liam had shown his true colours – and that was it. She could be angry. Which was better. Better than doubting herself, the constant questioning. She could hate him. And she was starting to.

'I mean, what was that about a baby?' she said, running with her fury now. 'He wanted a baby? Well, thankfully there isn't one. But that's what gets me, Isla. What was he doing, trying to trap me?'

'Trap you. Distract you. Who knows, who cares?'

'You're right. It's over now. Over, over, over.'

'You're well out of there.'

'Ten years,' Sophie said, her voice hoarse with anger now. 'Ten bloody years of my life. Wasted on him.'

'He's an idiot,' Isla said.

'He is.' Then a flicker of doubt. Her certainty wavered. 'Or maybe it's me that's the idiot. I should have seen this coming. I should have *known*.'

'You couldn't have,' Isla said.

'History repeating itself – I should have seen it coming.'

'Don't do this to yourself,' Isla said. 'How did you leave it with him?'

'I told him that was it. I didn't love him any more. That's actually how I felt – as if a switch flicked and *bam!* – it was gone.'

'That's good,' Isla said. 'That makes things easier.'

'I'm not giving him the opportunity to fool me again. No way. And what he's done to Rebecca – all that time I thought it was her trying to drive a wedge between me and her dad, she was, in her own way, doing her best to tell me what was going on. Trying to do me a favour.'

'Her view of men must be pretty shot.'

'Exactly. He took her to that party, when I bet he was hoping something would happen. He let her see him with Melissa – or at least made no effort to hide it. It makes me furious.'

'Poor kid.'

'Yes. Never thought I'd say that – but poor kid. I did this to Véronique, and I did this to Rebecca. And it feels crappy, knowing that now. I'm not trying to play the innocent, and you know I've never pretended to be that.'

'What he did was worse, though,' Isla said.

'I think so too. And I've learned. He hasn't learned a thing.'

'Chasing the sun,' Isla said. 'And now it's burned him on the bum, just like he deserves.'

Sophie laughed.

'I'm glad you're here,' Isla said, taking her friend's hand.

'I'm glad I'm here too.'

That evening, Hattie invited Sophie to help with the final stages of the quilt. The three of them sat there in the living room, listening to Louis Armstrong, stitching, sometimes talking but at other times barely saying a word. And by the time it was finished, and they were ready to go to bed, Sophie felt a little stronger. She'd sewn a little of herself into the quilt that night, and Hattie and Isla agreed that that was exactly how it should be.

Chapter 26

Sophie drove back to Bristol feeling more able to face things with Liam. He had sent several text messages, but she hadn't read them. This wasn't something she wanted to discuss in a few typed characters. Plus she'd needed the space, completely away from him, so that she could work out how for sure she really felt.

When she got back to the house, she had to stop for a moment on the front doorstep. She took a few deep breaths, composing herself. There was none of the usual pleasure of coming home. She was coming back to a home that was coming apart at the seams, and being there, being with Liam, would all be different now.

Inside, she found him in their bedroom. He was bent over by the wardrobe, packing his things into a suitcase.

'Hi,' he said, turning to see her. 'I wasn't sure when you were getting back.'

'Well, here I am,' she said.

'I sent messages.' There was pain in his eyes, as if he were a wounded animal. His skin was tinged with grey and he hadn't shaved.

Sophie felt nothing. No sympathy, no regret.

'I got them. I didn't read them.'

'Right,' he said. 'I understand.'

'You're going.' It wasn't a question, and she certainly wasn't going to try and change his mind. Liam leaving was the right way for this to end. It was all coming apart, everything they'd built.

'Yes. I'm renting a room at the university, while we work all of this out.'

It surprised Sophie, and she shook her head. 'I think you must have misunderstood me.'

'What do you mean?'

'There's nothing to work out, Liam. You cheated on me, you've already broken the vows that we took, and for all I know you may still be doing it.'

'No,' he said, firmly. 'I've ended it with Melissa. There's nothing going on between us any more.'

'Perhaps that was a mistake – you could probably use a safety net. Because we don't have a marriage any more. That's for sure.'

'Come on, Sophie,' he said, pleading. 'Ten years. We can't just throw it away. I love you.'

'And I loved you. Which is why it's so hurtful that you – and it was you – have chosen to throw this away. I know things weren't perfect, but I wanted to work on them. I wanted to give our marriage a proper chance, because there's already been enough hurt in this family.'

'We could still work at it. We could go to counselling,

find a way to move on.' He looked increasingly desperate. 'The future we talked about? We could still make that happen.'

It saddened Sophie that in breaking up her marriage she was also letting go of becoming a mother, for now. She had loved the idea of having a baby, slowly starting to believe that despite her own dysfunctional family she might have what it took to be a good mum. But to bring another child into a home where they might be hurt the way Rebecca had been? It didn't bear thinking about.

'You let me believe you wanted a baby, you encouraged me even, and all the while you were sleeping with someone else.'

'I thought Melissa was a one-off,' he said. 'I thought I would be able to get it out of my system. As I said, something about her reminded me of you, and I wanted to understand—'

'God, this soul-searching is almost more than I can bear,' Sophie said. 'You did something that was wrong, Liam. Accept it. And please don't try and sell it to me any other way. Because – in case you've forgotten – I've been there. I've been *her.*'

'I'm a different man now from who I was then.'

'Are you? Really?'

'Yes. And I can be a man that deserves you. I can change, believe me. I want to. For all of us.'

'Sleeping with her while trying to get me pregnant makes you a lot of things, Liam – most of them unutterable in polite company. But a man I want to stay with? No. A man I want to be the father of my child? No. It certainly doesn't make you that. That's going too far.'

'I want you to know that I wasn't lying to you,' Liam said. 'I did want us to have a baby.'

'That much I believe. But you wanted the ideal – it's the actual responsibility and reality that you don't seem to be able to handle. It would have fallen apart. Better that it happened now than have another child involved.'

'That's not true,' he said. 'You're not even giving me a chance.'

Sophie was distracted as a figure moving around on the landing caught her peripheral vision. 'Rebecca's here?'

'Yes,' he said, looking down. 'She's come to pack her things too. She's going to stay full-time with Véronique for a while.'

Rebecca was being uprooted, half her life messed around, and it was partly down to Sophie. She didn't want her stepdaughter to have to leave Bennett Street. She was collateral damage in a conflict she should never have had to witness. It hurt Sophie to think of how all this would impact on Rebecca, and there was no easy fix. Her love for her stepdaughter wasn't love that had come easily; it hadn't been born out of blood ties, but out of sheer perseverance. It was no less strong for that. The thought of losing Rebecca pained her. She wished there were something she could do to make it all right again.

'She shouldn't have been caught in the middle of this – for the second time,' Sophie said.

Liam's face fell. At last, Sophie thought she caught sight of a little genuine remorse in his expression.

'I want a divorce,' Sophie said.

'It's only been—'

She held a hand up to silence him. 'Promise me one

thing,' she continued. 'And this is more important than the terms we agree, or anything else. Promise me you'll be a proper father to Rebecca. Promise me you'll make this right with her. Work hard to get her respect back. Be there for her. Support her. But above all, for God's sake, promise me you won't do this to her again.'

'Sophie—'

Fury rose in her. 'I said *promise.*'

'I won't do it again,' Liam said. 'I won't.'

Chapter 27

Isla put on her running shoes and closed the front door behind her. She stretched carefully, wakening limbs that had been mostly resting these past few weeks, and then built up to a slow jog, her feet cushioned by the soles of her trainers. It felt good, running again. This morning she was going to meet Jo for breakfast in a café near her flat, and the thought of a croissant at the end of it all helped to spur her on.

This week, Isla's energy had returned. She'd even found herself starting something new – OK, so at the moment it was just sketches and doodles in her notebooks, but it got her out of bed every morning, gave her a purpose. She'd started writing a play. If she wasn't yet ready to get back on stage, that didn't mean that she couldn't still be part of the theatre world, in a different way.

It was time to get back to work.

As she jogged, she thought of Sophie – of the devastating

week her friend had had. They'd spoken on the phone every day, sometimes more than once, about Liam moving out and the first steps that Sophie was making in talks with a lawyer. Far from being broken, Sophie seemed stronger, more determined, and for the most part very composed. She went into work as usual, carrying on with her life as if nothing had changed. But then there were the late-night calls that consisted of little more than her friend's sobs. Isla just listened. She'd invited Sophie to come and stay again at the weekend and Sophie had finally agreed.

Isla ran over to Jo's road, and found her friend waiting for her on the street outside her block of flats.

'Morning,' Jo said, with a smile. 'It suits you, exercise.'

'Thanks,' Isla said, stopping and catching her breath. 'It feels good. I might even make a habit of it.'

'Welcome to freedom,' Jo said. 'Nothing like a crappy disease to make you appreciate your good days, is there?'

'That's true,' Isla said. She didn't think she'd ever take it for granted again, feeling well. Days like this were to be captured. They walked together to a neighbourhood café and got a table outside.

'How's Ava?' Isla asked.

'She's fine. She's loving school as usual, which is a blessing.'

'And you?'

'I got through the benefits assessment, thank God, though not without the stress bringing on that relapse. Anyway, I've been well enough this week to take her in myself, so that's been great. I had to go on crutches at first, and Ava got a bit of hassle from one of her classmates about it. Horrible little boy, he is. But anyway, she wasted no time telling him to mind his own business.'

'A strong woman, like her mother,' Isla said.

'She certainly has the makings of one.' Jo smiled. 'Resilience. She's got that in bucketloads. She's had to deal with a lot, with me being ill, and Aiden working so much to support us all. But when I start to worry, wish I could give her a carefree childhood like mine, I remember that all the time she's learning something. That life sometimes take a little working at, but it's worth it.'

'That's very true,' Isla said. 'There's something special about Ava. She already understands some things I'm only just starting to. She'll be the smartest girl in Reception class.'

Jo laughed. 'Perhaps. Certainly the sassiest.'

'I'm glad you're feeling better. It's good to see you laughing again.'

'It's good to *be* laughing again, believe me. That last relapse was tough.'

Isla felt for Jo, but thought of herself too – the language that was now part of her life. The relapses that might become more frequent, in time, something she'd need to work with and keep talking about. She felt grateful to have a friend she could do that with.

'Listen, Isla. I wanted to say – it was really kind, what you did, taking Ava in to school,' Jo said. 'I appreciate it.'

'It was nothing.'

'I hope I never have to repay the favour,' Jo said. 'That you'll stay well for so long I won't be able to. But, if that's not the case, know that I'm here for you. Me and Aiden both. If ever you need a hand.'

'Thank you,' Isla said. She and Jo shared a moment of silent understanding. Isla didn't have to be alone. She'd found someone who knew what it felt like to have your body let you down. She'd found someone who knew all that – and was stronger for it. The future, with the physical changes it might well bring, no longer felt like a lonely place to be heading towards.

That Saturday, Sophie went over to the cottage. Being with Isla and Hattie felt like sinking into a warm bath after the pain and upset of the week. She'd already told Isla on the phone that she wanted to carry on doing the things on her friend's list. Nothing had changed there, just because she was starting divorce proceedings. In fact helping Isla fulfil some of her dreams would give her the focus that she badly needed right now.

She was beginning to see that breaking up with Liam wasn't an ending but an opportunity. A chance to reinvent herself. Perhaps now she could be the woman she'd always wanted to be, not the one who took the wrong path at twenty. She could live the way she wanted to, without being weighed down by guilt. She didn't regret the past ten years, but she felt increasingly ready to let them go.

Yes, there were those moments in the middle of the night when the loneliness hit. When all she could think of doing was calling Liam and giving in, asking him to come back home. But she'd called Isla instead, and those moments were getting fewer and further apart.

That morning, they drove into town, to tackle another item on Isla's list, one that tested the boundaries of Sophie's comfort zone more than any of the others so far.

'I'm not pushing you into this, am I?' Isla asked. Sophie looked through the car window towards the arts venue. The circus skills workshop was advertised on a large poster outside.

'No, you're not,' Sophie said, shaking her head. She had a gentle fluttering of nerves in her stomach, but compared to the anxiety she'd been experiencing lately it was nothing. 'I want to do this.'

'You're sure?'

'Yes.'

'You're really sure?' Isla repeated.

'Yes.'

'It's just that you once said – and I quote – "swinging upside-down from a flimsy little swing is absolutely not my idea of fun".'

Sophie laughed. 'You remember that? Well, perhaps I've changed a little since then.'

Isla smiled. 'I think you just might have. Right. Let's go in and get ready, then. The trapeze class starts in fifteen minutes.'

Isla took her friend's hand and squeezed it. Together, they got out of the car and went inside.

Later that afternoon, Isla and Sophie stopped by at Isla's grandmother's bungalow, a short walk from the arts venue. Sadie opened the door, and a smile lit up her face.

'What a lovely surprise,' she said. 'Come in, come in.'

They settled in the living room on a sofa and armchair covered with colourful crocheted throws. 'Oh, I do like having my granddaughter back in town,' said Sadie. 'And you too, Sophie! What a treat. To what do I owe the honour?'

'Actually, we've got something to show you, Granny,' Isla said.

'Oh, yes?' Sadie leaned forward in her seat, curious.

'We've had quite an interesting morning,' Sophie said,

bringing out her iPad. 'I can't remember a time when I've been quite so terrified, or laughed so much.'

'We went to a trapeze workshop,' Isla explained. 'I thought you might be interested to see.'

Sophie passed Sadie the iPad with a video of Isla up on a trapeze. 'Isla was a total natural. After a couple of tries, and a minor panic attack, I decided I was better off as official photographer.'

'Oh, how wonderful!" Sadie said, looking at the video with sheer delight. Isla showed her how to pause and then play again. 'You really went for it, didn't you? It must be in the blood.'

'I loved it, Granny,' Isla said, beaming. 'I've actually signed up for a follow-up class already.'

'That's great,' Sadie said proudly. She hesitated, then asked, 'And you felt all right?'

'I felt absolutely fine,' Isla assured her. In fact being up in the air, weightless and free, had been the best feeling in the world. 'I felt better, if anything.'

Sadie looked relieved. 'Good. You know Hattie's always been rather embarrassed about my circus years. Never let me show her the photos, even. I suppose it must have skipped a generation.'

'Photos?' Isla said, curious. 'All these years and you've never mentioned there were photos of you in the circus?'

'Plenty of them,' Sadie said. 'It was five years, after all – starting when I was your age.'

Sophie caught Isla's eye and smiled, clearly impressed.

'Best way I could've spent the time. I got to travel, and each day was an adventure. Only reason I left was because I met your grandad. He was from the real world, you see, and there's not much crossover between the two. I couldn't be travelling around and expect him to wait for me. I knew he was special, from the start. Special enough to make the sacrifice for.' She glanced over at a photo of him, and fell silent for a moment.

Isla reached out and put an arm around her.

'Thank you, love. But this isn't about him, of course. This is about the time before.' Sadie went over to her bookcase, and brought down an album. 'Now – I hope neither of you is in a hurry,' she said. 'Because, my, oh my, have I got some stories to tell you.'

Chapter 28

'Hey, Berenice,' Rafael called out. She was struggling with an old-fashioned leather suitcase, and he hurried over to the door of the bookshop to help her with it.

'More books, I'm guessing?'

'Yes, just some I thought you could use.'

'Thank you.'

'Keep your favourites, but sell whatever you can. Last thing I want is for them to clutter up your house the way they've been cluttering mine.'

'I appreciate it,' he said. He bent to open the case but she held a hand over the clasp.

'They can wait. They're not going anywhere.'

'Sure, OK,' he said.

'Tell me, how are your family doing?'

'Better, I think.' Rafael also hadn't had a request for more money from Patricia for a while, which seemed like a good sign. His mother had sent through the occasional brief update, and there'd been no mention of anything being wrong – it wasn't much, but he'd learned to take no direct mention of a crisis as an indication that things were OK.

'That's good. How's Santiago?'

'Well. He's been enjoying school. Look – my mother sent me through this photo.'

Rafael showed Berenice the photo of Santiago holding up a handprint picture he'd made. When Rafael had first seen it, he'd felt a burst of pride – Santi was growing up so quickly, and looked confident and happy.

'What a lovely boy. He looks very much like you and your brother did, in the other picture you showed me.'

'He's a special boy. I hope he can have a good future.' Rafael couldn't think of his nephew without feeling torn, worrying that without his father, or Rafael, there to keep an eye on him, he might soon be dragged under just as David was.

'You'd like to be there with him,' Berenice said, picking up on his mixed feelings.

'Yes. I often think I should be there to help. It's hard on Patricia, it's hard on my mum, too.'

'You are helping them all by being here.' Berenice said. 'Dont forget that.'

'And what about you?' he asked. 'You had a doctor's appointment this week, right?'

'Yes, just routine. I feel bad for wasting their time, really.'

'I'm sure they don't mind. Oh – wait, before I forget – I found you a plant at the market,' Rafael said, getting it from his small kitchen. 'Feel the leaves. So soft, like rabbit's ears.'

She touched them gently. 'How nice. Reminds me of my parents' garden. Keen on gardening, they were. I'll plant this one close to my window, so I can keep an eye on it.' She smiled, but Rafael detected a certain sadness in her eyes.

A few minutes later, a wave of customers came into the shop, and Berenice and Rafael said their goodbyes. The afternoon was busy. Crime novels were impulse-purchased, enquiries made, romance books mulled over and bought as presents, a few rarities requested from regular customers were ordered up.

Finally, after he closed the shop, Rafael went over to the suitcase and opened it. As he'd expected, it was full of hard-backs – the first thing that hit him was the familiar musty smell. They were old but well cared for, no trace of the dust that donated books normally came caked in, and the pages, while yellowed, weren't crinkled or creased. He lifted up a copy and opened it. Then another, not believing what he had in his possession.

These were first editions – he didn't need his computer to know how valuable they were. They were books he'd longed to have in the shop ever since it opened. Berenice had given him a literary goldmine, and she'd left, without saying a word about it.

Rafael locked up the shop and stepped out on to the chilly canalside. He turned to head for his apartment, then paused. He needed to be sure that Berenice knew what she was doing – that she hadn't simply underestimated the value of the gift she was handing over. He hadn't been to her house before, but he knew where it was – she'd pointed it out from the bookshop as it was only across the canal. She lived alone in a handsome unmodernised apartment on the ground floor. He didn't want to disturb her, but took a chance and knocked on her door.

She answered, and seemed a little unsettled.

'Sorry to call by unannounced,' he said softly.

'Don't worry.'

'I just … well, the books, Berenice.'

'Not just any old books, are they?' she said.

'Not at all. I'm grateful – of course I am. I just wanted to be sure that you really know what you're handing over here.'

He glanced behind her. The flat was almost empty of belongings, boxes half-packed around her in the living room.

'Is there something you haven't told me?' he asked. 'It looks like you're moving.'

'I think you'd better come in.' She stood back and motioned for him to step inside into the hallway.

The basics were there, the pieces of furniture that made a home habitable, but there were no pictures on the wall, none of the shelves of classics he'd always imagined might line her living room.

'There are still a couple of places to sit, just about,' she said, with a smile.

'The books you gave me – they are worth thousands of euros, Berenice. I don't think I should really take them from you.'

'I know what they're worth,' she said. 'And I give them willingly. I can't think of a better place for them to be going.'

'And you're sure you want me to sell them on?'

'Yes, yes, don't whatever you do feel you should keep them for my sake. I don't want them just sitting on your shelves. No sentiment, please. All I ask is that these books give you wings.'

Rafael tried to read her expression.

'That's all I ask. That you sell them, and use the money to follow your heart.'

'You're sure?'

'I'm sure.'

She smiled, but there was something different about her eyes, a slight glassiness.

'Something's changed,' he said.

Her eyes went a little red around the rims, and she put her hand on his. 'Nothing's changed, Rafael. We all have our time.'

A lump came to his throat. He knew what she was going to say.

'And I just got the news this week that my time is nearly up.'

Chapter 29

A week after they'd tried out the trapeze, Isla and Sophie met in a quiet residential street in one of the cheaper areas of Bristol. Isla had been idly flat-hunting online for a few days now, and she'd decided to take the leap and go and see somewhere. The sums didn't add up yet, but she wanted to see what was out there, get a sense of how she might live once she was able to leave the cottage.

'Thanks for coming,' Isla said, passing her friend a take-away coffee. 'The estate agent hasn't arrived yet.'

'No worries. Nothing I like better than flat-hunting – it's the only time you can legitimately nose around other people's houses, isn't it?'

'I hadn't looked at it that way,' Isla said, laughing. 'There I was thinking you were doing me a favour.'

'It's both. How serious are you about renting this place?' Sophie asked.

'Semi-serious. Interested in finding out more. Here's the situation – obviously, I don't have a job. But Mum's hinted I could get some part-time work at her shop, whenever I'm ready.'

'And the deposit?'

'I've sold off a load of clothes and jewellery, plus some old stuff I found in the attic, so I've got that together.'

A car emblazoned with an estate agency logo pulled up alongside them, and a young man lowered the window. 'Isla, is it?' he called out. 'Sorry to keep you.'

He led them inside the Art Deco block, through to a ground-floor one-bed flat, with large glass doors that opened on to a pretty courtyard.

Isla found herself drawn outside. The pot plants and small herb garden were carefully tended, and jasmine and clematis climbed on a wooden trellis. She pictured herself there – she'd be able to grow the flowers she wanted, and if she was unwell, and the heat got too much, she'd have a cooler patch to retreat to.

The estate agent led them through to the pretty turquoise and white tiled bathroom, and showed them the bedroom. Each room was large enough that she'd be able to move around easily.

'It would work, in the future, wouldn't it?' Sophie said. 'If there are bad days.'

'Yes,' Isla said. 'I'd be able to get around. Even if I was on crutches.' There. She'd said it. 'Or in a wheelchair.' And again. She felt a rush, as if the words themselves had given her power over her life. It hadn't been as difficult as she'd thought. Saying the words hadn't made it any more or less likely to happen – and it somehow it took the threat out of them. 'It would be nice to have the garden.'

'I can see you being happy here,' Sophie said.

Isla felt the same. It was a place she could see herself having independence, and freedom, even if her movement was restricted. It was a vision of the future that felt deeply comforting.

'So can I,' she said.

'So, how was the flat?' Hattie said, when Isla got back. 'What did you think?'

'Beautiful.' She still found it a little strange saying the next word, the shift in her priorities that it revealed. 'And practical. It would be very practical.'

'That's good,' Hattie said. Her eyes gave away her mixed emotions, though. 'Are you going to go for it?'

Isla shrugged. 'I don't know. It's lovely, but I haven't made up my mind yet.'

'It's quite soon, isn't it?' Hattie said softly. 'For you to be moving out.'

'I don't want to put my life on hold. I'm thirty, and I'm feeling pretty well. I want to be independent, not relying on you all the time.'

'I know that, I just worry,' Hattie said. 'If you fall over again ... if something were to happen—'

'I'd pick up my phone and ask for help. Just as you or anyone else would.'

'You think I'm being overprotective,' Hattie said. 'And maybe you have a point.'

'Perhaps a little bit,' Isla said.

'I guess I've got quite attached to having you here.'

'And I've liked being here,' Isla said, smiling. 'It was what I needed, while I got things back together again. But I'm ready to move on now.'

279

Hattie chewed her lip and seemed to be holding back tears.

'That's a good thing,' Isla reassured her mother, putting a hand gently on her arm. 'That means you've done your job.'

'I know. Look at me. How silly. Said goodbye to you years ago and here I am struggling to do it over again. It shook me up a bit, all of this. You don't expect it to be your child that gets ill first.'

'I know, Mum,' Isla said. 'But I'm OK. Really.'

Hattie drew her daughter in towards her and held her for a while. 'I want you to do what makes you happy. That's all I'll ever want for you.'

Later that week, Sophie dropped by at the cottage after work, with a bottle of wine and some chocolates. Isla took her through to the kitchen and got some glasses out of the cupboard.

'Did you think any more about the flat?' Sophie asked.

'Yes,' Isla said. She'd thought about it a lot, weighing up the pros and cons of having her own place. She was ready to get back to being more independent again, and she meant everything she'd said to her mum when they'd talked. But there was something about the long-term nature of the move that didn't feel right – she knew that once she was in that flat she wouldn't want to move out for some time. The past half-year had taken her mind and body by storm, and each month had led her to a different place, emotionally. It was too early to predict where the next six months or year might take her – and she realised she didn't even want to. She didn't want to commit to anything at this very moment, not even a lease.

'I said no.' The moment Isla had said it, she knew it was the right decision.

'Really?' Sophie said. 'You seemed so keen.'

'I was. And hopefully one day I'll move into a place just like it. But not now. The timing isn't right.'

'How come?'

'I don't want to tie myself down right now. I've got the rest of my life to make sensible, future-proof plans. Who knows, one day this disease might well tie me down whether I'm ready for it or not.' The thought didn't fill Isla with joy – how could it? But she was starting, slowly, to accept the possibility that at some point her world might become a bit smaller. She could see the sadness in Sophie's eyes, as she seemed to reflect on that possibility too.

Isla took a breath and continued. 'I want to use this time, Sophie, while I'm strong and well, to be carefree a little while longer. If that's just a few months, then so be it. And if it turns out to be thirty years, then I don't think I'll regret a thing either.'

Sophie smiled proudly. 'Good for you.'

'I know things are going to change,' Isla said. 'I'm not in denial any more. Soon I'll have to start planning for the long term. But in the meantime there are other things I want to do. I'm not ready to let this illness dictate how I live. Not yet.'

'I can see that,' Sophie said. 'And who knows what's next for you? I don't think either of us saw the events of the past few months coming.'

'Not at all,' Isla said. Sophie seemed to be dealing with Liam's betrayal well, but she couldn't help wondering how it might be affecting her deep down. 'How are you feeling at the moment, about everything? Liam?'

'Good, actually. Bennett Street's going on the market.' Sophie looked happy, relieved even.

'You're OK about that?'

'We both need to move on. That house was our home, every room there reminds me of Liam. Of what we had, of what he threw away.' Isla glanced vulnerability in Sophie's eyes for a moment, but then she quickly composed herself. 'Even if I could afford to – which I can't ... ' Sophie said, pragmatically, 'I wouldn't want to live there on my own.'

'Where will you move to?'

'I'll rent somewhere for a while, before I make any big decisions. It'll probably be a two-bed, so there's an option for you to consider.' Sophie smiled warmly.

'Now there's a thought.' Isla said. She recalled how happy the two of them had been once, living together – how easy and uncomplicated it had all been.

'But first things first,' Sophie said. 'I've got a different kind of proposition for you.'

'You have?' Isla asked, curious.

'Yes. Well, we're not quite finished with your list, are we?'

Isla gave a smile, but it was one of resignation. 'I know. Broadway still beckons ... one day.'

'And the other one?' Sophie asked.

'It was learning to tango in Buenos Aires,' Isla said. 'So I'd say equally out of reach right now.'

'Are you sure?'

'Yes,' Isla said, amused that Sophie was even asking. 'I might have flogged a few things on eBay, Soph, and built up a small pot of funds from my mum and granny, but I'm not really in a position to afford that. It would take thousands to get us both out there. I can't afford a long-haul flight.'

'Who says you're paying?'

'You are kidding, right?' Isla said.

'No, not at all.,' Sophie said, shaking her head.

'But – how?' Isla asked, incredulous.

'Let's just say I have a feeling I might be able to rustle up that money from somewhere.'

'What?' Isla still couldn't get her head around the idea of Argentina being anything more than a daydream.

'Really. There have to be some good things about my life caving in. And the thing is, Liam's guilty conscience seems to be paying out quite willingly.'

'Wow,' said Isla. Excitement surged in her. 'You're really serious. I can't believe it.' Her head was spinning – red wine, dancing, getting to see life in a whole new continent. Then thoughts of the practicalities involved in the trip crept in. 'But what if . . . what about insurance? And what if I get sick again, Soph, before we even leave? I don't want to let you down.'

Sophie seemed determined that nothing would stand in their way. 'We'll work it out. Somehow. Trust me.'

Chapter 30

On Thursday night, Sophie put away the folders she'd been working from on the children's ward, thinking ahead to how she would fill the long stretch of empty evening. It was a new experience for her, being alone in the house, with nothing in particular to do when she got back, beyond the necessary chores.

Rob came up to her, and rested on the edge of her desk.

'Everyone's busy,' he said to Sophie. 'Everybody. Am I really the only one who's not married and settled around here, and even if so, is it really impossible to combine that with a quiet drink on a Thursday night?'

'Not everyone's busy,' Sophie said.

'They are, I promise you. And I wish it wasn't true, because this shift has been a killer and I could really do with a bit of time to unwind.'

Sophie had seen Rob rushing between patients all day, while she'd supplied him with sets of results that, for the people he spoke to, could sometimes be life-changing. She could see it all in his face now: behind that smile, he carried the responsibility of every child he'd treated that day.

Sophie coughed awkwardly and shuffled some papers, feeling oddly like the awkward teenager she'd once been. 'I'm not busy ... as it happens.'

'You?'

'Yes, me. What, is it so strange a concept?'

'No ...' he floundered. 'It's just, you know. You're usually the first to dash out of here once you've finished your work—'

'Not tonight,' she said. She felt a stab of sadness at the memory of having something to get back home to. But her life had changed, and it was time for her to change with it.

Rob was putting on his coat. 'Well – if you really are free ... will you join me?'

Something seemed different about him, and she thought she detected the slightest waver in his voice.

'Sure,' she said, slipping on the shoes she'd cast off under her desk and then getting to her feet. She hadn't gone for a drink with work colleagues for what felt like years. Family life had always come first, and she'd found it easy enough to say no. She hadn't even felt as if she was missing out; it was just one of the many sacrifices she'd made without even considering it. But things were going to be different now.

Sophie and Rob walked to the pub, which was lively with other post-work drinkers. Rob bought her a drink and they sat together in a quiet corner.

'So how come you're free tonight?' he asked. 'I mean, ignore me if I'm prying . . . just curious.'

She toyed with the idea of a white lie, but then thought of how she'd have to follow that tomorrow and the next day, with each of her colleagues. Her new start would begin today, and it would begin right here, with the truth.

'Me and Liam have broken up,' she said. The words, stark and simple like that, sounded unreal. 'We're getting a divorce.'

'Are you serious?' Rob seemed as startled as she felt. 'What, just like that?'

'After what he did, I'm not sure there really is another way.'

'Wow. I'm sorry,' he said. 'I won't ask questions, but it sounds like you've had a rough time of it.'

'A bit. And you can ask, it's OK. It turns out all that fooling around with your sister's friends wasn't quite as innocent as Liam made it out to be.'

'Really? Oh, God, that's awful. I don't think Kate knew about it . . . she would have said something.'

'I can't bring myself to care any more, to be honest. If it hadn't been her – Melissa – it would have been someone else, I'm sure of that.'

Rob let his breath out slowly. 'He's an idiot.' He paused, and his grey-green eyes met Sophie's. 'Losing you.'

'Hopefully he's finally realised that – but it's much too late.' Sophie laughed. Her laugh had become lighter – she didn't feel weighed down by bitterness or resentment any longer.

'How are you coping with it all?

'Oh, I'm a mess,' Sophie said, honestly. 'I'm thirty and

I have no idea what I'm doing with my life – where I'll be living, what tomorrow will bring. But I'm grateful for what I have. And everything is going to be all right, one way or another.'

'You're right,' Rob said. 'With all this in mind, I think it's definitely time for another round.'

Sophie hadn't exactly planned to stay there till closing time. And she certainly hadn't planned on drinking quite as much as she did. She and Rob were walking home through the back streets, arm in arm, singing some old Oasis song and weaving a little towards the kerb. A little voice in her head nudged at her – *what are you doing?* – but she ignored that. Because a) she wasn't really doing anything, and b) who was that voice, or anyone else, to tell her what she should or shouldn't be doing?

'Bennett Street,' Rob said, as they turned the corner to take in the curve of elegant white houses. 'This is you, right?'

'It is, until it finds a buyer.' Sophie smiled. 'Street of dreams. Or at least it was for a while.'

It stung a little, knowing she would have to leave, but she knew now that the world was full of streets, of houses, of flats, and each one felt like home to somebody. Being happy wasn't about a postcode, or bi-fold doors, or a period fireplace.

'I'm rattling around in it at the moment,' Sophie said. 'I haven't got used to coming home to an empty house yet. Not at all.'

'I'm sure it won't be long,' Rob said.

'Until what?'

'Until someone else snaps you up.'

'Oh, I don't know,' Sophie said. It was the very last thing on her mind at the moment.

'Any man would be lucky to have you, Sophie,' Rob said.

She blushed at the unexpected compliment. Rob wasn't usually the type to speak as openly as that.

It wasn't that Sophie had never thought about it. She'd sometimes wondered about Rob, even while she was still with Liam. It had flickered across her mind more than once – how it might be to kiss him. But she'd told herself that doubts, fantasies, were for those people who hadn't taken the path that she had, who hadn't stirred up the water so much.

'You're gorgeous. Funny, smart. Kind. If you hadn't been with Liam I would have asked you out a long time ago.'

Oh, bloody hell, Sophie thought. Now she really had waded in far deeper than she'd intended.

'Really? I didn't realise . . . I mean I assumed it was just a drink, tonight. I thought—' Her cheeks burned.

'Don't worry,' Rob said, shaking his head and smiling. 'I know I'm punching above my weight. But you can't blame a guy for trying. It's been a long few years waiting and wondering if anyone else would ever match up to you. And now you're single again I'd have been a fool not to have at least let you know.'

'You really mean that,' Sophie said, struggling to take his words in.

'I'm surprised you didn't notice,' Rob said. 'Maybe I hide my feelings better than I thought.'

'I never noticed,' she said.

'Anyway, this is getting embarrassing now,' Rob said. 'I'll say goodnight.'

He kissed her gently on the cheek. Sophie turned just a fraction. It was the slightest shift in the angle, but it was enough for her lips to meet his.

Chapter 31

Later that evening Sophie sat down in the Bennett Street house. She'd just got off the phone to Isla – she'd had to call her the moment she'd walked through her front door. She was still buzzing with the excitement of her kiss with Rob and had had to share it. Sophie wasn't sure what, if anything, it would lead to, but already it had reminded her that another future was possible – that her life didn't have to revolve around Liam any more. She was free. The energy of that freedom led her to do two things that had been on her mind for the past few days.

She opened her laptop.

The first email she wrote was a draft of her resignation. Her life was shifting, and the things that had once given her security now weighed heavily instead. She had given years of dedication to the ward, but now it was time to let go.

The second message was to Rafael. She'd found his email address on the website for the Floating Bookshop. She knew she was putting her friendship with Isla on the line by writing this message, but her gut was telling her to do it, and she'd learned to trust that a little more lately.

Hi Rafael, it's Sophie.

It's been a while. I hope you don't mind me contacting you out of the blue – and if your life has moved on since we met, then that's understandable. But I don't think you ever forget the person who brings your best friend to life, who makes them the happiest you've ever seen them. I certainly haven't forgotten you, and the way you and Isla were together. You had something special.

Listen, while I can't tell you everything, I have to tell you something. Isla didn't leave you because she doesn't love you. If anything I think she loves you even more now than she did then. She had her reasons for letting you go – she wanted to protect you. She wanted things in your life to be perfect.

But I have a feeling they probably aren't, without her. I know my life without her wouldn't be half as great as it is with her in it. She'll hate me for telling you, but when she was in Amsterdam she found out that she was sick. She found out that her life was going to have to change, not now, but in the future. She didn't want you to feel sorry for her, to feel that you had to look after her.

Her diagnosis has taken us in unexpected directions, though. Isla and I have been busy. You remember the list, right? Isla wants to live out the dreams on her list while she's still fit and healthy (which hopefully she will be for many more years), and we're making progress. Next month we're going to Buenos Aires.

I just wanted to tell you not to give up on her.

Love, Sophie x

She closed her laptop, wondering where the message might lead, what consequences for her friendship there might be – but confident that she'd done the right thing.

Then, finally, she went over to her antique bureau. She opened the top drawer, and then the one below. In there, at the back, was a folded piece of paper. She glimpsed a few of the words. *Learn Italian*, it said. *See the Northern Lights*.

She opened it and smiled. It was time to take another look at her own list.

Rafael was alone in his apartment that evening. He'd just read Sophie's email and was trying to make sense of it – decide what he should do. What did Sophie mean, about Isla being sick? But as he thought about it, rather than try to work out what it could be, he just thought about how little it mattered. How what he took away from the email was the positive message – that Isla was still living out her dreams, as best she could – and that there was a sliver of hope that she might still care for him.

As he was working out what to do next, his phone rang.

'*Mama.*'

'Rafael. It's me. I didn't want to call you – but things have got so bad.'

'What do you mean? I sent through the money . . .'

'Patricia has spent it all already. I don't know what on – you know how she is, Rafael. She's not responsible. I went around there yesterday. The little boy still doesn't have the things he needs for school.'

'I'll wire some money out to you in the morning.'

'It's not just the money, my love. David is worried – says his son needs a proper father figure, and he can't be that until he gets out.'

Rafael felt a stab of guilt when he thought of his nephew, growing up in the same environment that he and his brother had, with even less stability, if anything.

'I know I shouldn't say this,' his mum went on. 'But little Santiago misses you. So much. He's asked when you are coming to see us. I don't know what to say, Rafael. I know you have your business to run, but the thing is we need you here too right now.'

Isla and Sophie had spent the past three weeks preparing for their three-week trip to Buenos Aires. They'd compiled online recommendations and booked accommodation, given themselves some options for tango courses, taken a couple of introductory lessons at home to give themselves a head start, and then plotted out a rough itinerary for the trip.

They'd even gone along to some introductory dance lessons to pick up the basics, and Sophie in particular had really taken to it.

With two nights to go until their flight, they were sitting together over dinner at Sophie's house. Something had been on Isla's mind for a while, and she decided to raise it. If she and Sophie were in this together – they really had to be in it together.

'We're going to one of the most glamorous cities in the world, to have the trip of a lifetime,' Isla said. 'And you know what I can't get out of my head?'

'What's that?' Sophie asked.

Isla thought of the extra bag she'd have to pack, not that she was taking daily medication. 'I'm going to have to explain to security why I'm carrying a load of syringes.' She'd imagined the conversation she'd have to have, and the potential humiliation of it all.

Sophie smiled reassuringly. 'Don't worry about it. You won't be the first person.'

Isla was aware of that, but it didn't ease her embarrassment. She didn't want to have to be singled out as different, less still give reasons and explain about her illness. 'Maybe not . . . ' Isla said. 'But it'll be the first time I've done it.'

'It'll be fine,' Sophie said. 'You'll have your doctor's letter with you. And, more importantly, you'll have me. So if they start asking any searching questions about your drug addiction, they'll have me to answer to.'

Isla smiled, and felt instantly better. Sophie was right – she'd be there, and together they'd find a way to take it in their stride, laugh about it. 'I'm feeling a little braver already.'

'Good. Want to hear something funny? My brother called this week,' Sophie said.

'Oh, yes, what did he say?'

'He told me our parents were delighted to hear about the divorce. Seriously, Isla. Only they could be this over the moon about my life falling to bits. They think I've finally done the right thing.'

'And don't tell me – they want to see you again.'

'You've got it.'

'What do you think about that?'

'I don't know. Is it horrible to say I haven't really missed them? Not the way I should have. I've actually found it sort of liberating to not have them around, passing judgement on everything – and that started long before Liam, by the way.'

'No chance they might be open to seeing things from your point of view now?'

'I don't know. I doubt it. And I don't know if I really did do the *right* thing – I did the thing that was right for me, just as I did when Liam and I got married. I haven't made some significant moral decision here, just a personal one about what I am and am not prepared to tolerate. Their world is so black and white that I don't think they'd ever understand that.'

'Maybe in time,' Isla said.

Sophie shrugged. 'Maybe in time.' She paused. 'Tell me more about you. The list. What progress?'

'I've been thinking about Number One,' Isla said.

'New York?' Sophie was surprised.

'Yes. Don't worry. I'm not labouring under any illusions, I know that I'm not going to be performing there any time soon. Hard as it is to read the reviews, I have done, and I'm glad for them that it's going well – honestly I am. I invested enough in the production to take pride in the way it's being received over there.'

'Well, that's very grown up of you,' Sophie said. 'A whole lot more grown up than some of them were back then, by the sounds of things.'

'I don't believe in holding grudges, and maybe Greta had a point – the time wasn't right. Ultimately it was my decision and I understand now that I did need to come home, take stock.' Isla shrugged. 'But that doesn't mean giving up. If you can't join them, beat them.'

'And how do you plan to do that?'

'I'm writing a play,' Isla said. 'Halfway through.'

'You're halfway through and you never even mentioned it?'

'I'm entitled to my secrets,' Isla said. 'I'm actually really enjoying it. It gives me the same kind of buzz I used to get on stage.'

'You're not going to give up on acting altogether, though, arc you? I hope not.'

'No,' Isla said. 'I'm just pressing pause on it for a while. I don't think I could give it up even if I wanted to. It's in my blood.' She smiled. 'But this is different. Something new – and it feels like something I might be able to do, you know, if and when things change.'

'I'd like to read it one day. When you're ready,' Sophie said.

'You'll be first in line.'

'Great. And for now,' Sophie held up a copy of *Anna Karenina* that had been languishing on her bookshelves unread for years, 'this is going in my luggage.'

'You're doing it,' Isla said. 'You're starting the items on your own list.'

'Yes, I am. It's time. And there's going to be no stopping me – just you watch.'

Chapter 32

Rafael had booked Berenice's favourite canalside restaurant for the party, and decorated it with bunting. He'd invited all of her friends and family. He'd organised the band, the cakes, the drinks.

It was all that she'd asked for. Her one request, after all she'd given to him. 'Throw me a funeral party. One that I can be there for.'

He'd never found a gift so difficult to give. Yet now, watching her talking and hugging her close friends and family, unhurried and happy, he felt honoured that he'd been asked to provide it.

It was his last night in Amsterdam, for a while at least. His plane tickets were on his bedside table at home, ready along with his passport for his long journey tomorrow. His bag was packed with clothes for the warmer weather and he'd handed over the running of the shop to a close friend for three weeks.

When he came back, Berenice might be gone. The

doctors had given her a month, at best. So this is it, he thought, watching as Berenice smiled and laughed on the other side of the room. Where that woman he cared about stood, there would be nothing but a gap in all her friends' lives. He didn't want to lose her. He would miss her kindness, her humour, her insight – a hundred things. But if she had to go, how right it was to remember her like this.

'You did a good thing, organising this,' a woman said to him, offering him her hand to shake. 'I'm Joni, Berenice's cousin, by the way. We all knew that she wanted to do this, but none of us knew where to start. How do you go about celebrating the death of someone who's still here – so much alive? But she insisted, didn't she – she didn't want some dismal thing, but a celebration of life, with her still here in the middle of it.' There were tears in Joni's eyes, but she brushed them away.

'She's doing it her way,' Rafael said, 'like everything else. She's talking about wanting to send her ashes up as fireworks. Did you know that?'

Joni laughed. 'Funny thing is, I'm not even surprised. She always said you were special. That you understood her.'

'She's special to me too. A lot of people here are going to miss her,' Rafael said.

'She's ready,' Joni said. 'That's what matters. She's done what she wanted to do in life, and what more can any one of us really hope for than that?'

The next day, Rafael walked up the steps and on to the aeroplane, his head aching a little. Last night might have been a party, but it had brought out sadness in all of the guests, and it had left him with an ache.

He took his seat on the plane, next to a woman in her

fifties. She looked nervous, and reached out her hand, taking his.

'You don't mind if I hold your hand, do you? I get in a right state on flights like these.'

'Sure,' Rafael said calmly. 'That's fine.'

'Just for now,' she said, with a smile. 'Not all the way to Mexico City.'

Isla and Sophie arrived at their apartment in Buenos Aires and Sophie sat down on the bed, testing it with a gentle bounce. 'Not bad,' she said.

It had been a long flight out to Argentina, and they were both tired, and jet-lagged – but at the same time they couldn't wait to get out and explore the city they'd landed in.

Isla opened the colonial shutters and sunlight flooded into the room. 'Not bad? Take a look at this.'

Her friend joined her at the window, and together they looked out from their balcony over the square. It was bustling with locals buying fruit and vegetables at the stalls below them, and a scattering of tourists lingering by shops selling brightly coloured wooden trinkets and paintings of tango dancers. There was something in the air here, Isla thought, something that she had once thought she'd never experience again – life, and an embracing of the moment.

'Let's go out dancing tonight,' she said.

'You sure? You're not too tired after the flight?'

'Don't . . . ' Isla said, as kindly as she could.

'Sorry.'

'I'm fine. And if I'm not – I'll tell you.'

'OK, OK. I promise to stop acting like I'm your mum.'

'I appreciate that.' Isla said it with a smile.

Sophie went back into the room and started to unpack, hanging her clothes in the antique wardrobe.

'Some smoking-hot clothes there,' Isla said, admiring the strapless dress her friend was holding. 'So am I assuming that out here you're single?'

'I suppose I am, yes,' Sophie said, sounding it out. 'Feels very strange to say that.'

'How did you leave things with Rob?'

Sophie smiled. 'Open.'

Isla leaned back against the dressing table. 'That's it? Open?'

'Yes,' Sophie said, laughing. 'We had fun. And maybe we will again.'

'Wow. You're good at playing it cool.'

'Maybe that's because I am genuinely OK with however things go. I don't need to be rushing into another relationship, Isla. I've spent ten years in one, and it's hardly left me with a thirst for more of the same.'

'It wouldn't have to be the same, though. In fact you'd be supremely unlucky if it did turn out to be.'

'I know. And it's like I said, I'm not saying no to anything right now. I'm just not committing to a yes either. I'm also wondering, I guess, if my attraction to Rob isn't about another thing too.'

'Oh, yes?'

Sophie smiled. 'Nice as he is, I'm also quite keen on his job.'

'Interesting.' Isla laughed.

'I'm serious, Isla. Being a ward clerk was never my ambition, you know that – and now I've left, I don't want to go back. Nothing wrong with it – there was a lot I found rewarding over the years—'

'But you used to dream bigger,' Isla said.

'Exactly. And I'm not sure quite when, or why, I stopped.'

'It's not too late,' Isla said, encouraging her.

Sophie paused for a moment. If she said it out loud now, it would be real. Isla would hold her to it. Instead of feeling nervous, though, it only made her feel surer. 'That's what I've been thinking,' she said. 'I want to go back to medical school. Finish what I started all those years ago. If there's one good thing to come out of what Liam did, it's that he seems desperate to put money my way in order to soothe his conscience. I've got two options – say no, which in some ways I'm tempted to, believe me, as nothing in the world could make me forget about this – or take it, and use it to move on. Won't bring back the last ten years of my life, or get them back to the way they used to look to me, but it could go a long way towards helping the next ten years look brighter.'

'I think that's a wonderful idea,' Isla said. 'I've always said it – but I'll remind you of it now. You'll make a great doctor.'

Sophie smiled. It meant a lot to hear those words – to have someone else believe that her dream was possible. Even more than that – that reaching for it was a good idea.

'I know it's a long journey – but if I don't do it, I'll always regret it. And if I've learned anything this past year, it's that I don't want any more regrets.'

'Is Mexico your final destination?' the woman next to Rafael asked.

The stewards and stewardesses were settling the last few passengers and getting ready for take-off.

'Yes,' he said. He'd travel overland from Mexico City – up to his family's town.

'Anyone special there?' she asked.

He shook his head. Then he saw it – this wasn't what Berenice had meant. *All I ask is that these books give you wings* – that was what she'd said. Mexico wasn't meant to be the end of this journey. He would still go there – he wasn't about to let anyone down. But there was somewhere else he needed to be first. In her message, Sophie had given him enough to hope for. Her words had helped him glimpse a future with Isla again. But it was only here, now, on the plane – that he'd really started to believe it might be possible.

Now he saw that if he didn't trust his gut feeling, he might regret it for the rest of his life.

He didn't want to be that old man, sitting on his own in the bar, wondering what could have been. He knew what he wanted – and it was Isla. The last thing he thought about at night, the first thing in the morning. He longed to be close to her again, to touch her, to laugh with her. To spend time doing nothing at all with her – that was what he wanted more than anything.

'Actually, no,' he corrected himself, turning to the woman. 'I'm flying on from Mexico. I've got one more journey to make.'

Sophie and Isla were eating dinner in Buenos Aires's San Telmo square, the bustling cobblestoned plaza filled with people promenading or getting ready for the evening of informal tango dancing to start up. The sky was growing dusky, and two men stood on a ladder stringing up lights on an overhanging wire, so that the performance would be lit. Couples, from teens to octogenarians, chatted and practised steps while they waited for the live music to start.

'Glad you came?' Sophie asked.

'Yes,' Isla said, smiling. The upturn of her lips came from deep within her, a contentment, a burst of confidence and hope that had been with her ever since they'd arrived.

It had felt like such a crazy leap to be making, and yet now she was here she felt at home. OK, so she had a suitcase packed full of medicines and syringes, rather than just the shoes and handbags she might have had in there a year ago, but none of that had made as much of a difference as she'd feared it would. She felt liberated. Not from the disease – she accepted now that that freedom would never come, that the diagnosis had become another strand of her identity, like an ex-boyfriend she'd rather forget, or the unkind words someone had uttered to her at school once, now lodged in her mind. She couldn't detach it from herself, any more than it could choose to make its own way, separate from her body. But she was almost free now from fear. And, more than the regular injections, or the hospital appointments, it was fear that had been keeping her captive. Fear that had been insisting that only catastrophe lay ahead of her, and that all pleasure was now consigned to her past. Here, with Sophie, she didn't feel anything more than herself – and to feel like herself, her thoroughly imperfect self, riddled with flaws and vulnerabilities, but also towering with strength and courage, was the best thing she could imagine.

'You look miles away,' Sophie said.

'I guess I was. Just enjoying the moment, I guess.'

Their steaks and two large glasses of red wine arrived at the table.

'Were you catching that waiter's eye?' Isla asked.

'No!' Sophie blushed. 'Well, I couldn't really avoid it.'

'So Liam's well and truly ...'

'Absolutely,' Sophie said. 'But never to be returned to.'

'Good,' Isla said. 'I'm sorry that I'm not sorry.'

Sophie smiled. 'I kind of like being on my own,' she said. 'All this time I've been afraid of it, and you know what? It's got a lot going for it.'

'Of course it has,' Isla said.

'I don't feel lonely. Not at all,' Sophie said.

They ate their food and chatted, the evening warm and no one seeming in any particular hurry.

When the waiter collected their plates, Sophie glanced over at the dance floor. The music was starting up. A classic Carlos Gardel tango tune, that the locals and tourists both seemed to recognise, sending them migrating towards the centre of the plaza. The waiter asked his boss something, then came over, putting a hand out to take Sophie's.

'You want to dance, don't you?' Isla whispered.

'No – it's fine,' Sophie said, shaking her head politely at the waiter's request. 'I'm not good enough ...' She'd only had two lessons. 'And my friend ...'

'You should, Soph. Don't worry about me,' Isla said. She would be up there herself, on her own if necessary, if only the numbness in her feet this evening didn't make her feel she might stumble if she did get up.

Sophie gave a shrug and a smile, and reversed her decision before the waiter turned to go, taking his hand. The two of them walked out into the plaza, and he took her gracefully into his arms.

Isla let the music envelop her, sweeping her into a bygone time, and she delighted in watching her friend move on the dance floor, her red shoes a flash of colour as her experienced partner whirled her in ochos and turns, leading her and making each move look effortless. She felt the tiniest twinge of envy at the way her friend's movements flowed – and then relaxed back into enjoying the spectacle for what it was – a dozen or so couples, some known to each other, others virtual strangers, enjoying the warm air of the evening, and the long night of dancing and talking that lay ahead. Isla swayed a little to the music. She wasn't there, she thought, watching the dance floor. But she was here. She was completely, one hundred per cent here.

Rafael saw her sitting on her own, gazing out over the square. Her hair was pinned up, exposing the nape of her neck. Isla was wearing a dark red dress, low at the back. He stood still for a moment and followed her gaze out towards the dancers, until it settled on Sophie. Rafael watched Sophie's elegant movements and smiled to himself. She was a good dancer – and a good friend, who had helped him get there. But there was only one woman he wanted to be with right now.

He'd made it halfway across the world, and now she was metres away from him. The woman who reminded him what it was to be alive. That made him forget about the troubles in his past and the uncertainty of his future. And right now he felt intoxicatingly alive.

She turned, and her gaze met his. She blinked in disbelief.

No backing out now. No backing out.

'Rafael,' she said. She got to her feet. 'Rafael! What on earth are you doing here?'

She was smiling. Thank God, she was smiling.

*

They finished the carafe of wine in the half-hour they sat there. Sophie was caught up in dancing. They occasionally caught sight of her, but she seemed so lost in the moment Rafael wasn't sure she'd even noticed him arrive.

Not that it mattered. Rafael wasn't here to see her. He hadn't left the flight he was supposed to be on, and bought tickets for the next available seats to Buenos Aires, to see Sophie. He'd done it for Isla.

'You're insane,' Isla said. 'You came all the way out here, to see me?'

'Yes. I did. And I'd do it all over again.'

'Why?'

'Because you're all I can think about, Isla. I wanted to be here with you for this – the things on your list. I want to be there for you, while you do the things you want to. Because you're what I want. Without you in the city, Amsterdam isn't home any more.'

She smiled, and let herself take his words to heart just a little. To accept that they were, however incomprehensibly, about her.

'You think I'm being dramatic. I know. But I'm just being honest.'

'Thank you,' she said. 'But there's something you should know—'

He stopped her. 'Then tell me, in time. But know that there's nothing that could make me change my mind.'

Inside her, there was a softening. The parts within her that had remained taut – because she feared if she let go she might fall apart – loosened. He had come all this way. He was still thinking of her, now, months after she'd left. And then, the realisation that sealed it – the one that made it all more real.

Why wouldn't he?

Because she wasn't a bad deal. In fact, she was pretty sure now that she was the best thing that could ever happen to him. She'd show him happiness, and pleasure, and laughter and adventure that he couldn't even imagine yet. She'd show him what it was to smile every day, for as long as she could.

She looked up at him, and then her gaze dropped for a second to his mouth. She leaned forward, and he met her in the middle, kissing her. Their lips met, and the last traces of her fear dissolved. Her body wasn't hers any more; it was already merging with his. Life was no longer about the little pieces of her, of him – of anyone. It was about the big picture – about what happened when those pieces fell together into a whole.

Her thoughts were lost in a fog that was part music, part swirling warm evening, and part pure exhilaration. The future wasn't hers to take. It was theirs to build. They would make it together.

Epilogue

The day that your life changes for ever, chances are there won't be a sign announcing it. You'll wake up, brush your teeth, drink your tea, anticipating the familiar pattern of a regular day.

When you get that news, that package, whatever it is that disrupts your quiet, predictable day – you're going to need time to unwrap it, and have a good look at what's inside.

Not everything in life comes clearly labelled – the most delicious-looking peach turns out to be mouldy on the underside; that wrinkled, dark passion fruit looks and tastes a whole lot better once you get inside. Whatever you find in that box, sit down and look at it for a while. Take it out, touch it – show it to your best friend. Show it to your mum. Cry about it. Laugh at it. Learn what it is to live alongside it.

Then take off the label that came with it and make your own. A new one. Choose the colour, choose the words, the size of the writing. Show it to as many people, or as few, as you like.

You can plot, and plan and design yourself the perfect life. The one you thought would fit. You can tick every box, do everything on your list. And then life changes, and you change, in a way you never expected.

It turns out that the thing that makes you happiest was never on that list at all.

That much Isla knew now.

Acknowledgements

Writing a book is a team effort, at least for me. I get to do the typing, and the daydreaming, and the character sketches, and the plot outlines. I drink all the coffee and I'm probably the only one who lies awake worrying about what is going to happen to each of the people I've started to care about (and I worried a lot about Isla). But behind the scenes I'm lucky enough to be supported by professionals, friends and family who help make it all happen.

To my editor, Manpreet Grewal, thank you for the many ideas and workable solutions, and for always helping me see that I can do it. You're the best. Also to my agent, Caroline Hardman, who has been there since the very start of my career, and still walks me through every part of the writing and publishing process calmly with creativity, insight and unflinching commitment – thank you.

To the brilliant team at Sphere, in particular Thalia Proctor and my copy editor Linda McQueen, who did so much to help the story read better. To Stephie Melrose and Rachel Wilkie in publicity and marketing, Jen Wilson, Anna Curvis, Sara Talbot and Ben Goddard in UK sales, Rachael Hum and Victoria Cheung in export, and Tom Webster in production. To Little, Brown in Australia and New Zealand – in particular Louise Sherwin-Stark, Melinda Dower, Melanee Winder – who give my books a life down under. Thanks also to Tracey Winwood for designing a beautiful cover.

To the readers and bloggers who have supported me from the beginning – you know who you are.

To my mum, who is both a great reader and a talented (and willing) toddler-tamer, and stepped in to help dozens of times. To my sister Kim, and good friend Ellie, for providing expert medical knowledge. (Any remaining factual errors are all mine.)

Finally, to James, for a thousand things that you are and all that you enable me to be.